Indu Balachandran had a 30-year career in advertising, growing from copy-trainee to Executive Creative Director at J. Walter Thompson. Her best-selling first book *Don't Go Away, We'll Be Right Back—The Oops and Downs of Advertising* took readers on a roller-coaster ride through the world of advertising.

Indu switched to travel writing, and has published articles in *Travel Plus*, *The Lonely Planet*, *iDiva*, *The Sunday Times* and reviewed seventy eco-friendly destinations all over India for *Travel To Care*. Her writings have featured in five anthologies of short stories. She lives in Chennai and writes humour columns for the *Sunday Hindu,* and prize-winning contest slogans for ecstatic relatives. And fantasizes about doing stand-up comedy at staid Tam Brahm weddings.

She blogs at indubee.blogspot.com and can be contacted at indubee8@yahoo.co.in Follow her on Twitter@indubee

RUNAWAY WRITERS

Indu Balachandran

SPEAKING TIGER

SPEAKING TIGER PUBLISHING PVT. LTD
4381/4, Ansari Road, Daryaganj,
New Delhi–110002, India

First published by Speaking Tiger in paperback 2016

ISBN: 978-93-85288-28-9
e-ISBN: 978-93-85288-29-6

10 9 8 7 6 5 4 3 2 1

Typeset in Adobe Garamond Pro by SÜRYA, New Delhi
Printed at Sanat Printers, Kundli

For my two most valuable creations:

Kadambari

(who I thought would be writer, but turned into a banker)

and

Kanishkaa

(who I thought would be a banker, but turned into a writer)

Contents

1

'Choose a job you love, and you never have to work a day in your life.'

'Living space available for 9-month lease. Centrally located, fully functional, healthy environment with all supporting amenities. Call 9846635322'

It was this simple classified advertisement I wrote that started it all.

Now if you think that's a real estate ad, read that again, and you'll realize I was talking about leasing out my uterus to breed a baby.

I was writing this ad for a lark actually, scribbling down a line on a paper napkin in a pub. With surrogate moms being suddenly in great demand (what's with this sudden drop in fertility, Young India?), breeding other people's babies seemed like a cool new-age occupation to have, rather than slog as a home loan officer in Citibank—the job that I currently had.

But let me tell you, great things begin on the humble paper napkin. Email ids are jotted down; romances are traced back to hurriedly written telephone numbers on pub napkins. J.K. Rowling wrote her first Harry Potter ideas on a piece of white tissue. Hey, even that lovable 7-Up guy, Fido Dido, was born as a scribble on a restaurant napkin.

So I held up the paper napkin and read out my spoofed classified ad for baby breeding to my pals Kavi, Vikki, Lulu, Tarun and Shanks—I really had to shout it out over the roar of '*Summer of 69*', with half the pub singing along with the song. When I finished, my entire table broke into laughter and applause.

'Amby, you insane nutcase!' said Tarun. 'You really should make a living out of this.' 'Renting out her uterus?!' cried Kavi. 'Now what will the conservative Tam Brahm community have to say about *that,* Ambujakshi Balan!' I winced hearing my full name. But more on that later.

'No, idiot,' said Tarun. 'I mean Amby should make a living writing pithy lines like this all day.' He looked at me with palpable excitement. 'Amby, imagine you putting this line up on your Facebook update. You'll get 78 'Likes' within an hour.'

So here we all were at Chennai's 10 Downing Retro Nite, celebrating three events simultaneously: Kavi's birthday, Tarun's first no-smoking month, and my first month at Citibank. Oh, make that four events—it was also my *last* month at Citibank.

Now a mere month at a coveted job in a leading MNC bank is hardly the time when one says, 'I quit! I've had it with this awful routine. I need a new job.' But that's exactly what I had declared to my gang as soon as we'd found a table in the crowded pub. The hours were long, my boss screamed into phones all day, and my love for numbers suddenly seemed to have ended. That's why suggestions for alternative career paths for me were coming in fast and furious from my friends. I'd recently been reading this article on the huge demand for surrogate mothers in *Open* magazine, and a pub napkin was a good place to start jotting down new job ideas for myself. But my pals seemed to have more practical suggestions.

'Start a dog's beauty parlour in Bollywood,' said Lulu, influenced by her own mania for all creatures canine. 'Just imagine the money you'll make doing manicures for all those celebrity dogs with names like Popo and Sweetoo and Pugsy…'

Shanks' trademark gigantic sneeze (rumoured to sometimes start minor earth tremors in India) preceded his suggestion. 'Forget dogs. How about a clinic for cat allergies? I even have a name for it: Cat-astrophe.'

Vikki thumped the table. 'Hey Amby, I got it. You could make an entire living out of simply being a Professional Contest Enterer. We all know what a whiz you are with words. Start a website and charge hefty fees for finishing prize-winning slogans for people who are always wailing, "How come I never win in contests?" In fact, Amby, there's a holiday to Goa to be won in a contest. I read it in yesterday's papers—which may be just the opposite of your baby-breeding future career. Can you think of a snappy slogan for a revolutionary new contraceptive?'

I burst out laughing. 'Hmmm…okay.' I simply love this kind of word-puzzle challenge, and began scribbling again. 'How about this, Vikki: *Copulate More. Populate Less*,' I said, a few minutes later.

Vikki looked at me in complete awe. Before I knew it he would've told the whole world about it...living up to our nickname for him: 'Vikki-leaks'. As he quickly reached for a napkin to write down this potential holiday winner and sneakily enter the contest himself, the rest had broken into spirited singing again with a burst of '*Red red wine...stay close to meeeee!*'

That was also a cue for a new round of drinks to arrive at the table; not red wine but its close, poorer cousin beer, even though my own refill was still only Pepsi. My Tamil Brahmin community would be proud of this: I still drank and savoured only Pepsi, even if it was in unsavoury places like a pub. My family, though, was thinking I was away at 'Kavi's birthday dinner party' (correct) enjoying alu-parathas and home-made Punjabi pickle with her entire Sharma family around the dining table (incorrect), who were all probably hoping that my shining example of joining a leading MNC bank would influence their own wayward daughter, Kavi, to look for a similar 'good-respectable-job' in a bank (highly incorrect).

Kavi Sharma and I may have learnt our numbers at the same nursery school together, learnt our alphabets and how to spell b-a-n-k at the same junior school together, learnt the intricacies of money at the same Economics Honours college together, but to the utter dismay of Kavi's parents, their only daughter hadn't, like her best friend—myself—gone on to bring all these specific learnings in life into logical fruition with a 'solid' job at a bank. A multinational bank at that.

Kavi was, instead, stirring up eco-friendly soaps on her terrace in her fierce quest to save the world from further environmental waste. 'What about wasting away all your good education so far?' wailed her folks. 'I'm going to call Ambujakshi to see if she can get you an opening in Citibank. I am sure her recommendation will help.' This was invariably followed by a firm 'Don't you dare!' from their stubborn daughter, stirring up yet another batch of tulsi-jasmine fully biodegradable soap cakes—a hobby she was trying to turn into a business.

And even as Kavi's parents quite openly said—with one of the 10 Tamil words they had actually picked up in the 25 years of living in Madras, 'Why can't you be a bit more like the *chamaththu* Ambujakshi? (that single Tamil word for good, obedient, obliging). I suspect my grandparents, very secretly it must be added, were wishing, why couldn't I have been born be a bit more *chikni gori* like the pretty Kavi. My being dusky coloured had been a 'she is a bit dark, BUT…' feature all my life, since I was supposedly compensated with a pretty sound brain.

But what happens when a girl reaches the marriageable age in the arranged marriage scenario? But hey, I'll get to that later, as right now, it's about the job market, not the marriage market.

Well. Kavi's parents would be in for a great shock soon, when they heard that I, the good and obedient Ambujakshi Balan, math whiz and class topper, had quit a hallowed and respected career path, and was loitering in the by-lanes of uncertainty wondering what to do next in life.

Meanwhile, back at the pub, fate was at work, bringing a set of trivial happenings together, to suggest my new career destination:

1. The DJ had switched to the Beatles, and we were all singing along to '*The movie's gonna make me a big star...*'

2. Vikki had just received a WhatsApp text message, which made him guffaw and say, 'Who are these anonymous people who come up with these spot-on one-liners in our cell phones? Guys, just listen to this one...'

3. Lulu was looking towards the pub entrance, one hand on her heart. 'Oh my God, for a moment I thought that was Krish Kumaar walking in,' she said. 'He's just the HOTTEST film star *ever...*'

And then Tarun put some key words from the above dialogue together: spot-on one-liners, hot movie star, text messages...and exclaimed, 'AMBY! I've got it. I know the perfect new job for you! You should be the Tweet-writer for Krish Kumaar—I'm sure he could do with better PR.'

And that's how a brand new career path revealed itself to me. You have to admit it seems quite a cool new-age job to have: Tweet-writer for a Celebrity Film Star.

But before I tell you more about that, I have to borrow a sentence from *The Catcher in the Rye* (okay, I won't judge you if you never ever read this fabulous J.D. Salinger classic), but it's got this memorable opening line: 'If you really want to hear about it, the first thing you'll probably want to know is where I was born, what my childhood was like, and how my parents were occupied...and all that David Copperfield kind of crap.'

So here's a quick background sort of thing coming up...

2

'Don't raise your voice, improve your argument.'

I've always thought my name, Ambujakshi, was the Indian equivalent of 'Abigail'. I bet this is what you think 'Abigail' looks like: a dorky girl in pigtails with braces spangled across her teeth, and definitely wearing goody-two-shoes.

I remember feeling very sad in a self-conscious pre-teen phase of my childhood in Madras, wondering why my parents never gave me any of the trendy names of the early 80s like Divya, or Riya, or Ananya (there were four Ananyas in my class.) Or even if they wanted to go into those old elaborate Indian names from our classics, it could have been Kadambari or Lavanya or Priyamvada. But Ambujakshi? It sounded to me as clunky and utterly middle-class as a dark green Godrej steel almirah.

(But sometimes I thought they could have done worse. At least my name wasn't Alamelu or Abhayakuchaambal, fine old Tam Brahm names that were a fad during my grandmothers' times.)

Growing up in Raja Annamalaipuram, Madras (which was chopped to R.A.Puram) in No. 44 Pasumpol Perumal Street (again, pared down to P.P. Street), I too, had a shortened version of my name, frequently used by my aunts and uncles: Ambujam. Now I tell you,that was far worse than the full form!

My name seemed to go very well with the dreary

tamarind rice or idli-chutney that was invariably in my school tiffin box, but was promptly gobbled up by my best friend Kavi, the pretty Punjabi at school, who, much to my bewilderment, loved and craved for it so much. As much as I simply couldn't resist her delicious chole and methi parathas. That's what made us best friends in the first place. We helped each other go home with empty lunch boxes.

She was also the one who gave me my far more hip sounding nickname Amby, but I sometimes wasn't so sure, as it was also the name of our black, rather stodgy, fat-assed but immensely reliable family car, the good ole Ambassador.

Kavi lived two streets away, and the Sharmas loved me like their own. I was the good influence in their daughter's struggle with maths, our combined homework sessions, our exam preparations, and soon she even joined my Carnatic music classes—all the while managing to stay just a few ranks behind me, in my steady climb to the top of the class grade right through school.

Joining Kavi at the bus stop for our school bus every morning from kindergarten onwards, I was unaware of the liberal application of Pond's Talcum Powder on my face—this was my grandfather's own way of ensuring I looked as fair-skinned as Kavita—and at any rate, you couldn't belong to the average middle-class household in Madras without this most essential of all cosmetics.

I grew up with the typical smells and sounds of a middle-class Madras home: the whoosh of an impatient pressure cooker at 6 in the morning (it's a rule that rice and dal *must* be cooked and ready really early in Tam Brahm households, nobody has questioned why), and the familiar smell of filter coffee brewing—children could drink this only after they turned fifteen because, we were told, coffee could make you darker and, needless to say, was therefore totally avoidable in my case); and the frequent clang of my mother's steel 'biro' (impossible to decipher that we weren't saying a Tamil word, but our own version of 'bureau'!) as that was the repository of all our good things, from money for the vegetable vendor kept under old Kanjeevaram silk sarees, to a new cake of Mysore Sandal soap, should the current one in our bathroom be reduced to a sliver.

Kavi was a joy in my house; especially since she quickly learnt that here you had to drink water in a stainless steel tumbler 'from up'—that is, with the rim never touching your lips; that a banana had to be eaten by breaking bits off with your fingers, never by biting into it directly, and even if you accidentally brush your feet against a piece of paper, you must immediately dive and touch the paper, and touch both your eyes in humble apology to the Goddess of Learning. Little everyday things, but Kavi simply imbibed it all from my Tam Brahm household.

I used to look at Kavi's jovial dad, Ved Sharma, with some awe: he 'did business'—Kavi told me once; and for me, it was a rich man's vocation in itself, and one day when I asked my grandfather while walking to the bus-stop—can't my appa also 'do business'?—he laughed and said, no kanna, your father is a government servant. Not a fortunate choice of words to tell a 5-year-old: I was immediately plunged into gloom thinking perhaps my father was a sweeper for the government. I had once been taught what the pictures were on a 50-rupee note, ('this building is where our government works'), so I used to imagine my humble father, a servant, sweeping and swabbing the floors of Parliament House, as a portrait of Gandhiji (on the other side of the rupee note) smiled on encouragingly at him. Maybe that's why we weren't as rich as Kavita Sharma, I concluded.

I also whispered a terrible secret in my grandfather's ear once, that Kavi's father 'drinks whiskybrandy in the house.' My grandfather showed mock concern. Understandable, when the only alchohol consumption in our strict Iyer home was Woodward's Gripe Water (alcohol content: 3.6 per cent); something my baby cousin drank all the time when he was cranky.

Around the age of 8, Kavi and I both had our first big crush; both on the same man in fact.

He happened to be Mr Brown, the handsome funny class teacher from *Mind Your Language* which played every Wednesday on Doordarshan. We raced home on our bicycles after riding around Boat Club Road to be on time for this serial. But it seemed that the older we got, the younger the men who caught our fancy, and we became devoted fans of Doogie Howser, the prodigy doctor.

Well, maybe we both couldn't marry the same man, as in some of our earlier plans, but surely we could find two best friends to marry—like Doogie Howser and his good pal Vinny. That way, we'd all be best friends forever.

Our tastes in men began to differ after a while, when I thought Ridge, from the *Bold and the Beautiful* was the handsomest man on earth. But after a while, I decided I preferred funny, endearing guys to deep pondering men, and wished I could meet Jack Ritter some day from *3's Company*. Kavi by then was well into Aamir Khan, after watching *Quayamat Se Quaymat Tak* thrice over. Kavi was beginning to scorn my rather Western-oriented obsessions: from following Grammy Award nominees to Tom Cruise movies, while she became a complete Hindi movie fanatic.

And then the VCR machine entered all our lives. The debate was always about which video library was the better stocked: Rik or Tic Tac? And with a stealthy passing on of a borrowed movie cassette, from one household to another, we'd both be able to see a good movie at home by sharing the price of Rs 10 for two days' rental.

So apart from setting family TV time for some absolute unmissables—like the Sunday *Mahabharat*, we became addicted VCR movie watchers through our high school and college years.

It was around this time that my love for writing began to surface. I harboured dreams of writing a romantic bestseller, not the Mills & Boon variety, mind you, but a funny, endearing, hugely romantic novel with lots of witty conversations, with my patron saint of writers, Nora Ephron, as my guiding light.

I must have borrowed and re-borrowed *When Harry Met Sally* a zillion times. I knew some amazing one-liners and even entire dialogues by heart.

I loved the arguments Billy Crystal and Meg Ryan had: *'You see? That is just like you, Harry. You say things like that, and you make it impossible for me to hate you.'*

I loved the transition in a relationship from trying too hard to letting it just be: '*It is so nice when you can sit with someone…and not have to talk a word.'*

I loved the unclicheing of the phrase—Will you marry me?—to something so refreshingly romantic: '*I came here tonight because when you realize you want to spend the rest of your life with somebody, you want the rest of your life to start as soon as possible.'*

And my most goose-bumpy memorable part of all in the film. When Harry tells Sally:

'I love that you get cold when it's 71 degrees out. I love that it takes you an hour and a half to order a sandwich. I love that you get a little crinkle above your nose when you're looking at me like I'm nuts. I love that after I spend the day with you, I can still smell your perfume on my clothes. And I love that you are the last person I want to talk to before I go to sleep at night.'

I wanted to write romantic sentences like that.

I wanted to *write* more than even have a real man actually say such things to me. (In real life men don't. But Nora Ephron gets what they *should* be saying just so brilliantly right).

And then came *Sleepless in Seattle*. Sigh.

By this time I was deeply in love with love itself—the light-hearted romedy variety. I was going to be Ambujakshi Ephron. (My first name definitely, *definitely* had to change.)

However my proficiency in maths came in the way of my life's plans to hit the Oscars shortlists.

Maybe explaining complex concepts to Kavi through the years helped make any maths paper a *jujube* for me, a lovely Tamil slang for…well you can figure out that one.

Or was mathematics just a genetic hardwiring in my Tam Brahm DNA. At any rate after my Economics Honours degree in Ethiraj College, I was snapped up for a job in India's best market research company. My sparkling resume thus far—class topper throughout school, and the second rank in the University of Madras for Economics Honours—made getting a well-paying job a *jujube*. Now you get the meaning.

But even that three-year work stint was only for that 'job experience' fulfilment; as studying further and further was what our family did, in varying degrees of intensity. A Masters' degree in finance and administration was what had to be appended to my name next, and applications flew off to Ivy League universities in the US; Northwestern Univ in Chicago was chosen for the 70 per cent scholarship that came with it, and I was off.

Every now and then I wondered: And what of my Ephronic ambitions in life? When was I going to write that regular column in *Huffington Post* that would also be syndicated to magazines around the world? What about that debut romantic novel of mine that would take the publishing industry by storm? Which then would be lapped up by Hollywood—and I would be asked to write the screenplay? What about that special page I would be given on the last page of a glossy magazine called *Ask*

Amby where I would give snappy, fun advice to romantics everywhere and increase my reader base? What about TV appearances on chat shows where old schoolmates would see me and wonder, is that AMBUJAKSHI BALAN, that goody-two-plaits, somewhat dark, maths horror from our class in Churchpark? How did she suddenly get *this* way?'

Well, apparently I now bore somewhat of a resemblance to the actress Nandita Das, or so thought some kind-eyed people with rose-tinted glasses. I really wasn't so sure. People never do see themselves in mirrors as others proclaim them to be.

In my formative years, the mirror hadn't exactly been the favourite object in my room. After going through my life thus far being a rather horrendous Plain Jane, or should that be Plain Parameshwari, with two tight plaits looped around my ears, a pair of black-rimmed Turakia glasses so large that they safely hid not only my caterpillar-like eyebrows but also my eyes (large and fairly decent, but no one knew that…). I, the incurable romantic, was beginning to feel I would find a boy some day to love me only for my inner beauty.

Now that actually seemed quite gross, despite every gushing Miss Universe contender claiming that that's what was *most important* in a woman.

Inner Beauty? As in wonderful looking X-rays?

In my case, my parents had better attach my brain-scan while seeking prospective suitors, as apparently that was in pretty great shape, helping me win maths proficiency prizes year after year.

But a few days after I turned seventeen (and my

grandparents were beginning to accept that my dusky complexion wasn't going to be masked by Pond's Dreamflower Talc any more), my life went through a transformation thanks to two visionary men. I mean that literally: Lawrence & Mayo, the optician-magicians. They helped me fling away my brainy-kid defining 'sodabuddi' Turakias and I suddenly saw the world through tiny plastic lenses. And the world, too, suddenly saw my reasonably well-shaped black eyes below Eve's Parlour's expertly shaped eyebrows.

My torso, rather plump all through childhood and which my cousin attributed entirely to the ghee-ridden food in Kavi's house, was giving way to a slimmer teen version, thanks to a basketball obsession when we entered college. I was, I guess, beginning to look less like my namesake, my dad's old Ambassador car, the amby, and more like our newly acquired shiny Maruti.

By my eighteenth birthday, I was increasingly being told, by complete strangers in queues waiting for tickets, in supermarket shopping aisles, in wedding halls and once even in a lift, 'You look *so much* like Nandita Das! I just had to tell you...'

(The sentence used to describe me amongst relatives' circles was usually 'How did she turn out so dark, compared to her mother and father? And have you seen how thin she has become these days?').

Okay, okay, I won't pretend I didn't feel pretty flattered, who wouldn't, being compared to such a gorgeous actress like Nandita Das? Especially since I went through an entire girlhood looking totally nondescript even in a sea of totally ordinary faces.

Anyway, I guess any likeness to this dusky actress became more apparent with shorter hair; when I impulsively chopped off my thick long mane, so far swinging in a rope-like plait down my back.

My family wailed at the horrible 'bob-cut' I came home with, a few days before I left for the US. All that careful nurturing by my mother of my greatest asset, my silky, long, thick black hair! Nourished with warm gingelly oil and shikakai through a million Friday head-baths, through the years of being looped up in twin pigtails, to its classic single *otha pinnal* braid—just gone, with the snip snip snip of a heartless pair of scissors at a swank beauty parlour.

I had decided I couldn't be a busy student at an American university and be caretaker of two-and-a-half feet of thick hair as well. 'It will always grow back later,' was my argument to my distraught mother and grandmother.

Well here I was, back in India after mastering finance in America, with firm admonishments from my hair-nurturing mother that I had better let it all grow back nicely now. I suspect she was growing my chances in the Iyer marriage market along with my hair.

We were driving home from the airport after my arrival back in Chennai, with my brand new foreign degree henceforth appended to my name. I pondered about when exactly I would tell my ecstatic and proud family that a deep secret desire to be a writer had surfaced all over again, and was now sitting on my left shoulder in the form of a tiny grinning animated talking pen. And how editing my US university's campus news magazine had honed my writing skills. And how the short story I had written and won in a contest run by a magazine in Chicago, had the potential to be developed one day into a full-fledged novel. And that the novel may have the potential to be made into a play...and the play may have the potential to be made into a TV serial and the TV serial may have the potential to be made into a hit film...

And so, I was seriously wondering whether to enrol soon in a one-year diploma course in any good Creative Writing programme.

The thing to do, therefore, was to completely chill out a bit to think it all through...take a gap year now to see where all these exciting new creatively inclined plans buzzing in my head were leading me to.

Had my parents even heard of a concept called the Gap Year?

I may as well have said I was considering joining the Hooters as a saucy waitress, just for a change.

After a couple of weeks of settling in, I rapidly lost all my nerve about declaring my change of ambitions in life. There was too much fuss being made over my new degree and return to India and an array of exciting job opportunities, mine for the picking.

Meanwhile I bought a copy of *Screenplay Writing for Dummies*. I would just have to make my innate creative passion an after-hours hobby thing that I would do, alongside my sensible day job.

So I went right ahead and accepted a meaty job offer—

or should that be a plum job offer. (Considering I'd retained my vegetarian ways despite my rooming with meat-eating buddies at Chicago). I sailed through my interview, with all my shiny new credentials, and was shown my desk as a Citibank Loan Officer.

The office was swank. The people were smart. The pay was awesome.

A week down the line I loved my new job—as much as an artist like Rembrandt would have loved painting garage walls. My job felt mechanical beyond belief. The pasted smile on my face when people asked how I liked my posh Citibank officer job was starting to unpaste.

It was getting increasingly clear to me that our bank's slogan was the most appropriate thing ever: The Citi Never Sleeps. Neither did we. When did the workaholics of this place actually leave their desks here, and go home to their families and friends? In my case, to my secret writing ambition?

Biting into my order-in pizza, late one night at my office desk, I decided: 'Feck! I have to be doing something else with my life. At once!' (Note: With my innate inability to say bad words, this was how I coped in extreme situations—saying 'heck!' but carrying an overtone of bad by changing the first letter…)

My family would experience a group heart failure.

I had to go over carefully what I was going to say to them, very very gently, about my Gap Year plan, and get advice from my best pal on how to save my life from a certain impending death due to boredom.

Not that Kavi was in any way qualified to saving lives

unless you happened to be a whale; in the time I had been away in America, Kavi Sharma had decided that her compassion for animals now extended from dogs and cats to tigers, blackbucks and Ridley turtles. And after a long voluntary stint at a wildlife sanctuary, had recently joined a Danish group that was deeply involved in preserving the blue whale.

'Kavi, my life sucks. I simply cannot see myself spouting interest rates and easy pay-back drivel and smiling brightly at homeless hopefuls across my desk,' I wailed.

'You're lucky your parents aren't springing marriageable hopefuls at you every single day,' said Kavi. 'My folks are intent on finding me a male variety of human to occupy my life, rather than large aquatic mammals facing extinction. And there's always a 'nice haalthy bwoy from Chandigarh' they feel I must help procreate more of, not some dumb animals. And hey, they are wondering why you aren't knocking some sense into my head, and finding a solid well-paying bank job like yours...just advance warning, in case you drop in home for my birthday soon.'

Well, at Kavi's birthday bash, that memorable night in a pub, everything was set to change rather dramatically for me. With career advice from a highly inebriated bunch of good friends, as you saw in the opening of this story.

Thanks to Tarun's insane suggestion that I quit everything and join the PR unit of Chennai's hottest film star at once, I felt that my 'Gap Year' plan would at least be creatively occupied, as I tried to figure out my I-want-to-be-a-writer obsession.

Meanwhile I was actually going to be a Professional Writer! Well, of *some* sort.

Tweet writer. Facebook writer. Blog writer. Interview writer. Sound bites writer. Snappy-answers-to-stupid-questions-writer. Ghost writer for film star.

My gang had a very practical and workable plan when I said, 'And just *how* am I going to tell my family this bizarre piece of news about my career change?'

They all pushed away my Pepsi, and chorused, 'Have a *real* drink first, Amby!'

3

'You had me at hello...'

'Hey Amby. I want your life!'

I was hearing a LOT of this, wherever I went these days. This time it was a classmate from my college who rang me excitedly just as I was leaving for a major film shoot. One more envious person who had heard about my glamorous new job with the PR entourage of a famous film star.

Krish Kumaar. Now shortened down to a screen name: KayKay.

'You really have the world's coolest job, Amby. Where did you send your resume? Who did you interview with?'

Resume? Interview? Well!

I hurriedly said I would share my secret job-landing

techniques some other day, and jumped into my zippy new i-10 car. I had a long drive ahead to Chennai's film shooting district, Kodambakkam (the one that gave it its name 'Kollywood'.)

Come to think of it, my 'resume' was something Tarun texted to his friend Sailesh, head of PR for KayKay. In one short line, in half the number of characters of an average Tweet: 'Amby can come up with killer one-liners after drinking a couple of Pepsis!'

And the interview? The PR guys could've at least given me an official Tweet-writing test. Instead they pointed me towards KayKay's make-up van for the first, and also the final, interview. Who knew it was actually going to be that Momentous First Meeting!

Wait! I have to do a bit of rewind here first. To share some dream-sequence scenarios that have played in my head for years, featuring 'Momentous First Meetings'.

In my high school days, I would imagine 'the matched DVD scene'—shamelessly borrowed from Hollywood clichés you may notice, where the scene was a video library and I would place the film I wanted to borrow at the counter, and see a neatly manicured male hand (clean neat male nails are important to me) place the exact same ditto similar film on the counter. Two heads would swivel up, two pairs of eyes would say 'You too like *When Harry Met Sally*?!' Then we'd break into spontaneous smiles, music would swell up somewhere—and then we'd later, much later, tell each other: 'You know, that was the exact moment I fell headlong in love with you, my goddess of love, though I didn't know it then.' (That sentence itself was borrowed, word for word, from an old Mills & Boon romance.)

I would vary this scene with different film titles. It was the *Sleepless in Seattle* DVD that I and my handsome stranger would be borrowing on the same day, same time. Briefly it was the same episodes of *Friends*. (The One where Rachel has Feelings for Joey). Then it became *You've Got Mail*—back to delicious, funny, romantic comedies, always by the queen of screenplays: Nora Ephron.

Then I discovered a new Hollywood cliché. I decided dogs would bring me face-to-face with my future Handsome Lover. His Golden Retriever. My scruffy Beagle. Or his cute ugly Pug and my cute ugly Pug. (Nah, too much like a Vodafone ad). Back to his Golden Retriever. My scruffy Beagle. One would run after the other in a park, we'd chase them, their leashes would get entangled. We'd meet. Breathlessly we'd say our names to each other.

Well, what actually happens in real life first meetings is (after such a build up in one's head), the guy sees you looking like a smashed brinjal that's just been oiled and roasted on a fire (that's how we girls look when we go for a monthly scalp oil massage at Dimensions—now why the hell did our favourite parlour go unisex suddenly?) while the guy himself, on the next chair, is getting his nose-hair trimmed.

Okay, that's how my friend Lulu met a guy, in a unisex parlour and it later actually blossomed into a great romance.

In my case, neither the matched DVD scenario happened. Nor the dogs' leashes-tangled-up scenario.

It was *better* than all of that. And even came with a music-swelling-up background score.

The song? '*Every new beginning is some other beginning's end…*'

MY SONG. Currently on my Top 5 List of Bestest Ever Songs.

I had stepped into KayKay's make-up van for the first time, where '*Closing Time*' filled the chilled, conditioned air, and my stunned gaze crashed headlong into the meltingest, chocolatiest eyes in the universe.

'"*Closing Time*"—that's among my most fave songs!' I said at once.

Chocolate Eyes had White Teeth in close competition for best features. Wait a minute. There was the Divinely Touchable Hair in the race too. Of course, I'd seen this pleasant-faced hero, gussied up in crazy filmi costumes in posters around town, but seeing him in real life, up close…oh wow!

'Hello! You like the Semisonics too? I thought you kids of today wouldn't even have heard of this 90s band…'

Now why did I think that anyone *hiring* a Tweet writer would have talcum powder on his chest-hair, wear white shoes and a safari suit, read only Chetan Bhagat, and groove only to '*Kolaveri di*?'

KayKay looked urbane in his cool white linen collarless shirt (Rohit Bal?), spoke Doon School English, and had a copy of Julian Barnes' *A Sense of an Ending* lying face down next to him.

Already I had ticked off about five boxes. One more got ticked off as I noticed super neat nails.

Now he'd probably also be a fan of Seinfeld. And William books as a kid.

I wished I'd had time to put on my lenses after all, not just run out of the house in my stupid glasses. I wished I'd worn my more flattering black Zara top, instead of this baggy red T-shirt. I wished I'd had that new haircut I'd been postponing for about a hundred years.

I wished my eyes hadn't strayed to a bunch of yellow roses on the table before me, with a box of expensive-looking chocolates, with a card that said: *'It's okay to sin occasionally…xxx*J'

Okay, I am a compulsive reader. Of everything. I read funny signages, I read the newspaper packet that comes with a bunch of grapes, I read crazy hair dye ads on backs of buses. I read 12-year-old *Inside-Outside* magazines at dentists' waiting rooms. I read romantic notes written by other people to other people.

Hmmm. Did *KayKay* write this note with the flowers? Or did someone write this for KayKay? (Would my future job include writing KayKay's romantic notes to other women?).

'Come. Do sit down.' KayKay patted a cushioned stool next to him, neatly trimmed nails and all.

Half an hour later, we'd gone from talking about Julian Barnes to Rajesh Khanna to Ikea furniture to my broken French (he was fluent in it!) to where in Chennai one could get fresh buffalo mozzarella to the Teflon poisoning controversy to Nora Ephron—*hey* he knew who she was—to Dove hair conditioner to funny anagrams to the difference between basil and tulsi leaves to a cool trick to prevent pasta turning sticky to the 40 per cent off sale at Landmark to *When Harry Met Sally*. Which, of course, led right back to Nora Ephron.

So here was I, quite a private person in my own way, telling a man I'd met just half an hour ago my secret ambition in life: to be able to write a romantic screenplay some day.

And in return, got to know that Kollywood's sexiest, most sought-after star also had a secret desire. No, not the one concerning the roses and chocolates sitting 5 feet away from me. (I was *dying* to ask, but hey, I am a well brought up girl.) KayKay confessed that he'd rather be knocking a dinner guest speechless with his Spaghetti Carbonara than biffing a villian speechless in a fight sequence. KayKay loved to cook!

KayKay's firm handshake and devastating grin at the end of that First Meeting told me I had a new job.

Of course, 'Tweet Writer' wasn't the silly title that was going to be on my visiting card. That was the top secret part of my job.

My card would say: *Public Relations Executive, KayKay Moving Pictures Company*. And my job description included jazzing up Press Releases, writing out smart answers for magazine interviews (the magazine apparently 'interviews' Kaykay, in his make-up caravan between takes, but what they actually do is: simply send a set of questions to be answered by email; I then chat with KayKay on car rides to shoots, to airports, et cetera, and then quickly write up my own interesting answers in KayKay's voice on my laptop. And often even make up the questions, for some cool answers I want to add.)

And then there were those sudden sound bytes, to be included in radio shows, or in filmi TV programmes. I'd have some 'spontaneous lines' all ready for KayKay to say into cameras and microphones, while entering an awards show, or being interrupted during a red carpet walk to a film opening.

Meanwhile, my family had gone into catatonic shock over my resignation from Citibank. They said I had completely lost my mind with strange Western concepts called 'Gap Year' which only confused drug-addicted American students and hippies took, when they had no idea what to do with their lives.

They nearly had me exorcised by matted-hair mantra chanters, when I declared I was going to work for a film star. When relatives came calling, my parents were relieved I wasn't at home, as they had their own sanitized and respectable story: 'Ambujakshi is just temporarily helping out with some Public Relations communications work for a company in the entertainment sector, till she gets another bank job to her liking…' A face-saving explanation for my own reckless reason for quitting Citibank.

In less than a week, I had eased into my role as the 'secret voice of KayKay'. The head of PR was ecstatic. KayKay himself seemed merely amused that so many people were following his Tweets instantly. When I sent him 'draft

Tweets' for approval, or a concept note for a regular KayKay column, called 'Konversations', or a suggestion for his Facebook page, or a design idea for a blog, most of the time he'd laugh and say 'You're the expert, Ambidextrous Amby!' and carry on with his rehearsals.

I myself was astonished at the power of social media, and was waking up at all odd hours even in the middle of the night, to see which famous celeb was saying what in 140 characters, and how much their followers had grown since the previous day. My love for numbers was back!

No two days were ever the same in my new worklife. With a major blockbuster going on the floors soon, I was in the thick of a massive pre-release campaign—rushing from song recordings to location recces to still photo shoots, scribbling something down in my notepad or tapping into my cell phone notes constantly. My family caught occasional glimpses of me running in or out of my room. My pals thought I had fallen neurotically, pathologically, insanely in love with my new job.

So here was I zipping along in my new shiny white i-10 car towards KayKay's new film, *Facebook Kaadal* (Facebook Romance!) going into the shooting floor at last after weeks of prep. I reached my 'office' for the day: a studio with a massive set design for a modern-day film love song to be picturized with KayKay.

I stood astonished at what had been created all through the night by countless carpenters and painters. Two gigantic laptops, the size of huge theatre screens; one blue and the other, pink—were displaying Facebook pages!

The blue laptop showed the page of 'Sharan' and the pink one, 'Shalini'. Both their glamorous FB thumbnail photographs—each the size of a door—beamed out at us from the left-hand corners of the two screens.

A buzz of electricians and scampering assistants were following orders from a large pony-tailed foreigner, who had specially come from Hollywood to supervise this unique set and special effects. Repeating in Tamil whatever the white man said in English, was the tiny 5 foot 4 inch film director Pallanisami—who had a reputation for huge block-busters much bigger than his small frame would have you believe.

I had to sit down on the nearest plastic chair to get over this scenario.

Of course, not surprising that our diminutive imaginative Director-saar had come up with this unique love-song idea; after all it was a modern-day version of his earlier famous song-and-dance sequence that even I could clearly remember from my childhood days. In that late 80s hit film, the leading pair had pranced romantically around gigantic dummy typewriters, set up on a beach. If I recall correctly, the song began with the hero first sitting in a Typewriting Institute (Ah! our low-tech 80s!), day dreaming about the pretty girl in front of him…dissolve to a scene with amazing 10-feet-tall typewriters, constructed and set up on a vast beach…and the hero wooing the pretty girl by leaping on different keys to form the word—what else?—L-O-V-E!

Even as I watched fascinated, the song sequence was being finalized by the dance director with a stand-in hero and heroine. The actual lead pair, busy putting on make-up now, would later jump and twirl on sleek computer keyboards, as directed. I heard that special effects would later dramatically change the gigantic Facebook Status bar from 'Single' to 'In a love relationship' on both the laptops, as the song progressed. What a contemporary and with-it lot our South Indian film Directors still were…

Someone should send Mark Zuckerberg a link to this unique film song!

'*Suda-suda tea*, Madam?' Taking a steaming glass of the 'worst hot tea' as it was proudly claimed to be—the worst described the degree of heat, not the tea of course—I left the studio floor and made my way to the plush make-up vans.

Outside the hero's van was his now popular nickname KayKay, with Krish Kumaar written below in brackets.

About 50 feet away, a huge gaggle of excitable fans was being held back firmly by mustachioed security guards. The fans watched me enviously as I made my easy way past them all, with the security fellows even saluting me, and soon I was inside the air-conditioned comfort of KayKay's swanky retreat during shoots.

'Hey Amby!' said KayKay swivelling around his chair. His million-watt smile was enough to light up the make-up area; he didn't really need those array of bright bulbs around the mirror, I thought.

As always, KayKay made a very deep and direct eye-contact with his sensational brown eyes, with whoever he was talking to: from his leading lady to a chai-server to an inquisitive journalist to a demented fan…to me. Was it a trick he'd developed as a star, or was he born with it? There was something so utterly complimentary about that lock-in look of his; an act that said, *my eyes are listening to you and you alone.*

'Hey Kay!' I said, sitting down, holding on to my glass of tea, still steaming away. 'Have you seen where you're going to be prancing around shortly? It's humungously brilliant! I got bits of the song they were practising your dance moves to…*'Facebook kaadali, status yennadi…?'* Ha ha ha. (Which translated from Tamil to: *Oh Facebook lover, what is your status?*)

'Fabulous, isn't it! I tried to keep a straight face when it was played to me here an hour ago, by the earnest dance director…and we have some cool moves ready for that refrain. By the way, please give me your glass of tea, if you don't mind, and drink this fancy tea-bag thing instead,' said KayKay. This swanky make-up caravan came equipped with a gilt-edged tea service and superior Darjeeling blends, which I gratefully exchanged for my 5-rupee glass of over-sweet, over-boiled chai from the studio floor. I had barely taken a sip of it so far.

KayKay cradled the hot glass of tea in his hands. 'Can't imagine how you like that fancy, weak Darjeeling stuff—now this is real Indian chai! Hmmm, your lipstick marks are here on the rim, Amby, so I shall dreamily sip off the same spot too. Seems right out of a scenario from our film here, what say Ambujax!'

This was ridiculous…I felt a silly unwarranted *thump!* against the ribs around my heart. I hurriedly said, 'Now that's really cheesy, Kay! Save those moves for your pretty leading lady Shamini—and where is she by the way? I saw some frantic faces outside her van while coming here—apparently she's yet to show up for her make-up.'

'Oh, let her take her time, we have a lot of catching up to do anyway, Amby...come...sit you down closer to me here...'

Closer. Dangerous word.

So I safely moved my cushioned stool just a fraction of an inch forward, towards Krish Kumaar—the hottest, coolest star of Kollywood right now, with predictions like '*First Kolly, soon Bolly, next Holly?*', as a popular film rag headlined recently. And I began my day's 'work'. Tweeting for a famous star.

Hey look, if a star can hire a professional make-up man to make his face look better, why not a professional Twitter-girl to make his mind look better?

Not that KayKay didn't have a fine mind (and face) already—but we were there to add some sheen and sparkle and that's a job too. And quite an enviable job at that and it's so today and it's pretty challenging and needs clever brains and a lot of creativity and it's a specialist's job and it's the done thing all over the world and all part of the PR requirement and what's wrong with that and stars would be stupid not to hire an expert for this and it's a regular *writing profession* like millions of other writing professions and...

Whoa! Now and then a stream of defensive sentences about my job would enter my head and gallop away like a runaway horse. Of course, all of the defensive babble above are bits and pieces from several heated conversations with my bewildered folks at home; never really with my friends' circle. Friends cheered me all the way, for my bold move of quitting a bank job I hated, and taking up something that came so naturally to me. Even as my faithful buddies kept the 'secret': that I wasn't just part of KayKay's PR entourage; I was also the person behind all his witty one-liners, blogs and sound bites.

And the rewards of professionalism? 2,97,654 Twitter fans and growing.

'Ambujax…start thinking of how you and I are going to celebrate some round figures approaching soon. Your last night's Tweet after that party got a lot of re-tweets, and some more fans in the bandwagon!' *Hey not bad, KayKay was actually taking an active interest in his Tweets these days.*

KayKay read out aloud what I had tweeted out of his iPad yesterday:

Was at a high society party by the beach. Saw a lot of familiar face-lifts☺.

KayKay roared again, looking at his Twitter page. 'Ha ha! Amby, how did you come up with that diabolical Tweet—even if I may cheese-off Mrs Lovely or Queeny or whatever that hostess's name was, if she ever sees this line. When I arrived at the party, she began gushing like a broken pipe all over me, till you rescued me…'

I laughed too, recalling last evening's event, a lavish beach party on East Coast Road thrown by an ageing society diva with more sparklers around her wobbly neck than there were out in the sky that night.

KayKay, handsome, famous, single, was the perfect film celeb that party-throwing divas craved to have at their posh dos—guaranteeing a good coverage in all the Page 3s that week.

But there was another reason for choosing KayKay for this la-di-da party: the star's secret talent in whipping up Mediterranean food. If there was one thing that rivalled KayKay's prowess as an actor, it was his cooking skills. And Mrs Lovely Malhotra had been the first to capitalize on this little known fact: by cleverly inviting him to a live cook-out by the sea, where KayKay too would wear a chef's hat and have the cream of Chennai eating out his hand, so to speak.

So KayKay had made a reluctant trip out to the sea-facing villa after a full day's shoot, honouring a promise made at a weak moment long, long ago. Two of us from the PR group were expected to be there too, and we had tagged along with equal reluctance, but once there, I found plenty of amusing moments even in the hour that we spent there. The ageing faces of high society ladies propped up with make-up that I saw there also gave me ammunition to send out that somewhat mean Tweet about face-lifts.

Well, there was the other bonus: being blown away by KayKay's deft handling of the pasta counter. A dishy man that cooks! Oooh, how sexy is that...

I have to say I felt a major melting of heart too, along with the melting parmesan on my creamy penne with olives...

NOT that a single person in the world could have

guessed this peculiar squishy state of my heart these days. (Okay—that's not counting Kavi, my confidante).

Getting back to the van, the morning after the cook-out beach party—KayKay was giving me a brief for something that had to go out right away. 'Amby, the PR guys think it's the right time now to release my "look" for this film. What say we Tweet this picture out with my new designer beard that Toni has lovingly art-worked on my face?'

I waited till the suave picture of KayKay's new look popped up on his iPad. Wow! A work of art all right, by Toni, the wizard of hair and make-up—a skilled chiselling and modern rendition of what we once simply called a French beard. I stared at the picture, and wondered what line could go with this.

'Okay, I got this,' I said, tapping out a quick one. '*My new beard is growing on me...#kaykaynewlook.*'

'Perfect!' exclaimed KayKay with a high-five, his exploding laughter filling my happy ears. KayKay should be made a compulsory first row guest at all stand-up comedy shows; he's generous like that with immediate guffaws of encouragement. We attached the picture, and instantly 2,97,654 Twitter fans all over the world knew what Kaykay was feeling about his newly styled face.

'Saar! Shot ready, saar! Director saar is calling to set for doing Facebook dance rehearsal!'

KayKay got up and broke into his characteristic jig, and grinned his devastating grin at me. 'Ready!' he said. 'Come on, Amby, this is one dance you can't miss...'

I have to continue the story of the pursuit of my glam new life a bit later.

Right now, you have to meet two other amazing Writerly People who are waiting in the wings to cross my life, and who you'll be hearing a lot about, and who, in a parallel Writers' Universe, were going through exactly the same career angst as me. They are Bobby Verma and Mini Cherian.

I'll go with Bobby first. Bobby is a girl, by the way…

4

'Not all who wander are lost.'

DON'T JUST KISS AND MAKE UP.
MAKE-UP AND KISS.
Smooches without smudges! New Bella Lipstick

Bobby Varma, advertising copywriter and recent Cannes Gold winner knew she'd reached that exalted state of Creative Diva-hood, when whatever she presented at a meeting was taken seriously. Even when she was seriously joking.

Bobby (Babita Varma, actually) could tell by the look of mild discomfort in the eyes of the client, the Marketing Manager of Bella Cosmetics, that he thought the same thought of a million clients all over the world, when advertising agencies presented 'catchy' (sic) headlines: 'Hmm…the idea is good but is that line a bit *too* creative?'

While the rest of her colleagues from her advertising agency X-Factor thought: Wow. Bobby's done it again: she's come up with a really smashing ad.

Everyone in her agency's team sitting in the room knew that their stick-in-the-mud client would have very happily settled for a safe headline that went: 'Now in India! Non-smudge lipstick from Bella!' with a close-up of perhaps the actress Deepika pouting her pretty red lips. But then one would need the brains of a cabbage to write such an obvious line; and then there would be the possibility of the client suddenly turning around and saying. 'It's very good. But can you add some punch to it?'

Bobby's commanding height, and her broad-bordered Kanjeevaram cotton saree which made her appear even taller, had already taken the client's marketing team by surprise. It had never occurred to her boss Anil to specify that 'Ms BABITA Varma' was making the presentation. In their typical sexist way, the all-male client team had probably expected a stubble-faced fellow called Bobby in jeans to appear before them.

Bobby wondered whether to put the client out of his misery by showing him the Option 2 and Option 3 layouts of the smudge-free lipstick ads, and then deftly manipulate him into choosing the Option 1 that her agency wanted to run.

How different things had become ever since she won that most coveted Cannes Gold Lion! Despite the pressure it had put on Bobby to perennially produce award-winning work, she found a happy flipside to the situation she could never have imagined earlier: whatever she said in brain-storming sessions in the conference room was now treated with new respect; there were easier nods of agreement whenever she came up with a zany new idea. 'If Bobby wrote it, it must be good.' That was how everything was being judged now.

Bobby Varma, at the age of twenty-seven, had already been stamped 'certified award-getter' in the ad world; not just at the Goa Ad Fest, or the 3 As of I Awards or the Effie's or the Ad Clubs of Gurgaon or Gumidipundi, but at the ultimate Oscars of advertising: the Cannes Advertising Festival in France. A shiny Gold Lion in the Public Service Films category! And thanks to a particularly rich haul for India that year with twenty-eight awards in all, Bobby's face had suddenly appeared in every English TV news channel—her '15 seconds of fame'—as she had held the India flag and waved it about ecstatically with other prize winners on that exalted stage.

And to think she nearly got left out in the scramble for delegate tickets and all-expenses paid trip to the Cannes Festival in her agency.

'Hey, Bobby baby, what would you give to go to the South of France in June for 10 days, feast on the best advertising around the world, and party all night with pony-tailed creative wizards at the gala, even if your film doesn't even make the shortlist?' said Jai, the Head of Client Servicing, who'd popped into her cabin down the corridor.

'I would give my right, copy-writing arm for it...' said Bobby.

'Okay! Prepare to amputate and hand me that arm! Though you may need it to clap at Cannes when your film does make that shortlist, so hold on to it for a while...Because Bobby! You're going to FRANCE!'

In a haze of disbelief, Bobby had rushed home to get her passport, scramble for copies of photos, fill visa forms, in between cracking an idea or two in her head for pending ads, even as she raced for new togs to Anokhi for a smashing new ethnic skirt without even a glance at the price tag. Lucky day! They actually had a skirt that was pretty, and long enough for her large, XL frame. Standing 5 feet 9 inches in her flattest chappals, Bobby still felt like a Queen Latifa in any group, and a possible caption after her win suddenly popped into her head: 'Huge Success at Cannes'. Yeesh!

She even stopped off for a quick teeth-whitening at her dentist (okay, wasn't that being a bit presumptuous here, thinking of herself flashing a smile of victory in the slim, remote, improbable, outside chance of her film actually winning?).

Maybe, perhaps, why not, what if. But a girl's got to be prepared, right?

As it happened, she had to thank her own Head-God of the Creative Department, Anil Prabhu, for this unexpected Cannes bonus. Anil (not-so-secretly known as 'Anal' Prabhu by miffed colleagues, fed up with his famous tantrums) had written a film script for a ketchup which *only* had to be shot in the Tomatino Festival in Spain, and *only* by Tarsem, the world-famous ad filmmaker. But Tarsem's precious dates were *only* available in the exact week of the Cannes Festival—and a kicking and cursing Anil had had to suddenly drop out of the Cannes junket.

So there was one spare delegate ticket up for grabs in her agency: Who would now go instead? The moody, erratic art genius, Ronny Biswas?

Or that new tall chick who did that clever female infanticide commercial, Bobby Varma?

The news had spread fast around the office—largely due to the fact that Bobby had screamed so much when Jai told her to start packing for the trip. There were handshakes, hugs, demands for immediate treats, smiles, cheers, and yells of delight…just as there were looks of utter disbelief, unmistakable eyes of envy, grudging grunts of acknowledgement, and without doubt, uninhibited bitching behind some cabin walls.

Bobby's going to Cannes! *Bobby's* going to *Cannes??*

It had all actually begun when the Goa Ad Fest Gold Award had pitched Bobby's face into the lead story of *Brand Equity*'s 'The Young Unsung'—a feature on five hot new young creative talent in various ad agencies who were still unknown outside their own offices—but names to watch out for bringing in the bling from Cannes later that year. Bobby had been shot against the sea in Goa's Baga beach, in her white shirt and blue capris and huge sunglasses borrowed off a friend in the last moment ('You're a celeb, Bobby! You gottu wear Jolie-type celeb sunglasses now!'). By the time they returned to Mumbai flush with triumph and her agency's first ever Gold in Goa, the local papers were calling her too.

'Mumbai girl says it for the girl child' had headlined the city's *Mumbai Buzz* supplement. They came to take a picture of her at her office desk this time. Out of focus poster of Dilbert in the background. The prize in focus in the foreground. Despite planning to keep a sombre, thoughtful expression for the photographer, Bobby had suddenly laughed into the camera when a bunch of her pals burst into whoops and whistles around her cabin, at the photo session.

Her parents and sister in Delhi were ecstatic when she sent them the link to her story. 'Will it be seen all over the world?' asked her mother. 'You're wearing the dark green top I gave you! I just knew it would slim you down,' said her sister. 'Beta, did you get a raise?' asked her banker father.

Oh yes, she had. She had also got secret calls by head-hunters, asking her to send her resume at once 'as some hot agencies were looking.' In fact her raise may well have been in anticipation of calls from those poaching head-hunters…Meanwhile came the reshuffle on Creative Teams and Accounts. Bobby's name in all the most exciting brands to work on. Bella Cosmetics. Audi cars. Rowntree Chocolates. Capri Time-Share Holidays. Samsung New Products. Bobby was on a roll…

'Helloo? What's with that faraway look, Bobby?' asked Jai breaking into her thoughts at Pizza Hut. Bobby looked startled. 'Why, nothing…nothing at all, Jai…'

'Oh come on, Bobby, you're as transparent as a Lady Gaga costume. What's biting you?'

'My film, that's what biting me!' blurted Bobby in a sudden fit of confession. 'It hasn't run on a single main line channel yet, despite my daily fight with the media guys. Just in some unknown bloody midnight channel that's as much viewed as the back-side of the moon…'

'So what do you care, my winning wonder. It ran. Therefore it's not a scam. The only friggin' rule that rules our ad world contests all over the world.'

'Well, it's not just that, Jai,' said Bobby. 'There's something else about that film I made that er…that I, hmmm…I feel sort of, er…'

Suddenly Bobby wondered if she had gone insane. Why was she subjecting Jai of all people to this Confessions of an Advertising Woman? Jai who woke up every morning, went to sleep every night completely focused only on awards, awards, awards?

Whereas Bobby went to bed every night with an odd sense of regret over her potential international winner, for inexplicable reasons. Well, pretty explicable, actually if she put hand on heart and was honest about her sense of unease.

'Holy moly, Bobby!' yelled Jai, suddenly. 'Did you COPY this idea from somewhere? Tell me, we'll destroy every copy of that One Show Annual, The Creative Black Book…'

'WHAT! Jai I shall impale you with this two-pronged fork and feed your blood to dehydrated chameleons. Are you crazy? COPY an idea for a film? How dumb can you be to think how dumb I could be? NO, Jai. It's 100 per cent an original idea from my own head. But, er…hell forget it! Who's game to drive to Ice Station Zebra for dessert?'

And late that night the real reason for that unease came back to haunt her.

As her advertising world saw it, Bobby had made a startling film to change attitudes towards the girl child. Terrific. Only all those depraved monsters and son-worshipping bigots who mindlessly killed girl foetuses and who *needed* this change of attitude wouldn't have understood one single frame of that 30 seconds of esoteric, profound, hauntingly lit, aesthetically edited, brilliantly subtle example of an intellectual art-form called an award-winning public service ad film.

This truth made Bobby cringe with guilt.

But then came all that buzz in so many websites and magazines. Industry experts placing her film amongst 'strong contenders from India to win this year'.

And then came the unexpected turn of events with her boss Anil dropping out. And then came Cannes. And then came The Gold.

And then came the angst…

Her mom's phone call only rubbed it in further. 'It's a very nice film, Bobby, and I am very very proud of you, beta…and so many people in our building saw the film too, but I didn't understand it fully when they showed it in NDTV news. But don't worry, I'm sure all clever ad people will love it. And Papa wants to know, did you get another raise?'

Raise? Oh yes. A big big one. She also found herself with a very big low.

It was a low that hovered around for weeks. Her own mother hadn't understood the film. Her neighbour in the lift hadn't understood the film. Her office receptionist Julie hadn't understood the film. Okay, the film was not meant for them. Well then, was it meant for Ram Pyaari in a backward village of Rajasthan who ought to feel a pang of remorse for her earlier actions, and celebrate the next female that emerged from her body?

And now here she was, newly elevated to Creative Group Head of X-Factor Advertising, making the Bella Cosmetics annual campaign presentation. Wondering whether her own decidedly cheesy headline about 'Make-up-and-Kiss' was the one out of all the alternatives presented, that the client would say: 'Go ahead with it! I love it!'

Well, of course, the client did—after half an hour of skilled persuasion by her team.

In the lift going down after the presentation, hi-fives were exchanged. In the office, more hi-fives with her art partner who was already contacting a model co-ordinator for the shoot with Deepika Padukone.

But. The genuine high came later, much later, that evening going home. And it had nothing whatsoever to do with her advertising skills…

A 12-year-old's scruffy face grinned at Bobby through her taxi window. A tiny traffic-light books and magazines salesman on his daily rounds. 'Books, madam? Cheffery Aarcher book, madam? Magazine latest? *Femina, Outlook Traveller*? Condy Nasty?'

There it was! Her article in a magazine. *Eat. Pray.*

Louvre. By Babita Varma. Announced right on the cover page of a glossy travel monthly. Her fabulous discovery of Paris, in the extended holiday she took, immediately after the Cannes excitement.

Bobby's heart raced as she lowered the window, simultaneously reaching in her purse for a 100-rupee note to buy a copy from that grinning child, before the traffic light changed. (Jai asked later: 'Did you know you were supporting child labour by buying that mag? Baaad girl…') but Bobby's heart was hammering, flipping the pages till she got to her story. Her first published article in a swanky glossy. Not an advertising magazine. A TRAVEL magazine.

This is the writing that I was meant to do, *born* to do—not for matte lipsticks and milk tetra-packs.

This is the writing I want to do, love to do.

And that's how a brand new career path—Travel Writing—revealed itself to Bobby.

Okay, so you now know a bit about me, Amby (the banker quitting everything to be a writer).

And a bit about Bobby (advertising-copywriter, craving to be travel writer).

And again, before we go any further with me or Bobby, we have to see what's going on in the life of another kind of writer, Mini Cherian.

Not that I or Bobby or Mini even knew of each other's existence at that point of time…

5

'If you love life, it will love you right back.'

Violets are blue
Roses are red
If you wake up in a cemetery
It means that you're dead

Mini Cherian chuckled seeing her neat handwriting in the dog-eared diary. Did she really write this poem when she was just nine? Dark!

Mini was flipping through the old 'Indian Overseas Bank' diary, the one her grandfather had diligently collected at the start of the New Year 1999—part of an annual ritual when he'd visit three banks in the vicinity, and extract his promised free diaries for the year. 'Anything with broad lines' was always given to Mini to write her poems in, and Mini had filled up the fat diary with her prolific output of verse—sometimes nonsensical, sometimes profound, and usually outrageous, but perhaps not as Wordsworthian or Keatsian as her sweet literary grandfather may have imagined she was secretly scribbling away.

On the cover, Mini had even written an appropriate title for her book of short verse: *Mini-atures.* Hmm, not bad a title, even though the descriptor line below it: *Short*

& Sweet Rhymes was barely visible as it had been firmly scratched out with her black felt pen at some point of her teenage years.

Short & Sweet. Yetch! How Mini had balked each time someone described Mini herself with this saccharin sweet cliché. Years ago, when it had become apparent that Mini's petite legs wouldn't grow any longer, and the only way to increase her full-grown height of 5 feet 1 inch was to make her curly mass of hair stand up as far as it would go, Mini had had to accept the fact that her name was both a proper noun and adjective. All her parents' fault of course, for not choosing a name more powerful; like Maxima, for instance. She'd been doomed to remain tiny, just so that millions of people could believe how witty they were by saying, 'Mini is just like her name: Short and sweet!'

And of course this clichéd observation had happened all over again last night at Mini's latest book launch at Crossword. After the Chief Guest, a TV personality, Aakaash with-no-last-name, had 'released' the book from its red-ribboned trappings, a thunder of applause by clapping kids and beaming parents had broken out. And a fresh round of cheers as those expected words emerged from Aakaash's smiling face: 'I now call upon our best-selling children's book author, for a peek into what we've all been waiting for, *the short and sweet Mini Cherian!*'

And Mini had then tried to look as 29 years old as possible, wobbling on to the podium in her new Metro Shoes 5-inch stilettos (even as the large adoring crowd in the hall may have placed Mini's age at somewhere between

17 to 18). Mini had held up her colourful new book *Bak-Bak and Chup-Chaap*, the adventures of two crows, one manically talkative, and the other profoundly quiet—and then signalled her actors, two children costumed in splendid crow-heads hiding behind a book rack, to 'fly in' on to the stage to enact a funny 5-minute episode from the book.

As expected by her beaming publishers, more than a hundred books had sold that day. A long queue of eager parents and kids waited patiently in line for a personalized book signing. And boy, did that take time! While signing her own name consumed just half a nanosecond, writing out the full name of each child had driven her batty...what's with parents these days, searching in our ancient epics or delving through exotic ragas for multi-syllable tongue twisters like Ashvatthaman—that's with two Ts—Dakshayini, Neelambari, Suryavansh...

Mini had then mingled with her target audience over the tea party funded by the bookstore. The media had trouble trying to locate her in the crowd, as she looked hardly any taller than the bunch of 6- to 8-year-olds, the prime target for Mini Cherian's books.

'There you are, Mini!' said her dad, just as she was handing over an orange juice and brownie to a fat kid, who'd come back for his fourth helping. 'The TV guys have finally arrived! They've been shooting and interviewing some parents and kids too. Even I spoke into the camera, Mini...I told them nowadays hot cakes are selling like your books...ha ha.'

Mini reluctantly followed her father, and she could see

the startled change of expression on the cameraman's face as her over-6-foot lanky father led his dimunitive offspring past the brownie-hogging masses of kids, and proudly presented her. 'Here's the author of *Bak-Bak and Chup-Chaap*!'

Oh God, what on earth had her mad and crazy dad said to these guys, wondered Mini, even as she forgot every single line she had rehearsed that morning. She noticed the fat kid stuffing brownies had eagerly followed her and so most of the interview had gone with Cake-faced Kid jumping up and down behind to get into the frame too.

'Here, why don't you ask this little gentleman his views on reading?' said Mini, pushing the brownie monster forward into camera view—trying to flee back into the crowds.

'Wait, Miss Cherian! Just a few more questions…A parent here says your book on two crows is a "return to the innocence of reading illustrated books with an underlying moral content too." Was that your motive for writing this book?' Now what was that her publisher had particularly wanted her to say at book launches? Mini wondered. Oh yes. 'Engaging books like *Bak-Bak and Chup-Chaap*, about two funny, eccentric crows, will hopefully counter many young kids' obsession with Angry Birds on their comps…'

Mini faithfully parroted what her editor and publisher thought (Mini had actually written this book simply because she loved crows). But the reporter seemed so pleased with this answer. 'What's your next book going to be, M'am?'

A reluctant Mini was back under the cameras. 'Tell them about your childhood *Book of Verse*, Mini,' whispered her dad from her side, even as she was mumbling, 'I really have no definite plans yet...'

Too late. The camera moved onto the eager interviewer, who was already saying, 'And now Mini Cherian's fans will be delighted to hear this: coming up next is *Book of Funny Verse*, which she actually began writing when she was 8!' Mini whirled around to see her grinning father—oh God! When the hell did he tell them this? Or was it her over-enthusiastic publisher?

Mini tried to regain her composure as the cameras moved to her again and said, 'Oh that! Maybe my current readers are not yet ready for that one!' She'd definitely strangle Dad later for telling them this silly piece of information without her permission whatsoever.

Before her dad could tell them more about her nonsensical childish prattle written in old bank diaries, Mini quickly said, 'Well, maybe it's something I'll keep for when I'm about 80, when kids would have had enough of whatever digital ways stories directly enter their brains, and they go back to discovering a nostalgic way their grandparents once consumed books—by actually reading them.'

The TV crew seemed pleased with that ridiculous response. 'Tell us the title of this poem book, Miss Cherian!' they persisted.

'*The Book of Worse*' said Mini on an impulse.

And after even more face-ache-inducing smiles and juice-sticky-handshakes and brownie-faced hugs, Mini and her dad had escaped for dinner to their favourite Gujarati restaurant: their standard celebration haunt for every important event, The divine aam-ras put her back in such good humour, she gave up plans of strangling her father, the blabber-mouthed proud parent.

And while getting into bed exhausted late that night, Mini suddenly jumped up. Hey, where *is* that crazy old book of verse? Mini perched precariously on a stool in the middle of the night, and reached in the loft above for that school bag stuffed with notebooks and diaries—searching for that precious old Indian Overseas Bank diary again.

There it was! MINI-ATURES. Mini shook the dust off and began to read out some random 4-line verses loud, and chuckled over the grim twists her lines had usually taken in the last line. What kind of kid was she, with this sense of the macabre at the tender age of 9? She read out another one that she'd completely forgotten she'd written:

When Ben met his doc
He went in coughin'.
When Ben left his doc
He went in a coffin.

Ha Ha Ha! Obviously her dad had completely forgotten how viciously wicked some of these poems were, even if he'd been telling her for years to 'dig out those gems you wrote when you were nine or ten, Mini!'

Well she could be likened to her own childhood idol Enid Blyton then—a writer of innocent childrens' books to an adoring world, but with a dark side to her that people discovered years later.

So now here she was: firmly cast into a mode of author of 'wonderful children's books that we parents enjoy buying as much as our kids love reading them...' and other horrendously kindly tributes she'd been hearing over and over again for the last few years.

Mini knew her own petite childlike appearance hardly helped much. (Wearing a sophisticated shade of red lipstick and brown eye-shadow to the launch event had somehow made her look like she was dressed for a school play, rather than transform her into the 29-year-old she'd hoped to look).

And in a few hours, the Friday Metro papers would be carrying her picture with her latest book, surrounded by those pesky grinning kids, some even taller than her for sure. '*Bak-Bak and Chup-Chaap'*: Mini Cherian's new book for kids has much to crow about...would probably be its expected review.

And then Mini fell asleep dreaming about another kind of book she secretly hoped to write. What was that thing she'd read in *10 Tips to Kick-Start Every Would-be Writer*? One of them was 'Imagine and write down pithy one-liners that critics and reviewers may write about your finished book...'

So Mini, settled back on her pillow, started writing out imaginary reviews of her scandalous new book in her head:

'Freewheeling unabashed sensuality...'

'Steamy...till the very lust page of the book...'

Proper Grown-up Writing! No kiddy-widdy gibberish any more from Mini Cherian!

Wondering blissfully what her brand new and exotic pseudonym would be for her sensational foray into adult-novel-writing (obviously 'Mini Cherian, former bestselling author of kids' books' would never ever be appropriate), Mini drifted off into sleep.

And that's how Mini's new path to Grown-Up Writing began to take a definite shape.

So there you have it—three wannabe writers whose lives were going to get suddenly interlinked, thanks to cyberspace and a superior force at work.

Amby Balan, the much-envied ghost Tweet writer for a famous film star.

Bobby Varma, the much-envied Cannes-winning advertising writer with dreams of giving it all up for travel writing.

Mini Cherian, the much-envied bestselling children's books writer nursing a secret dream of writing for an entirely different audience.

Each of us living and breathing our dreams in three different cities: Chennai, Mumbai, and Bangalore. Each of us being frequently told by friends: 'You really have the BEST job in the world!'

Like I said, not one of us had any clue about the others' existence in this world—till an online pop-up ad on each of our computer screens brought us all together. On a magical faraway island.

6

'As you start out on the way, the way appears.'

YOU'RE A WRITER.
ABOUT TO BECOME WORLD-FAMOUS.
AND IT ALL BEGINS RIGHT HERE...

And below that enticing line, a luscious visual, urging us to click on...

A girl with a laptop, staring out into the Aegean blue, from a waterside café in Crete, Greece.

It was a manic Monday, and there I was, right in the middle of catching up on my 'homework'—Shah Rukh Khan's latest tweets (I always keep close tabs on KayKay's Tweeting competitors). That's when that pop-up banner above slyly appeared on the right of my screen. Writer? Famous? Greece? All three were trigger words for me, coming together all at once. Of course, that had me instantly hooked onto the Creativity Workshop advertisement—I succumbed, and clicked.

'AMBUJAKSHI! Didn't you say you had to be in Kodambakkam by 11? It's 10.45 already and your dosas are still lying cold on the table!' My mother's scolding voice climbed up the staircase, got past my room's closed door, to smack me on my ears.

With horror I realized I had been wandering about in a state of demented glee for over an hour at this website,

Creative Awakenings, and rushed right out of the house before my mother could corner me to eat breakfast. I replaced it mentally with a huge bowl of Greek salad with feta cheese, waiting for me in an exotic island, far far away from my predictable Tam Brahm dosa-chutney fare.

A Creativity Workshop in Greece for destined-to-be-famous writers! In that opening paragraph they were describing me, of course, even if they never actually used these words, 'Are you currently a ghost Twitter-Writer? Making a film star famous? Be a bestselling writer in your own right; get the fame *you* deserve!'

Well, what they did do in that attractive website was describe a person full of great writing potential, full of dreams to become famous, needing just the right push by established writing experts—at an extraordinary workshop set in the capital town of Chania, in Greece's largest and most beautiful island, Crete.

The dates for the 14-day workshop were 6 whole months away, but by signing on now, there'd be a saving of 100 euros, said a starburst on the home page.

Sitting undisturbed in my car, I quickly began checking out my iPhone for course fees and places to stay in Greece. Steep! But I knew I was going, no matter what the current scary exchange rate for euros to rupees was. I had to, I deserved to, I had worked for this, I had saved for this...I realized I was actually constructing arguments in my head for my family, who would begin to wonder if their daughter had become a rampant serial-job-quitter.

And despite the huge relief they may feel that I was dumping my mindless filmi job at last (a job that had been going on now way past that Gap Year), my plan to bust tens of thousands in a single fortnight on some fancy writing course was going to have them summoning new gods from the Hindu pantheon to make me see reason.

I could practically script out the dialogue for my dismayed parents.

Pa: Chania in Greece? Never heard of it. I am sure this is a fraud money-making idea; what is the sign-up fee they are asking for? I'm sure it is not refundable too. Just forget it!

Ma: But how can you just go away in the middle of the wedding season, kanna? Stop talking rubbish!'

Pa: Why Greece? Do you know how disastrous things are in the Greek economy just now? What did you do Economics Honours for anyway? Even now, I'm telling you—just get back to your good Citibank job; our new neighbour's brother-in-law works for the Treasury, and he too was shocked you'd quit the bank, and I've already given him your earlier resume, and…'

Ma: And when are you going to allow us to take the Seshadri proposal forward? I am warning you, this fine catch will just fly away…now you can keep that Greek-sheek holiday plan for your honeymoon, okay? Anyway, it's not nice for a young girl like you to just go off to a strange country all by herself…'

Young girl! Well just the other day it seemed like I was really really *old* at twenty-eight, according to a phone conversation my mother was having with her sister. What to do with this Ambujakshi's *ashattu pidivadam* (an evocative Tamil phrase for acute stubbornness)? Still unmarried, and nearing thirty; brilliant academic record, excellent family, but what was the use…I had foolishly given up my prestigious MNC bank job, and under the influence of bad company, was now working strange hours and hanging around with the 'low life' in the film industry of all things. Too shocking a profession to admit to the Iyer community, from which 'excellent matches for successful IT grooms from the US' continued to pour in…

Midway through my ride to Kodambakkam came a message from the PR unit that shooting was cancelled for the day, because of a massive power cut. So I sent off a quick message to Kavi to join me later for a cold coffee at Amethyst—the only place to be for its free Wi-Fi, and more importantly, for some semblance of breeze, as the heat was beginning to melt several parts of the brain, making further plotting of my confused life impossible.

Why was I running away to Greece, actually?

I hadn't confronted this question yet, but I was quite sure that when I told my confidante Kavi about this mad plan to change tracks all over again and join a writing workshop in a faraway island, she'd cotton on at once, and ask me some uncomfortable questions. About my *real* motive for running away from my job.

Chennai has a glorious past. A fabulous future. But no current #goddamnpowercuts

'Amby, that was quick! What would I do without

you?' KayKay's guffaw rang through on my cell phone, seconds after I had texted him this power-cut line 'for approval', to send out as his next Tweet. In Kodambakkam, apparently, the heat was making tar ooze out of roads. With busted generators and blown fuse boxes, film shooting had been abandoned for the day, and KayKay, chilling in his generator-backed AC make-up van, had messaged me for a Tweet on 'something to do with the lousy power cut.'

Writing that line was easy. Telling KayKay he'd soon *have* to do without me wasn't going to be—or was I being foolishly vain? He was KayKay after all and could hire some other ghost writer with a snap of his manicured fingers.

I ended the call, and I guess I looked a bit flushed—who wouldn't when South India's Hottest Star sends a kiss through his cell phone onto the lobe of one's left ear?

Kavi looked at me most amused, as we sat sipping our lattes at Amethyst. 'You're blushing like an apple orchard in May. So what did your *amoreux* say to you just now, Amby? And have you planned when you are going to break the news about Greece, and simultaneously break his heart too perhaps?'

'Shut up! He's no amorous lover, are you crazy? And no, Kavi. I really thought I should let him know right away that I have this Greece plan, 6 months ahead, but I needed to talk it through first with you. Anyway, I won't be meeting him today. There's a Boutique Opening and Fashion Show tomorrow; I'll tell him just before that. Or after that, actually. Or should it be somewhere in-between, very casually, in the middle of a conversation? Or what's the big hurry? Maybe a couple of months later...Oh feck, Kavi! WHAT am I going to say!'

'Well, whatever you do, don't Tweet him your break-up line, like that jerk Kunal did to Aarti. He sent her an sms implying it's all over between them, can you believe it!'

'Oh don't worry, I plan to be very matter of fact and cool about it. I'll just act my natural self...'

Which led to a sudden 'stand-by' Tweet that popped into my head: a stock of snappy one-liners related to actors and show business, or a pithy comment on life—I keep these ready for KayKay to send out at random. *Act natural. Now that's the best oxymoron in show biz...#nobizlikeshowbiz*

I typed this to store away into my iPad's notes marked KK Standbys; which made me wonder whether I should first keep a bank of about a Thousand Smart Lines for KayKay, and only then declare I was quitting my job as Chief Tweeter/Status Updater/Blog Writer/Smart-comebacks Writer for KayKay, the Super Tweeter.

But did KayKay really need me as I thought that he thought that he did? Kavi burst my bubble.

'Amby, don't kill yourself wondering how to tell KayKay. And don't worry, he won't be hiring another smart thinking Tweet-spouting gal just like you; KayKay will Tweet his own 140 characters like he should. You think he hasn't got the hang of it, just hanging around you? Life will go on fine for him without you...'

Kavi can be a cruel best friend to have sometimes.

Well, if Kavi saw some of the texts KayKay had been sending *me* and me alone over the past few months, she'd have even more reason to believe he didn't need ghost-writers.

Like the one he sent me when he was on a crowded stage, and he spotted me entering the far end of a jam-packed noisy hall, at a film's music release: *Beep!* went my cell and I read: *Looking for a quick release myself...*☹. Our eyes had met across 600 heads and laughed together.

Or. That other one he sent when I was sitting just 10 feet away, at the most boring script reading by a producer's team. KayKay texted me midway, even as he feigned great interest in a terrible storyline: *The director should shoot the script-writer, rather than the movie.*

Or how about *that* one, when I was actually sitting right next to him, at the front row of a fashion show. My bare arm touching his black silk shirt. *Mmmm. Someone here is smelling extremely dangerous. Wonder who??* ☺

Or. That loaded one. This was a handwritten note actually; I really shouldn't have run with it to Kavi's house to show her, but I thought it might amuse her.

You smiled in your sleep just now. Tell me more about him...

'AMBY! He watched you *sleep*? Waitwaitwaitwaitwait. WHEN did this happen??'

Well, who am I kidding? I had shown it to Kavi because I wanted to show off a bit; show off how creative (read romantic) KayKay could be himself. He'd actually drawn a picture of a cell phone on a paper napkin, and on the screen part of it, handwritten the 'text' above, and held it up to me.

When I woke up. Next to him. On a *plane.*

Since cell phones are switched off in a plane, this was his way of texting me mid-flight. Even as I had inadvertently dozed off on his shoulder (what did those gushing airhostesses who welcomed us aboard think?) on our way back after an exhausting music promo trip to Bangalore.

'Amby—you know what this means? You have now "officially" slept with him!' cried the incorrigible Kavi.

When some magazines started featuring stories on the power of social media, and how every smart and articulate film star was using these so brilliantly, I used to feel pretty smug and smart and articulate myself. Especially when many of my lines, I mean *his* quotes, got re-tweeted and re-re-tweeted. But when an opinion poll indicated that KayKay was among India's top three wittiest film stars, a funny kind of angst was beginning to set in.

Hey, those were my lines.

And then there were those days when KayKay would disarm everybody with a very quick comeback. *Not* written by me.

Like when I saw his face pop up on a local TV channel, coming out of a big celebrity wedding in the city, while I was at home nursing a bad cold. A chirpy TV reporter from *Kollywood Kalling* had caught him as he was leaving, and asked him, 'KayKay Sir, what kind of wife are *you* looking for!' To which KayKay had flashed his smile and said: 'I'm looking for a single girl actually. I really don't want another man's wife!'

Now that would lead to a strange mix of emotions: I'd

be hit with sudden admiration, and faintly upset too, that he came up with a clever thing to say, entirely on his own…

Kavi was so bloody right. Life would go on for KayKay…

By the next day, Part 1 of revealing my audacious Greece Plan was done. I told my parents in a scenario full of drama which went pretty much as I had scripted it in my head, reinforcing that I could write authentic dialogues for my forthcoming screenplays.

Now for Part 2. Telling KayKay. Maybe immediately after the rehearsals for the Chennai Fashion Week show, where KayKay was walking the ramp for the finale.

We were all at the Hyatt with a buzz of models and designers and press people for the final rehearsal before the big show in the evening. KayKay's voice broke into my thoughts. 'Wassup, Ambujax? You seem to be in another planet today…everything okay?'

Oh yes, I was very very far away…in a Mediterranean island. And not everything is okay, Kay. Especially as I don't know how I'm going to tell you I have to leave you soon….what I mean is, I have to leave this job *of mine soon…I need to go to Greece, Kay!'*

'Everything's cool, Kay!' I said instead. 'Just didn't sleep enough last night. I accidentally stumbled on *When Harry Met Sally* again on Star Movies—watched it for the umpteenth time till 3 a.m.'

Wait. My Workshop was six whole months away. I

would do the telling when I wasn't so wound up. As I followed KayKay into the hotel's banquet hall for rehearsals, I was trying to rehearse something myself too: a matter of fact declaration of my new plans in life, and how to say it firmly, unemotionally, to my celeb boss.

Probably the same way that Bobby Varma, advertising copywriter, was struggling too—for the right words to put in her resignation letter, after a fit of disenchantment with her job in Mumbai.

7

'I love my job. It's the work I hate.'

YOU'RE A WRITER.
ABOUT TO BECOME WORLD-FAMOUS.
AND IT ALL BEGINS RIGHT HERE...

The words from that enticing pop-up banner on her comp rang through Bobby Varma's head all through the day, sometimes even drowning out the words of the inane ad jingle that was being sung and re-sung for Sowbhagya Weekly Lottery. Bobby waited for the music director to declare 'Yexcellent!' to the singers, bringing an end to the torture; instead it was the inevitable: 'Please, one more take, vokay va?' Just as he'd been doing the whole last hour in this crammed recording studio.

Oh no, here we go again! Even though the main song was in Kannada, promising quick wealth with a single ticket of Rs 10, the end of the song retained the English slogan that had been this lottery's famous baseline for over twenty years; announced by a squeaky voiced child: *Weekly Quickly Lucky Lakh!*

Bobby thought, some day I'll track down this voice-over child (now surely a full-blown grown-up) and silence it forever with a heavy blunt instrument.

What the hell am I doing here anyway? Bobby wondered, supervising a crazy regional language radio jingle, when she didn't know the language herself? Shivering in the over-chilled dark studio, Bobby closed her laptop, fed up with the flaky internet connectivity that was taking her nowhere, and shut her eyes to escape to another dream world with blue waters, blue skies…

Blue, brilliantly blue Greece.

She couldn't wait to get back to the office and log on again to that delicious-looking website that had teased her from the screen—the Writer's Workshop in Greece. An advertising girl, a victim of advertising!

Two hours later, Bobby was racing into the lift at her office, X-Factor. 'Where have you been all day, Bobby?' A frantic client-servicing executive looked relieved seeing her step off the lift. 'Tried a zillion times on your cell—we need those alternative baselines for the bank, or can we just go with our client's suggested line, Bobby? Pleeease?? All our launch ads are being held up…'

Oh Jeeez. 'My cell was switched off, recording your horrendous Lottery radio jingle…and for God's sake do whatever you want with your client's baseline. I give up!'

Bobby's colleague had that constipated look of a guy who didn't know whether to push forward or backward, and stood rooted in indecision as Bobby whirled away, back to her cabin. Bobby generally never threw those annoyed Creative Director vibes at junior client-servicing people—like those other cabin-walas did, but this battle for a baseline had gone on for two weeks, and even someone like Bobby had had enough with the client servicing chaps on Acme Bank. Who wouldn't, after being made to do a dozen variations on 'Caring for you…always'? Who reads baselines, anyway? Who cares, anyway?

Apparently the bank. Always.

Sitting down at her desk again, Bobby wanted to suddenly laugh at the whole moronic issue of baselines—how clients got their chaddies in a twist, wanting what someone else already had—with a profound variation you wouldn't be able to see even with the vision of Superman.

In fact *Caring for you dot dot dot always* should become, by law, the one commonly shared baseline around the world for gazillion products ranging from nappies to hair-lice medications to toe-nail clippers to instant momos to industrial valves…(not forgetting banks) who wished to evoke an image of smiling, soft-hearted emotionally wrought and teary eyed service providers waiting like mothers to hug us into their ample bosoms and 'care for us'. What Bobby's pal Zac would call 'creating advertising with a condom on it'; or, let's-play-safe ads.

'Lottery Radio Spot done, Bobby? Hey, thanks so

much for that one—my client is going to feel happy you sat in on the recording…' Jai popped in and out of her cabin, but just the mention of the radio spot made that shrieky end of jingle line invade her head again. *Weekly Quickly Lucky Lakh!*

And hey, maybe I should pick up a lottery ticket today myself, thought Bobby. A lucky lakh would be most handy to say cheers-bye to this stressed-out advertising copywriter life—and click click! fly far far away to this blue paradise.

Crete. Largest of all the Greek islands. To sit there like this gal in a sea-front café, crafting evocative phrases to make a reader feel that were right there too. Even as a giant marker from the sky appeared and changed her destiny, obliterating the words 'Advertising Copywiter' next to her name, and firmly write in its place, 'Travel Writer'.

Babita Varma. Travel Writer.

Bobby mentally began designing a cool new visiting card for herself.

Bank Gothic? BABITA VARMA. TRAVEL WRITER.

Or her good old favourite American Typewriter?

Babita Varma. Travel Writer.

Or…why not keep her own bold signature scrawled right across—*Babita Varma?*

And then she eagerly began to read more details of the Workshop; whether there was a special course for a particular aspect of writing. Travel Writing of course.

Well she did have that one published piece *'Eat. Pray. Louvre'* in an upscale travel glossy already; something she wished she could frame and keep with as much pride as her Golden Cannes Lion decorating her agency's reception area…

'Bobby! Conference Room brainstorm. In 5 minutes!' Oh no! Bobby wished she had hung around the ghastly recording studio a bit longer, and escaped this session altogether. Anything was better than being roped into this 'gang-bang' as Zac called it where all the creativest of creatives of the office—and she was now one of them, of course—would come up with initial thoughts on the upcoming Fairness Cream new business pitch. Quite a challenge—how to be politically correct; promising what apparently every dark-skinned low-self-esteemed girl in India craved for—without landing the ad agency in the dock at the next 'We the People' TV debate, being mauled by enraged women activists.

Ditch that pitch. That's what Bobby wanted to say to everyone. Who the hell wanted to work on a Fairness Cream in these enlightened times, anyway? Simple answer: the manager, the entire client servicing team, and most of all, the chief accountant at the Head Office. Because it was a Rs 14 crore business up for grabs.

Bobby minimized the luscious page extolling 'Why Greece touches every writer's soul…' on her MacBook, and made her way reluctantly into the conference room. Ah, the downsides of a Cannes award win! Bobby, certified award getter, was her agency's Most Wanted. What seemed flattering at first ('Can we have Bobby just sit in for a bit on this campaign review? Can Bobby just knock off this brand name for a toffee, as our client has rejected about one million of them so far? Can Bobby just supervise that lottery jingle?') was making her work bizarre hours every day.

And then there was this other stupid thing—a nice-girl reputation—Bobby *never* throws attitude.

Right now Bobby wanted to just throw up. Not the greasy medhu-vadas she had eaten at the studio, but her job.

The finality of that sensational thought suddenly gave her a burst of manic energy. After this meeting, she'd check the notice period one needed to give to quit. She'd wrap up the animatics for research for that herbal cough remedy, dragging on for months. She'd finish that simple, quirky, 'bound to win an award' film for Insurance, just to give a break to a budding young filmmaker. She'd write 2 million new brand names for that new toffee…

'I knew Bobby would find that conclusion amusing…' Jai's voice in the conference room suddenly broke into her thoughts. Bobby realized with a start that the silly smile on her face had been taken as a reaction to a slide of a large pyramid in that power point presentation. What's with these suits of the office drawing pyramids for everything! Bobby and the rest of the creative guys in the room were looking at the graphic rendition of 'sociological ramifications of fairness cream usage in B2 towns' with the same enthusiasm of a poet seeing an engineering diagram of a double-glazed capacitor. Jai took the cue and brought the presentation to a rapid close. 'Okay guys, storm away! Here are post-its for scribbling every crazy thought—and can someone call Subway? What'll you have guys, sandwiches for all?'

'I'll have garlic rolls with Greek Tzatsiki please,' said Bobby.

Two hours later, Bobby staggered back to her cabin, more determined than ever that The Letter had to be written.

The question: what's the tone of voice? A sentimental 3-para thing, a dear-John letter of break-up, filled with I-love-you-yet-I-must-leave-you kind of emotionally wrenching stuff?

Or. A quick, government job one-liner, with a 'due to personal reasons, I wish to resign from the services of X-Factor, after duly serving my two months notice period'?

Bobby was afraid it would ultimately become the first option. How could anyone who hated clichés end her career in advertising with a clichéd one liner? Sigh. That meant she'd be up half the night writing and re-crafting the sentences, getting soppy with her gratefulness, thanking everyone in sight including the office cat, like an Oscar speech.

And so we leave Bobby with her struggle for words, ending what she thought was a life-long affair with advertising, for a new lover—travel writing...

But it's time to see how that same pop-up online ad for that Greece workshop would throw another young writer's life into a completely new spin.

Mini Cherian. Once-upon-a-time, famed children's books author.

8

'Life has no remote. Get up and change it yourself.'

YOU'RE A WRITER.
ABOUT TO BECOME WORLD-FAMOUS.
AND IT ALL BEGINS RIGHT HERE...

Mini stared at the right side of her iPad. This was definitely A Sign! How come the irresistible 'click here' button had led to a fabulous picture of Greece, just when NDTV news was talking about Greece's election results? How come this ad appeared on the very morning she'd read this cryptic clue in the Times Crossword: 'U in a Greek zoo, drunk (4)' and had filled in 'OUZO' in an instant?

Here it was. The life-changing Workshop of her dreams. Where Mini Cherian, India-famous kiddy book writer would dramatically transform into Mini Cherian, world-famous adult erotica book writer, in just 14 days.

Of course the tame name 'Mini Cherian' would have to go. Her name would have to be far more Erica Jong ish, or maybe an exotic international one-worder; hmmm...Minerva.

Hey, that's not a bad one. Minerva. Goddess of poetry! Wasn't she from Greek mythology? Uncannier and uncannier, these connects to Greece today. Mini rapidly typed in 'Minerva' on Google and found she was from Roman mythology: the goddess of poetry, wisdom, crafts, magic...That was significant enough a connect to have, and the more she thought of it, the more she liked her brand new pseudonym. She could see her first novel, a hot crimson colour jacket, with the title in black, in Braggadocio Italics, perhaps something sinfully irresistible to read, like *'Promiscuities. By Minerva'*. Perfect.

Mini looked again for details of what writers could get out of this Workshop. Of course, there was nothing that flagged off 'Adult Romantic Fiction Writing', but there was this promising line: 'Get kick-started on that bestselling novel that's in your head! Learn the tricks of the trade from established writers of fiction in different genres, be the kind of writer you've always dreamt of being.'

Mini needed some adult guidance now for pointers to at least get away from erotic writing clichés. Such as this short story opener which ran through her head sometimes...

The doorbell rang.

'Madam, did you order a pizza? Or have I come to the wrong house...?'

'I did order it. A very spicy one. But I'm afraid I may not have the cash to pay for it...' she said, already unravelling her bathrobe.

Bye bye talking crows and crayons. Hello carnal chronicles. Greece was calling her for a make-over in her writing...

But. What about a make-over for herself, right now? Standing 5' 1" in her bare feet, with the face of a teenage cherub, it wasn't one bit appropriate for the *Sex and the City* author Candace Bushnell-like personality she hoped to project at book launches, nor suitable for the stark black and white portrait she hoped to have gracing the back of her forthcoming novels.

At least her dad, who gave so much of himself to her all through her life, could have given her a basic necessity: his 6-footer genes. Unfair! She should have at least reached her mother's height of 5 feet 3 inches, and to expect a spurt of growth now at twenty-nine was hopeless. Six-inch heels got killing after a point, and leg-extensions hadn't yet been invented—so she would have to settle for some seductive eye shadow and a haughty, superior expression maybe, to stop looking like a pre-pubescent moron at her interviews…

'Mineeee! Get here at once! Our petunia babies have bloomed!' Mini raced to her bedroom window and saw her father's mud-streaked face looking up from the garden, flushed with joy. 'Be down in a minute, Cheerio!' Mini yelled back. Mini glanced back at the clock in her room. Past 3 already! And Cheerio (Mini's name for her dad, Cherian, so christened when she was 2) was still mucking about the garden, instead of getting ready for the family wedding at the other end of town.

Mini wondered when would be the best time to tell her dad her life was about to head Greece-wards. She could already guess what he'd say: 'Mini! But you are nearly world-famous already! What on earth can a writing workshop teach you? This is for idiots who are still writing school essays; not Mini Cherian, published writer since the age of nine!'

'Cheerio, I'll see those petunias later…time we got dressed! We have to get going to the church in 10 minutes!'

And soon the father–daughter duo would make their appearance at another painful, but unavoidable family wedding. Annoyingly cloying bejewelled aunts (tagged with her father's forgiving phrase: 'well-meaning') would descend on them, with several alliances for that poor thing Mini, nearly 30 now, isn't she? But what can that helpless father, Cherian, do all by himself without a wife, finding a suitable groom for his daughter?

Mini hoped a pearl chain and dangly earrings were enough to add a 'dress up' element to her simple salwar-kameez. Even as her dad was pulling on his only full-sleeved white shirt—'NO tie, sorry Mini, anyway I just can't find the only one I have…'—they were whizzing away to St Patrick's Church in their beloved, ramshackle tempo-traveller. A vehicle used for transporting potted plants was hardly the fancy vehicle to arrive at a fancy upper-crust Malayali Syrian Christian wedding, but the posh relatives were pretty used to this sight by now, father and daughter arriving at weddings as if they were going to the local market.

'You couldn't find your only tie because you used it to hold up a canvas-cover over those orchid beds, Cheerio!' laughed Mini.

'Is that right? You mean I have to get a new tie if you get married some day, Mini? Speaking of which, *molay*—please remember to smile blankly, and repeat sure, sure, of course, of course, and keep moving on, when those aunts descend on us both with marriage proposals. It's just pointless getting into arguments with them any more. So I even practised a fake smile of gratefulness to flash at them this evening.'

Mini looked at her father and laughed again, with a rush of blinding affection. Her mad, mad dad; the best in the whole wide world. Ironically, it was these very same concerned and sympathetic aunts who had bitched so nastily once: 'That worthless Vinod Cherian who doesn't go to "office" even though he's an engineer; just sitting at home all day and doing some gardening or something.'

While his wife Mrs Sarah Cherian went to work. Slogging like a man, poor thing.

And yet, for the world that Sarah and Vinod Cherian built for their little girl Mini, nothing could be better. Sarah, brilliant chartered accountant with a job that kept her on the move with frequent travel. Vinod Cherian, civil engineer who quit his job, as he would rather raise plants. And their little girl.

But who in India had heard of a stay-at-home dad? A house-*husband*?

And the most dismayed and disapproving of all were Mini's grandparents. Both sets of them. While Sarah's own parents thought of her as a 'cold, ambitious career woman, simply neglecting her house', Cherian's parents were embarrassed by their 'foolish son who stopped working and is cooking at home…'

The Cherians couldn't care less what the world thought; and it was in this secure bliss that Mini too grew up in; and why her favourite book was *The Story of the Emperor Penguin*. Here was their own family story! The Mother who worked so hard and went out to secure food for her family. The Father who dutifully and devotedly nurtured first the egg, then the baby, at home.

When Mini's summer project in Class 3, 'My Daddy the Emperor Penguin' was put up on the corridor notice board, everyone was astonished at this 8-year-old's story-telling and drawing ability. Except the disgruntled mother or two standing in front of the notice board. 'Oh, her own father must have helped her do this. You know he just sits at home? Doesn't have a job or anything…'

Because 'Proprietor, Planet Plant' was hardly a job.

Years ago, Mini's father had turned his green thumb into quite an enjoyable pastime, supplying plants for a few homes around the area. The inspired name for this venture was from little Mini, something she came up with when she was just six : 'Cheerio! I thought of a name for your garden: PLANeT PLANT! Written in her crayons in charming multicolours, with a small 'e' so that it almost read Plant Plant, this had in fact become the logo, and later painted onto a board by Cherian himself.

So when Vinod Cherian wasn't out grocery shopping, or ironing Mini's Friday sports uniform, or searching for material for her history project on Egypt, or making notes from TV food shows on new kinds of stuffed parathas, he was busy potting marigold cuttings for delivery to their new neighbours down the road.

When a leading MNC hired Sarah Cherian, her pay nearly doubled. So did the travel. The day Sarah got her appointment letter, the Cherian family went off to eat at their favourite Gujarati restaurant; the one they went to for every kind of celebration, big, medium or small.

Sarah raised a toast, and the three of them clinked their glasses of jeera water together. 'First of all, here's to

Planet Plant! Cheerio, we can now afford to hire you a Chief Assistant Gardener Boy. English-speaking! At last you'll have someone to bully in the garden. And you can start that patch for growing organic vegetables at once.'

Which also led to a series of fortunate events.

Mini's short story 'The Vegetable Wars'—a fight between two armies of vegetables, one bigger and better-looking, with smarter 'uniforms', fortified with chemical pesticides, Chemix; and the other smaller slightly rag-tag army, but fed with natural nutrients, Organix; with the Organix vegetable army emerging triumphant, naturally—won her her first Writing Prize when she was just 8.

And then a talkative lady in Seat 17 B, made that story famous. A woman seated next to Mini's mother on a Calcutta-bound flight said she was always looking for young writing talent for her new publishing venture. Sarah mentioned Mini's prize-winning story. And within 10 months of that lucky meeting, Mini's *The Vegetable Wars* was sitting in Landmark: printed, published and steadily picked up by kids and parents alike.

Mini Cherian. Published Author. Age 9.

As envious parents at school PTAs learnt from the notice board, the school was proud of 'The School's First Ever Author of a Book, a Student in Class 4'. Suddenly all credit went to the father; the parent who was so involved with the child's upbringing and her studies, nurturing her writing talent, while that career-minded mother of hers just cared for nothing more than her fancy job; it's a wonder she hasn't just upped and left them altogether.

Till the day that prophecy came true.

Mini's mother went away on a business trip, and never came back.

Ironically, Mini's father didn't notice a thing when it first came out right in front of his eyes. He was so busy copying down the recipe for pumpkin soup on the TV screen, that the BREAKING NEWS flashing at the bottom of the screen never caught his eye.

Delhi-Blore Flt 101 crash lands

Delhi-Blore plane crash: no survivors

Some things got permanently etched in Cherian and Mini's minds after that. Cherian was rummaging in a basket in the kitchen, wondering if 'one onion' in the pumpkin soup recipe meant a big one, or a lime-sized one would do. Mini was wondering how to use those twirly wood shavings that fell off as she sharpened her colour pencils—maybe make them into skirts for little girls in the collage?

The quiet lady from next door had uncharacteristically burst into the house: 'Mr Cherian! Wasn't Sarah on her way back from Delhi today? Have you seen the TV news?'

Pumpkin soup. Pencil shavings. Both became associated forever with the death of Sarah Cherian.

Late that night, Mini had wondered if the bigger you were, the more tears came out of you...she had felt the wrenching salt-flavoured grief of her father, wetting her own cheeks, her hair, forming a damp patch on the shoulder of her green frock...While she herself, wide-eyed and bewildered, seemed to have dried up altogether.

Cheerio. It's all right. The story will suddenly change now. Mom will be back, she will walk in.

But Sarah Cherian never came back.

Vinod Cherian parked his Traveller tempo alongside a gleaming and swanky Innova at the church compound. Mini looked towards the church in dismay. 'Cheerio! We're late again. The service has already started!'

'But we wouldn't want to disappoint our clan, would we, Mini *molay*? We are expected to be awfully late, for every wedding we are invited to.'

Mini watched her coy cousin Deepa enjoined in holy matrimony with Jacob, though 'matri-money' would have been a better way describe it. Cardamom plantation was marrying coffee plantation, inherited wealth was marrying blue chip stocks, antique Kerala gold jewellery was marrying a 6-bedroom family tharavadu in Kottayam.

The bearded priest was now waving a cloud of incense from censers swinging from his arm, chanting ancient unintelligible verses, prolonging the ceremony even further. 'Why do only Malayali Christians have this strange chant? Our weddings are all Greek to me...'

'It's Syrian, Cheerio!' laughed Mini. 'But you're pretty close...'

Mini was jolted back to her own world. Greek! Another Sign! Why was everything pointing to Greece all through this day?

On the way back home, Mini would definitely have to bring up the topic of the Writer's Workshop.

'Cheerio, speaking of Syrian and Greek and everything…guess where I plan to head off to soon for a Writers' Workshop!'

I'm hitting a pause button here on the lives of Mini Cherian and Bobby Varma—even as they plot and plan and scheme and dream their way to a magical destination by the Mediterranean after taking some life-altering decisions.

Meanwhile, I'm taking you back to a muddled, befuddled, confused, deranged creature called Amby in Twitterland—and the annoyingly handsome king that ruled my life there…

9

'If your ship doesn't come in, swim out to meet it.'

Ironically, I had joined this PR job with one preconceived conclusion about KayKay:

'What a complete loser!'

Good-looking devil and a rocking celeb star with a hot bod and all. But in my mind, an absolute dumbo.

I mean a guy who hires *someone else* to write his Tweets??

Maybe he gets tongue-tied and can't give interesting answers at interviews. And that rumoured highly educated background? Must be one of those 'sports quota' creatures that get into fancy learning institutes but are duds in the personality and word-skills area.

Meeting him face-to-face had, of course, changed that around completely. After getting past the fact that his eyes could melt rocks, and turn sturdy knees to jelly, I could see he was as articulate as they come these days. Now why wouldn't such a person put a mere set of 140 characters together on his own, like a Shah Rukh Khan or a Madhavan did, every day?

To get an answer to that we have to go back a little into KayKay's life when tweets were just bird calls and nothing else.

Right from the age of about 9, KayKay had decided what he wanted to do in life in order to become world-famous. And for his tenth birthday, had even asked for a special present: a box of 100 visiting cards printed specially with his name and profession.

Krish Kumaar

The world's greatest

FOOD TRANSFORMIST

(KayKay had considered calling himself Food Transformer, but transformer sounded too electrical, so he transformed that word itself to transformist).

Whenever uppuma was made at home by his mother, it was never a mere uppuma by the time it reached the table: KayKay had transformed it into Semolina Cakes—a simple trick of stuffing uppuma into small bowls and turning them upside down neatly on each plate.

The idli was never just an idli; it became Cuddly Iddly, with smiley faces on top made with two peppers for eyes and a mouth made of a coriander stem.

Boiled potatoes turned into snowmen-like Potato Wallahs, with a small potato resting on a large potato, and toothpicks for arms.

And chappatis were turned into Chap-Maps, or country shapes; as KayKay's scissors snipped away at a bunch of chappatis, turning them into an Australia, an India, an Africa, or a China. Not a very popular idea with his mother, as many bits of her perfectly round chappatis landed in the dustbin, even as dinner was turned into a family geography quiz, guessing which country each person was eating.

But guests coming home for dinner were quite charmed by his Incredible Edible Egg: where boiled eggs were cut in half lengthwise, and made to look like small white mice sitting around on a plate, a piece of cheese in the middle. Each had a tiny tail made of boiled spaghetti, and yellow eyes of lentil seeds. Which rendered them quite inedible actually (as even non-vegetarians didn't fancy eating mice), even though they applauded the little boy's artistry.

Then cricket completely took over as his number one passion right through the teenage years, and his tenth birthday visiting card became just a funny family anecdote.

But from college days, KayKay began spending many hours in the kitchen again, this time not to 'transform' his mother's cooked dishes, but to actually cook exotic new things himself. Even as his worried parents wondered whether to take him seriously when he said he was now planning to make cooking his vocation in life.

What about his consistent good grades in his B.Com? What about that MBA plan that was to follow? *Cooking?* That's for chokra-boys who were zero in academics!

KayKay began scouting around the internet looking for the best culinary courses around the world, shortlisting Le Cordon Bleu and Lenotre in France as the world famous culinary univs he'd like to go to. Nevertheless, an authoritarian father sent him firmly off to sit for the CAT exams. Considering the bindaas way he went off to do the exam, just to please his dad, KayKay was totally surprised to see he'd actually made it to the interviews.

Meanwhile, Le Cordon Bleu's glossy brochures came in. Over 40,000 euros for the Grande Diplome Course? Whew. Plus living and board expenses. That would be roughly over 40 lakhs. Now where was he going to get that kind of money. Certainly not from an uncooperative dad!

Coming out of the CAT final interview, which surprisingly seemed to have gone pretty well, KayKay made his plan. Why not do that goddam MBA. An IIM MBA was a highly affordable course at under 5 lakh anyway. And then see where that leads to…maybe that high-paying corporate job, marketing one of the top four coveted brands in the industry: sugared water or scented soaps or triple-action blades or instant coffee.

And after a couple of years of wearing this Marketing Professional hat, he'd have saved enough moolah. Enough to fly off to Cordon Bleu and wear a chef's hat instead.

Not that KayKay shared this larger plan in his life with his parents—supremely thrilled that their only brainy, smart, sensible son was finally taking the expected course in life. And rejoiced when he announced his acceptance into the most prestigious of all MBA programmes in the country: The Indian Institute of Management.

And that's how KayKay ended up standing with a bunch of his classmates under a big tree in the vast wooded campus of IIM Bangalore, watching with much amusement, the shooting of a major Bollywood production, *3 Idiots.*

Aamir Khan. Madhavan. Sharman Joshi. Three brilliant, far from idiotic stars had descended on their campus for a month-long shooting stint, along with a huge crew of directors and technicians and actors for what seemed to be a guaranteed block-buster. There was already such a buzz in every film magazine about this film adaptation of Chetan Bhagat's *Five Point Someone*, the bestselling novel about IIT life.

And during an outdoor sequence featuring the three stars plotting some crazy campus caper, KayKay along with his friends decided to generally hang about and watch the proceedings—if nothing else than to report back to his excitable mother, a devout fan of Maddy.

And then something happened. An assistant director on the sets, in charge of the shooting of *3 Idiots*, was panning his camera to take in some of the campus's real student bystanders hanging around the sets, when he spotted KayKay. The rather good-looking face of KayKay.

While a completely unware KayKay continued to chat, smile, laugh, turn left, turn right and walk away back to the hostel, the camera of the assistant director intently focused on this 'face in the crowd' with increasing excitement. What a find! What a face-cut! What a body!

Soon after, a handful of people in a preview theatre were scrutinizing every angle of a student named Krish Kumaar, second year MBA, IIM Bangalore. Several times a man named Pallanisami, a much revered Director of Tamil films, asked for a re-run, or a pause, or a zoom-in. 'Excellent chaaice. And fair also. Is he Naarth Indian?'

'Well saar, he is half Kannadiga, half Maharashtrian saar, but growing up in Madras only, and speaking good Tamil saar…' The talent-scouting assistant director seemed to have done some secret sleuthing too, finding out details about his handsome new find.

'Can he dance?' asked the Director, happy that his long and intensive search for a 'new-face' hero had ended. 'Never mind, tell Shiamak Davar just he must come at once here only, and give special classes to this boy…'

Such was the power of Pallanisami-saar. No one ever said no to anything he asked for. Except Krish Kumaar.

'NO! I have absolutely NO interest in joining the films. No, never, sorry sir—no, no, I can't even just meet you, sir…NO, I'm really sorry. Now if you'll excuse me, I have a class to attend…' KayKay had laughed so hard later telling this incident of a strange phone call to a couple of his pals in the canteen, and that really was that.

Till one day three weeks later, he heard there was a visitor to see him in the main lounge. KayKay saw five men rise the minute he entered, as though he was a political hero of some sort. The man coming forward, hand outstretched, seemed vaguely familiar.

'Good evening Mr Krish Kumaar saar. Myself Pallanisami, Film Director, and how are you, saar? Remember I was speaking to you one day on phone?'

And despite another session of amusement, protests, disbelief, firm refusals, and several polite shakes of head indicating no, no and absolutely NO, KayKay was going back to his hostel room in a daze, staring at a visiting card in his hand ('please call us when you are telling us yes, Krish Kumaar saar') wondering what the hell that unbelievable offer of money was all about.

As he drove off out of the campus on his bike on his fortnightly visit to his cousin in the city, he thought he saw a new sense of respect and awe in the salute of the IIM campus security guards. When he turned to see them talking excitedly among themselves, he wondered if they had anything at all to do with welcoming that celebrity Director saar into the campus, and locating KayKay for that meeting in the lounge.

KayKay's cousin threw back his head and laughed. 'This absolutely beats that story of that fancy woman relentlessly pursuing you to model for *Fair & Lovely*!'

'*Fair & Handsome* if I may correct you,' said KayKay, nevertheless shuddering at the thought. KayKay remembered how some persistent model coordinator from some ad agency had stalked him for over a month, after spotting him at a cricket match—till it seemed she had other intentions too, despite him communicating quite clearly he had no intentions to ever become a model.

But when his cousin heard what was on offer; that is, if KayKay would simply say YES and star in Pallanisami's next big block-buster, he gasped in utter shock.

One *crore?!*

'KAYKAY! This is INSANE! Is this what even brand new stars are paid these days? And don't they want to first check out if you can even act in the first place?'

'Oh, apparently the Director had already found out I've done a bit of theatre and debating and stuff...not that any of it matters in any way; and they even seem to think that my so-called "screen test" is done too—that sly video they took of me without any permission whatsoever, while I was hanging around the *3 Idiots* shoot!'

'Have you told your parents this crazy piece of news?'

'Are you nuts? Only a couple of my pals in my class know, which I now totally regret, as I have been subjected to crazy leg-pulls ever since...' said a nonchalant KayKay, as he and his cousin set out to grab a beer and a pizza.

And then the next day, a Le Cordon Bleu culinary school email arrived, asking if he was still interested in enrolling in the next September intake. And KayKay looked at the fees structure again, and thought about what he'd reply: that he'd probably take up the course in about two or maybe three years from now. After he'd done with this MBA. After he'd accumulated a sufficient bank balance. After a couple of years of slog in Levers or Gillette or Nestle or Whatever...

Or!

How about if he simply picked up the phone and said YES to that bizarre bountiful bag of big money that a certain Pallanisami was dangling in front of him!

A year from now, the film would be done. A year from now his bank balance would be bursting with health. A year and half from now, he'd be in Le Cordon Bleu.

And in a move that created an unprecedented buzz on campus—(and sent his shocked mother off to the family temple to beg the gods to come to the rescue of her imbecile son, and nearly sent his father to the emergency ward of Apollo hospital), KayKay quit his prestigious MBA programme.

And *Kollywood Kalling* broke the news: Pallanisami ends his big search for his new-face for a yet to be named blockbuster.

Krish Kumaar. With a short snappy screen name: KayKay!

'But I was never ever serious about a future in business management anyway, Pa! In fact I told you very clearly I was doing this MBA only to work for a couple of years or so, didn't I? I was always thinking of getting into Cordon Bleu, you know that—so what's the big deal if I make that happen much much faster...'

'But to give up at IIM Bangalore just one year before finishing the course?'

'Because I was NEVER really interested in an MNC firm, Ma! Don't worry, I am not making films my future career or anything of that sort. Just ONE silly film, that's all. Then I take the money and run. And I may still make you proud as Chennai's leading chef...' KayKay winked at his wailing mother, as she applied some holy vibhuti ash on his forehead, after her latest visit to the gods to plead for her son's return to sanity.

As his cousin laughed and said on the phone that day,

his mother would probably expect his first film to be called *One Idiot*—even as she rued the day that stupid film unit had chosen her son's campus to make their stupid film…

And so a new star was born. KayKay. Even as *Kollywood Kalling*, *Ritz*, *Screen*, *Glitterati* and other local magazines splashed the rising new star's handsome face across their cover stories, the director Pallanisami was, in a well thought-out plan, prepping up the 'body of KayKay'. The city's leading personal trainer Dhananjay was acquired to create the mandatory 6-pack, while KayKay's dancing muscles were stretched by Shiamak Davar's trainers, at an intensive crash course in mastering cool Kollywood moves.

There was much hype around the 'accidental discovery of KayKay'. Being an IIM-MBA final year dropout added to the *Ooooh WOW!* with which girls of Stella Maris college read about him in *Chennai Times*' filmi columns.

The build up to his very first film *Chennai Chips* was perfect. The city's leading advertising agency was signed on. A big teaser campaign on what this intriguing title *Chennai Chips* could possibly allude to had everybody guessing. An online contest added to the pre-publicity. What on earth was this all about: Potato Chips? Banana Chips? Or was it Chips at the Casino?

Soon the movie's hi-tech gadgetary and Bond-like action scenes planned gave everyone a clue: Micro Chips! In a wildly imaginative and bizarre tale, Chennai's Electronic City became the place where the greatest minds gathered to create the world's most advanced chips. And

KayKay, the brilliant young electronics genius was pitted against the forces of evil that was out to terrorize the world with a chip that goes missing, capable of unbelievable mass destruction.

Chennai Chips was a box office smash hit, as predicted. Not like the unpredictable KayKay though; who despite his regular assurances to his parents that he was going to be a one-film wonder, and then quit...happily gave in to the flood of film offers coming his way. And signed on his second film: a fun-filled romantic caper this time called *Facebook Kaadal.*

'*I take my films seriously. But never myself!*'

KayKay's astonishing debut success was by now going national, with this cover story headline in *Filmfare*. With the Hindi remake raking in even more than the regional language dubs, KayKay was creating a major buzz in Bollywood too, and rumours were rife about him replacing a well-known tantrum-prone Bollywood star in a hugely publicized coming blockbuster by UTV productions.

Only KayKay's closest pals from IIM Bangalore knew exactly what that meant, when KayKay said 'he didn't take himself seriously'.

At first he was so refreshingly different from other ego-infested heroes and heroines one had to constantly deal with, but now here was the other extreme—a star who really couldn't care less about maintaining or boosting his starry image, the minute he stepped off the sets.

He shunned all interviews. He never went to filmi

award shows. He didn't cut ribbons at boutique inaugurals. He didn't preen on the ramp at the Chennai Fashion Week. He didn't make guest appearances at book launches.

He didn't Facebook. He didn't Tweet.

So what made KayKay suddenly join the glossy cover-story race and social media tamasha? One reason could be the rabid persistence of his PR manager.

The other reason, of course, was the PR unit accidentally finding a one-liner spouting gal and interview make-over artist. If he could outsource all this tweeting-shweeting to some eager over-enthusiastic writing chick, why not? So thought the laid-back KayKay.

Well, lucky for the PR gang of KayKay that the person they hired was happily going far beyond her job description. My market research background was something they couldn't care less about, as long I wrote 'good wordings for KayKay saar'…but research was what I wanted to do, once I had put KayKay on the popularity track.

I decided to make a formal power-point presentation to my rather amused boss one day. It had taken me about three days of intense Tweet-immersion to spout my findings from our starry world.

'The two big warring Khans, Salman and SRK, are quite trigger-happy with their fingers on cell phones, and have their favourite phrases popping up regularly. Salman can be annoyingly teeny-bopper sms-y like with 'NoIPL team fr me jst being human and mvies'. And the frequent 'OMG!' For all that oozing machoness, OMG is such a girly thing to say, don't you agree? It's also Piggy Chop's constant expression. With exclamation marks galore!!!! And SRK cannot stop telling us how he loves his kids, loves his kids, loves his kids. But can turn out a mean phrase whenever he wants to; mean as in super witty; SRK NEVER wants to be anything but the nice guy in his Tweets.

'And John Abraham talks of himself in the third person! John feels this and John thinks that…erp. But there's nobody quite so Tweet-obsessed perhaps as our tech-savvy Priyanka Chopra: and wants to thank every glorious thing that comes her way, especially entire cities that love her, with 'Thnk u Bangalore! I so luv you' 'Thanx Kolkatta!!! OMG. Luv the luv you're givin me.' 'Back in my own city! Mwaah. I love it the best!!' and that sort of thing.

'But what of our ultimate Big Daddy of Blogs and Tweets? Amitabh Bachchan is so meticulously propah, he actually numbers his Tweets! Like he began with T1 and we are now on T 3000 or something…I wonder if he's making it easier for a person writing a mini novella based on his Tweets. Maybe called a Tweetella.

'And as for our awards-shunning hero Aamir Khan, the less said about him, as he says very little. Despite being a pioneer in the social media game some years ago…'

'Then there's the most Tweet-friendly of all stars from the South, Maddy, with a constant update of interesting nuggets of what's happening during his shoots.' I concluded my presentation with a table of who tweeted, who didn't, amongst the top 20 stars of Bollywood and Kollywood.

'Whoa, Ambujax, that deserves an OMG!!!!! from me, with five exclamations. As girly as you think that is. How did you figure all this out so fast already?' exclaimed an astonished KayKay.

'It's my R & D for the job, Kay! We must know the field we're playing in first…'

'Well, that makes one of us,' responded KayKay with a wink.

My boss may not be taking himself seriously. But I chose to…

10

'A secret is something you say to one person at a time.'

I don't know if I mentioned that in our gang, the Information and Broadcasting Minister was Vikki Anand. Nobody could figure out how in the world 'information' just naturally propelled its way towards Vikki; he came to know about stuff in other people's lives even as it was being manufactured.

And what's the use of information if it wasn't broadcast at once?

It had been a while since our entire gang had met up—

which was mostly blamed on me, as I was all the time zooming away with KayKay even on advertising shoots—cars one day, cell phones the next—always shot in many exotic foreign locales like Mauritius and Thailand. Our gang did miss being together and hearing the latest outlandish utterings of Vikki. Finding we were all in town, Vikki sent out urgent messages to our WhatsApp group to meet up at Chamiers Café at 7 p.m., and Kavi was already on her way to pick me up.

I abandoned a fun piece I was writing on KayKay's behalf (called '20 Quick Ones with KayKay', where he had to answer 20 rapid-fire questions from a leading Sunday magazine with snappy answers…well guess who made up most of the questions too along with the answers?). As I jumped into Kavi's eco-friendly Noddy's car lookalike, Reva, we wondered what Vikki was dying to spill to us now.

Vikki was already sitting with Lulu, Shanks and Tarun in our favourite 'Friends' type Central Perk-sofa at Chamiers. The problem with that lovely big sofa was, lots of other Friends-type gangs in Chennai also decided it was their favourite meeting place too, and it was a triumph to find it free and ready to grab.

'Hi Vikki-leaks!' said Kavi. This brilliant nickname for Vikki was perfect, as disseminating secrets was his great purpose in life. Some day Assange would get Vikki to work for him.

'Okay, okay, call me names, my lovelies, but have I got some extremely classified (or should that be assified?) information for you! And remember you heard it here *first* on Vikki-Times Now, the No. 1 breaking news channel, for anything the nation wants to know…' Vikki did a perfect imitation of a certain extreme-aggression news anchor we all loved to hate.

And Vikki broke the big breaking news story to us: *KayKay is gay*.

At least Vikki was cautious enough to make us huddle forward before he whispered this outlandish news. Which made me immediately yell, 'RUBBISH!' so loudly, the entire restaurant, including some posh shoppers in the gift store alongside turned to stare at our group.

'Shhhhhh! Calm down, Amby…I know this is your beloved macho virile metrosexual boss and all, but I swear what I'm saying is true. And it's bound to get out some day soon, and Amby, how come you yourself didn't guess so far…?' Vikki continued his whispered revelations, even as the rest of my pals broke into 'How do *you* know?' 'Say more!' 'Who's the lover?' 'WAIT. I can guess!' 'WHAT! Can't be…' 'Impossible!'

'Vikki-leaks! You dare not leak this nonsensical piece of lie to even one other person, okay? This is insanely untrue. He is most certainly definitely undoubtedly surely straight. I should know…'

'Aha! And how would you know with such certainty, Ambujakshi Loyal-Ghost Balan? Is there some *personal* circumstantial evidence you have to the contrary? That you never told us about yet? No problem, we'll get it out of Kavi the confidante then. Anyway, your KayKay could well be a swinger too, you know…'

'Don't be such a SICKO, Vikki. Well, what about all

those dalliances with his leading lady Shamini? Have you forgotten those...'

'You yourself told us he is simply not interested in that simpering dimpling Shamini, Amby! And that it's Shamini herself, and her even more conniving, accompanying Amma, that is keeping all those romantic rumours alive in the magazines.'

Kavi and I looked at each other again and again in disbelief. True, Vikki-leaks often told us inane stuff going on around town, but most of it would actually turn out to be true, even if we never took it seriously. But hey, this was my *boss* we were talking about here. And a rather hunkworthy, crush-inducing boss.

Of course, it took us all little time to guess WHO Vikki was going to reveal as the love interest. Who else but KayKay's fiercely talented, out of the closet gay buddy/stylist/hair-dresser/recent house-guest. Toni.

House-guest! It was me who had told Vikki and the rest that the dashing Toni had taken a temporary break from his Mumbai commitments and clients, to be here in Chennai exclusively on call for KayKay's next few packed months of film shoots. And me that had said Toni was moving into KayKay's rather ample bachelor beach-villa at Neelankarai on East Coast Road. And also me that had said Toni was having problems with a well-known relationship with a young rock musician back in Mumbai right now...So our dear pal Vikki had simply come to some logically stupid assumptions here.

'Vikki, I do admire your great sense of rumour. But this isn't funny at all! Are you jumping to conclusions here based on what *Amby* told you?' demanded Kavi.

'Ha ha! No, not our dear confidential secretary, Amby. I do have my sources in the industry you know…'

By the time I got back home to my half-written assignment due the next day, some of the harmless, silly *20 Quick Ones* were taking on weird double meanings.

For instance, one of them was Q: What's your favourite look for men? A: Tall, dark and hands-on! (Omigod Toni was a super tall 6 feet 3 inches, and rather dark…). Q: Your view on marriage? A: Bigamy is having one wife too many. Monogamy is the same'. (A quote from Oscar Wilde. An utterly gay man at that).

This was getting ridiculous. But I must admit that I was pretty much on edge the next day in the make-up van, when I overheard Toni and KayKay making a weekend getaway plan to Pondicherry—and they didn't even ask me if I may care to join them. (It's only polite. I was standing right there.)

Okay they were zooming away in KayKay's fancy Yamaha VMax bike, and it wasn't anything new they were doing; checking out some eclectic new French food joint near Auroville, as they often had before on shoot-free days.

But. Why was Toni saying, 'There's a superb B&B villa run by a French couple near the beach. I'll book a room there.' *A* room. He never said *two* rooms. Yipes! I was turning into Ambujakshi Holmes now, looking for clues in every tiny thing they said or did to confirm an outlandish assumption…

'Amboos, why so quiet today, darling?' said Toni to

me. 'Tell me, what do you say to this menacing scarface look I'm planning for KayKay's spy thriller coming up called *Rakshasan* soon. I'm planning this vicious gash all the way from here, (touching KayKay's temple) to here (tracing the finger down to his chin) all across this gorgeous face…' Now why was Toni's hand lingering so long on my boss's face, even as a nonchalant KayKay kept busily talking into his cell phone throughout?

'Er, am sure it'll be a pretty awesome look, Toni, and could you just ask KayKay to check this printout and see some nutty answers to stupid questions I've done for a Sunday magazine feature? It's due to be sent out today—and I have to dash off for an urgent meeting just now with the PR gang in the office…'

With that I hurried away—even as I ignored answering an incoming call from that pesky Vikki. Undoubtedly to ask me if I had 'seen and heard' anything to confirm his crazy news.

Yes I did.

No I didn't.

Damn! Why was this all upsetting me so much??

No matter what, it wouldn't do at all for the hard-working PR gang to hear of this foolish rumour now; they were already in such a manic frenzy over the forthcoming release of *Facebook Kaadal*. And of course it suited them happily to do whatever they could to keep the so-called off-screen love interest between simpering Shamini and casual KayKay alive.

'Ah, there you are at last, Amby!' said a smoke-billowing Sailesh, head of the PR unit. I had seen him just five days ago, but he seemed to have doubled in size since then. He was looking so rotund and pressurized, Sailesh could easily turn into a huge hot air balloon and go floating over the city, carrying advertising messages. For the upcoming film, of course.

'Sit! Sit! And I need some brand new ideas from ALL of you to promote the film, do you hear me? Things never done before, do you hear me?'

What about a floating human hot-air balloon idea, Sailesh? I wondered silently.

The stressed out team looked eagerly at me; hoping I'd say some miraculous things that would stop Sailesh chewing their heads off.

Soon the ideas generated in the room ranged from the utterly obvious (create a Facebook page, called 'Facebook' on Facebook, and put up juicy teaser updates about the film) to the utterly ridiculous (get Mark Zuckerberg to come to India for the premier, and therefore, get world-wide news coverage).

One random idea that I came up with was instantly actioned, and I was even made to rush off and get it going at once: a photo feature in a leading glossy magazine, where KayKay and Shamini would be costumed as various Famous Secret Lovers from real life—only the layout would follow a Facebook kind of format, with a profile headshot of both, on the left, and a large posed picture of both right across the double spread, like the typical Facebook cover picture.

I went to tell KayKay and Shamini about this, fortunately not when they were together: while Shamini gushed, KayKay gagged.

Who really was delighted was Toni. 'I love it, Amboos!

Famous Lovers have been done to death, quite literally, with all those fictional Romeo–Juliet, Laila–Majnu kind of pairs. The "secret" adds a delicious element of rumour, scandal and adultery to it!'

We began writing down possible Famous Secret Lover pairs to get their costumes going: Marilyn Monroe and John F. Kennedy, Diana and Dodi, Whitney Houston and Michael Jackson (Oh yes! Why not?), Edwina Mountbatten and Jawaharlal Nehru, Rekha and Amitabh (perhaps not, we'd stick with dead people maybe, or Hollywood types, far away from our libel courts), as we jointly brainstormed for ideas, sitting around KayKay's van.

That crazy Vikki rang me up in right in the middle of all this and when I told him I really couldn't chat then as I was busy thinking of Secret Lover pairs for KayKay's urgent shoot, the wicked Vikki promptly suggested why not a famous secret *gay* lover pair too? Even the Toni-boy could get himself into costume for that one. Like how about Oscar Wilde and his whathisname Secret Lover—you can find it on Google search…

Very funny. I quickly cut the call, and went back to my work.

By the time we began our Lovers' shoot four days later, I was begining to wonder if the reason I even got this crazy idea in the first place, was to firmly put KayKay back on the heterosexual path, in my mind—even if it was with another woman altogether, and a very pretty woman at that. Right through the trial costuming sessions, everyone was thinking the same thing: Shamini had this remarkable face that could transform and become so many different good-looking women, just with the right make-up and Toni's collection of made to order wigs.

Shamini, I could see, was in some kind of wish-fulfilling heaven, playing different kinds of besotted women to a highly besottable KayKay. She went from being a blonde, pouty, red-lipped, glamorous Marilyn to a laughing, swimsuit-wearing, devil-may-care Diana, to (the idea started off as a joke, but it actually worked!) even a seductress in a big black wig as Monica Lewinsky. It became impossible to turn KayKay into Bill Clinton, so we had just the back of him, holding that suggestive cigar in his hand—enough for anyone to guess who he was.

Toni, we all declared, should get the Oscar for make-up: as he excelled in creating a remarkable likeness to each famous pair. KayKay, I thought, made an incredibly handsome JFK.

Shamini's mother was the most ecstatic of all, watching her daughter transform into her various seductive avatars with KayKay ('They are having such chemistry, no?') and was probably already thinking of names for her future grandchildren.

Meanwhile *Kollywood Kalling*, the gossipy online mag that regularly reported shenanigans of the glitterrati, was going to town with juicy snippets about the lead pair—many of them gently dropped into willing ears by none other than the mother and star-daughter pair I suspect.

And then there was that small but loaded piece about Toni too. These days I was slyly logging on at least twice a day to this website, checking for the latest—and there it was. In the most popular Chitra's Chitter Chatter column:

Is it ta-ta for Toni with his Pali Hill lover boy? A little birdie tells me that Bollywood's most talented style guru is in no 'hari' to get back to Mumbai yet! Which, of course, was a clear reference to the well-known rock-guitarist Hari Prem, with whom Toni had been openly linked with for over three years.

Whew. Nothing yet about Toni finding new love interests in Chennai. Vikki-leaks was talking through his hat. What was I expecting to read anyway; maybe something like: 'It's all o-Kay again in Toni's love life!' Aaargh. I was really getting pukey with my own imagined headlines…

I had a bunch of one-liners kept ready for KayKay to tweet as teasers to our Lovers' feature, like *Love ceases to be a pleasure when it ceases to be a secret #secretlovers.* But wondered about that funny grin on KayKay's face and read crazy meanings into it.

Meanwhile, why was every comedy serial on TV popping up with a gay pairing suddenly? Even the latest episode of *Friends* that I was watching one evening with Kavi had Ross and Joey cosying up to each other on a sofa! (The one with the Nap Partners).

One day, Kavi put me in a spot suddenly asking, 'So Amby—isn't your Greece plan just three months away now? And how long are you going to postpone telling your boss about it? And what do you care now, anyway?'

Why did the last of those sentences have a gigantic question mark rising out of her and hover about in the air?

True, I still hadn't said a thing to KayKay. Whereas telling the folks at home about Greece had been pretty smooth after all, as it had a great flip side to it: I was leaving the low life at last. and my family could start making up fresh euphemisms about 'what the girl does' for their groom search engine. I pretended not to notice, but since the day I told them I was resigning—almost three months ago, there was fresh purpose to my parents' fantasy of me in a nine-yard saree, coyly smiling like a successful case study in a bharatmatrimony.com ad.

But at my workplace? KayKay's queer work schedules (now why did I have to use this word?) and my perpetual race to catch a billion simultaneous publicity deadlines and travel around for shoots in various exotic locales AND tweet witticisms in between intakes of breath left me with no opportunity to do the deed.

Omigod. How had nearly a hundred days passed since I postponed telling KayKay I was quitting?

Now what was that carefully worded speech I made up months ago—why don't I *write* down these things?

11

'When life goes out of control, just say "twist in the plot" and carry on...'

'Kay, I've decided to quit!'

There, I said it. The moment I saw my boss the very next day on the sets.

Even I was a bit alarmed at the insensitive and brutal way it just came out. The other carefully thought-through option running through my head most of the night began with pleasant generalities. Leading to convoluted apologies. Went into persuasive arguments. Then some articulate reasoning. And finally, defensive protests.

What was more shocking was KayKay's characteristic laugh that followed my abrupt exit-line. 'Good! I was just wondering why you hadn't already!'

WAIT. Who just changed the script here??

Seeing my eyes widen with complete disbelief, KayKay laughed again, 'Sorry, my Ambitious Amby! I confess I have been snooping on you…and know ALL about that Writer's Workshop you're heading off to. Crete in Greece, right?'

While my mind raced to KayKay hacking into my laptop in unguarded moments, or eavesdropping on my conversations (How? Unless he was a part-time lizard who lived on our drawing room wall, or a moonlighting waiter at Amethyst where I meet Kavi all the time…) the simple, and rather ridiculous explanation was: I'd briefly left a 4-page printout of the Writer's Workshop, along with a *Lonely Planet* on Greece in his make-up van—in full viewing range—more than three months ago. 'And even though I don't have your advanced math brain, I did put two and two together…' grinned KayKay.

He had known about my Greece plan for months!

'Okay, now that I know that you know that I know, you MUST tell me about it in detail some day…'

Oof.

KayKay could've acted a tiny bit chalant here (there should be a word like that—as an opposite to nonchalant, the word that best describes KayKay), just for the sake of my self-worth. He could've looked like the distraught Richard Gere in *Pretty Woman*, when Julia Roberts said she was going away to San Francisco to study and better her life. He could have clutched both my hands and said, 'No, Amby *no*! You are my right hand, my shadow, my thought-completer, my voice, my alter ego, my confidante, my cohort, my accomplice, my adjunct, my double, my ditto…'

Worse. He didn't even look slightly concerned when I declared impulsively that I wouldn't be in the next day, as I had a family wedding to attend. I wondered if I should add that my parents were introducing me to several interested parties in the Iyer community. Or bluff that a shortlisted eligible would be attending the wedding too, and recklessly add that that's the real reason I was quitting. Not that writing course, which *may* happen after, who knows? A very quick engagement right away and marriage almost immediately…

I was getting hyper-panicky-desperate for a reaction.

He simply breezed away with 'I've been to Greece! It's magical. Don't ever miss out on Santorini. Hey, we got to talk about this later! I could even teach you some Greek words. *Yia sou!*'

And strode off to prepare his ridiculously pumped up muscles for an utterly hideous fight sequence, for which he had to be made-up with a stupid fake scar. By that stupid effeminate Toni.

By the way, all those rehearsed speeches in my head involving persuasive arguments and defensive protests et cetera didn't really go wasted. When I rang up Kavi later that night, I told her I had gone through a highly emotion-packed drama concerning my boss and my resignation.

Sometimes one has to lie to even one's best friend to save face.

Maybe as a counter to all these confusing happenings, I suddenly morphed into my good, *chamathtthu* Tam Brahm girl avatar. And said casually over dinner that night that I *may* come along to that third cousin's wedding after all, as I could try and ask for a day off.

I may mention here that in the past few months, the relief my family felt over my decision to quit that 'embarrassing filmi job' was so great, they were on over-drive again in their world-wide web search for a fine Tam Brahm groom.

So when the parents had asked, 'after this Greece-sheece business is out of the way, can the Seshadri marriage proposal be slowly taken forward?' I did a vague nod of head, indicating 'er, well, okay, why not...' just to get them off my back. It did make me extremely popular at home.

I was still feeling peeved as hell that KayKay had laughed away my rather short resignation speech so casually...I would show him that even though Greece was three months away, I had far better things to do in life these days than be obsessing over writing stupid stuff day and night for him. Somewhere, some time, I would also let it be known that a rather fine 'boy' had already been found for me, and that I would be meeting him one of these days.

So I texted him as soon as I woke up. '*Reminder: Not coming in today. Important family wedding to attend with my parents*'

To which I got this prompt reply. '*So Ambujakshi Balan is on display! Text me as soon as some catchable catches are spotted in the gathering...*'☺

'Ambu! So what have you decided? Are you coming with us?'

I knew that tone from my mother could only mean: 'You *better* come with us...' so I yelled back from my room 'Yes, yes, Ma—I'm coming to the wedding...'

'Good! Wear the orange and gold Kanjeevaram silk, NOT your usual plain black tangail. And I've brought the navaratna necklace and matching bangles from the bank locker. And the jimkhis. And don't forget a *pottu*—where are those coloured bindis I got you from Luz...and PLEASE tie your hair up in a neat ponytail...'

The last part of that instruction I mimed along. Every single family outing, family puja, family function, temple visit, relatives' encounter, especially those sudden surprise visitations at our doorstep—brought forth that wear-a-pottu and tie-up-your hair command from my mother.

I transformed from the 'bob-cut' Amby, Page 3 party frequenter, to a ponytailed and jasmined Ambujakshi, Iyer-wedding attender, faster than one could say *virundhu sapaad* (the fabulous Iyer kalyanam-lunch: the real reason I was showing great signs of eagerness to go for this wedding). Particularly since it would be catered for sure by 'Mountbatten Mani's' wedding service—a nickname acquired after the patriach of this group had allegedly served an amazing payasam (so says the legend) to Lord Mountbatten himself! The grandson, appropriately called Mount Srini, was continuing his family tradition, and it would be foolish to forgo an opportunity to pig out at a traditional South Indian wedding feast.

'See? How good you look in orange, that's your colour, though you could have worn your diamond earrings with your jhimkis, no? If you don't wear them for these functions when will you ever wear them?'

Because they have stems the size of drainpipes, and won't ever get in my earholes. But even if I'd worn these every Tam Brahm girl's must-have 6-diamond-stoned piece of basic necessity, every relative was still going to look only at my gold necklace and bangles and ask me, for the umpteenth time, 'Ah Ambujakshi—so you are wearing your gold winnings!'

You see, I won gold. Real 22-carat GOLD—one whole kilo of it, in a slogan writing contest by Saravana Homeneeds Store.

A couple of years ago, a crazy rhyme I had scribbled on a contest entry form (I love shopping in Saravana Homeneeds because…in 15 words or less) had won me the first prize in a department store's promotional contest, sending waves of shock, envy and disbelief among everyone who heard this news; who would then instantly wail one of these reactions:

'What! Do they actually give these prizes? I thought all contests were a scam!'

Or. 'What! How come I never ever win anything?'

Or. 'What! How much is all that gold worth…lakhs or crores?'

Only my ecstatic family and close pals weren't really surprised I won—yet again—as writing pithy lines for all kinds of contests and winning something or the other had become a happy pattern in my life. I had won a Prestige pressure cooker for Mom (when I was just 14!), free tickets for the movie *Appu Raja*, a month's free provisions at Spencer's, a set of four Horlicks mugs, a Godrej steel almirah, (the most coveted prize so far), a VIP strolley bag, a year's subscription to *Readers' Digest*, and a kilo of Lions Dates.

But a kilo of *gold!* That simply blew everyone away. An exaggerated version of my contest-winning ability was immediately splashed in a leading Tamil magazine *Kumudam*, much to my family's dismay, and my grandmother must have waved several evil-eye eliminating concoctions around my head, should the power of jealousy ever affect my life.

Nevertheless, my ratings shot up in tamilmatrimony.com, secretly subscribed to by my grandfather. As middle class as we were demographically, my Master's in Economics, good prospects at joining a leading MNC bank, my genealogy which included several illustrious granduncles in the ICS that made mine a 'good family', had pitched me into the Yay Von Category of prospective brides for You-Yes IT professional Tam Brahm boys. (That's an A1 highest ranking girl for the US boys' marriage market, if you didn't get the Southy accent here.)

Horoscopes enclosing photographs, inboxes with jpeg attachments galore, began flooding our mail boxes, both the wooden one on our gate, and the cyber one in our comp screens. And one fine day, I was expected to wear my multicoloured navaratna necklace, chunky gold jhimkis, diamond earrings, my gold bangle set, pull my hair into a jasmined ponytail, wear a *pottu*, and say 'Yes'. Probably to the one right on top of the list of Eligibles: Arvind Seshadri, Head of New Global Markets, Nokia. Currently based in Finland. Age 31. 6' 2", St Stephen's topper, followed by MBA, Carlton School of Management, Minneapolis.

But when I had said 'Yes' instead to a film star's PR entourage, they had witnessed with great dismay, my endless whirl of Page 3 parties, film launches, music launches, IPL after-cricket-match parties, and studio shoots, exotic foreign location shoots, and more parties…

My marriage prospects ranking must have dropped from A-1 to Z-26 in the Tam Brahm marriage market, I imagine.

Now even if my family tried hard to hide this shocking entry into the 'industry' no conservative South Indian Brahmin family girl would get into, I was spotted by disapproving Aunties and Uncles in several parties—in where else?—Page 3 of *Chennai Times*. Sometimes in the background with a dashing KayKay upfront, sometimes right next to him, with even my name in the caption below.

I hated this part of it actually, and always tried to hide or run away seeing those camera-toting guys in every

Kollywood event, but they'd catch me unawares sometimes…And what were conservative Tamil middle class Mamis and Mamas doing, slyly looking at Page 3 pictures anyway? When I asked this question at home one day, I only got a fresh round of scoldings…a litany sprinkled with *'sariyaana ashadu'* (complete idiot), and '*buddhi kettupochu*' (brain got damaged).

And just when they were beginning to wonder if they had lost me to the 'filmi ullagam' forever, fearing my shocking new vocation was getting to be my long-term career path, here was I, suddenly back on the market, with a decent career change ahead in the field of writing.

The family had gone back eagerly to hunting through albums for the best photographs of me, to send to the top-billed 'prospect'. The Boy. Arvind Seshadri. Hopefully still available.

Pictures of me winning gold medals (not the kilo of gold—my parents are not that crass!) at school and college, and definitely the one of me smiling brightly at our family holiday in Ooty, facing the sunlight, I may add, where I magically looked as white-skinned as Katrina Kaif. Off they went to the Boy's family in the old-fashioned way—in an envelope, stamped and addressed in my grandfather's neat handwriting.

The picture they sent back of The Boy to my parents wasn't one of those studio shots, as much as mine wasn't one of those of typical elbow resting on a gothic column portrait, wearing a Kanjeevaram saree and gazing into the future at a spot, top-left on the ceiling. By the dictates of modern alliances, only casual pictures were sent: one of him in a totally snowbound backyard in Helsinki (oh my, his company gave him such a big house!) and another of him in a black suit—close up—addressing an international forum; (he's a public speaker: gold star for that!) and one laughing, with three other buddies at a weekend fishing trip near Helsinki, where he actually looked his best in all three pictures sent.

The Boy appeared to be holding up a large fish that he had just caught. But that one photograph was cleverly hidden away by my discerning grandfather—now which Iyer boy would go fishing? Anyway it doesn't specifically *say* that he is a non-vegetarian, said my grandfather, re-reading his bio-data just to be doubly sure.

I had, of course, dismissed it all at home with 'I am definitely not getting married till I am thirty-one and a half! So why are you showing me these pictures, Ma?'

But later I had secretly scanned and cropped only his face: the one of him laughing with his buddies on a fishing trip, and then shown it to Kavi, just for a laugh myself, mind you...Kavi had reacted with 'Amby! He's not bad at all, so just keep him on the back-burner for a while, will you? DON'T say an outright no, not just yet...'

So here was I ready to go to family functions once again, even willing to 'be seen' at a vast exhibition area akin to a village shandy where prize cows are paraded and picked—also known as a community wedding hall.

And even though The Boy and The Girl hadn't even met, a vivid picture of a big billboard at the entrance of Woodland's Wedding Hall, announcing 'AMBUJAKSHi weds ARVIND' embellished in marigold words embedded amongst roses, had been forming in my parents' optimistic heads.

My relieved parents gave me pleased glances in the car. In my wedding regalia, I was bound to be viewed most favourably by my community all over again…I was *maaneram* (a polite word for darkish, but not dark) BUT my face cut was good. I was dusky BUT was excellent in academics. I was wheat-complexioned BUT I could make rasam and vendakai poriyal rather well.

(How come they never said AND instead of BUT when they appended my plus points to the latter half of those sentences?)

At the wedding, I would probably meet Arvind Seshadri's maternal uncle's daughter-in-law who was related to my second cousin's sister-in-law, whose neighbour's son went to school with Arvind, and knew all about his family, and even visited him once in Helsinki where he is 'doing so well'…and who knows? I could even be given many glances of appreciation as I swished about in my orange silk in the large marriage hall.

Hmmmm. So I would do my Greece Writing Workshop thing. Then I would shut myself in my room for a whole year, writing my chart-busting novel-cum-screenplay. A *Bridget Jones's Diary*-like book for sure. With super-romantic dialogues for sure. With some scenes set in Greece for sure.

Meanwhile…somewhere along the way, perhaps Arvind Seshadri, no. 1 on our shortlist, would move onto the front-burner. He'd visit India on some global forum again. Nokia had the fastest growing market in India, I heard in NDTV Profit.

We'd meet in a casually arranged 'outing' at Park Sheraton's Dakshin restaurant. I'd find out he finds Seinfeld the funniest man on the planet. He'd be polite to the waiters and take charge of ordering the food, without dithering away with the annoying 'anything is fine by me'. (I tell you, restaurant behaviour is a very good indication of a person's true character). He'd be a great listener. Too. He'd have neatly trimmed nails. Too.

Just as I was plunging my own bangled hand into the delicious *bisi bele bhath* served on my plantain leaf at the noisy wedding dining hall, I heard my cell phone beep. I rummaged about with my left hand in my handbag and saw a New Message.

All the best as you settle down into a parent-approved deranged marriage. Oops. I meant arranged marriage ☺.

It was KayKay.

(Now why did that that pleasant scenario of arranged marriages and happy families described two paragraphs ago suddenly vanish, like the payasam being served in tiny plastic cups?).

DERANGED marriage?? How did he come up with something so pathetic? I read the message again. How did he come up with something so hilarious?

Damn KayKay for disturbing me on my rare day off. One day I wasn't there to follow him around, writing his stupid lines, and he becomes desperate trying to reach me and get my attention. One day I take off from that faltu fecking fake filmi world, and I am missing being there.

Oh, how I hate KayKay. Oh, how I love KayKay.

'STOP!' My payasam cup had been refilled three

times over already, and I hurriedly prevented the server from sloshing another ladleful in.

I attributed a muddled feeling in my middle to gross over-eating. NOT wannabe Tweeters sending messages between takes. Tweeters who were unsorted still over even their gender-preference, or their priorities in life…

Wait .Was *I* the confused one here.

Okay Mr Terribly Witty KayKay. Add this too to your list of nicknames for me: Ambiguous Amby. Mixed up jumbled flustered disturbed Ambiguous Amby.

My parents returned from the wedding charged in their pursuit of the Suitable Boy, and were happily trying to progress 'talks' further. I would sometimes hear snatches of 'the girl and boy should meet very casually—who can push these youngsters into anything formal these days?—but by God's grace this one will work out…'

Or my ever-hopeful dad would be saying to some eager relative, 'Even after marriage the girl can easily go back to her last job in Citibank—surely there is a Citibank in Helsinki also? Anyway what she is doing now in the media field is only temporary you know…'

'Media field'. What a decent euphemism for my current occupation!

Well, as it happened, the said eligible Arvind Seshadri popped up one day on my friends' request on Facebook.

Well. Well. Well. So this was how today's traditional arranged marriage got its make-over as a modern love marriage, was it? To be really accurate, one should call this the beginnings of a 'Like' marriage.

Girl and Boy become casual friends on Facebook. Girl puts up new profile picture—44 of her friends hit 'Like'. One of the 44 is the newest friend on Facebook, the Boy. One of her old pals from school writes under Comments: Wow! That's a smashing look in your cool new haircut! And someone hits the 'Like' for that comment. Mouse-over to see who. It's The Boy. Aha.

Then the conversation between Girl and Boy moves to the private messages section on the FB page. A few *Hi, how're you doing?* kind of general exchanges happen. Many secretive views of each other's albums happen. (Good time for both boy and girl to hastily remove some ridiculous pictures with beer mugs in hand, singing like unhinged loonies at a pub. Or those unflattering ones with half closed eyes and one's tummy popping out taken by a pea-brained moron in the gang and tagged, without seeking one's permission whatsoever.)

And then the mildly flirtatious dialogue moves from Messages to Mail. Then from Mail to Skype. From Skype to a fine dining restaurant. Till the announcement is eagerly made on both sides of the boy-meets-girl tableau:

It's a Love Marriage!

Meanwhile back at the ranch. Everyone was applauding the amazing way the Secret Lovers feature of KayKay had turned out. Everyone was singing my praises: most notably the ecstatic starry-eyed Shamini.

Again a kind of churn in my digestive region was beginning to set in that even Hajmola couldn't cure…

So I found a weird way to make amends for myself- I went a bit beserk hitting random 'Like' buttons on various pictures from Arvind Seshadri's Facebook albums.

Then I recklessly wrote to him in his private Facebook message box. 'Off to Greece in a few weeks for a Writer's Workshop! A whole fortnight in Crete, learning how to plot a bestseller ☺.'

Now before I hit the send button, I became vain enough to first change my profile picture—certainly a more flattering one, shot by Kavi at the East Coast Road Beach some Sundays ago. I hoped it conveyed to prospective viewers, an air of an aware, much travelled woman of the world, in an idyllic setting by the sea…

Two other writing-hopefuls were also right then putting Greece travel plans into place. Bobby Varma and Mini Cherian.

Bobby, instead of tackling the thirteenth ad film script she swore she'd finish before her notice period at the ad agency ran out, was staring at her iPad trying to decide whether or not an envy-inducing Facebook update concerning Greek getaways was a good thing or a bad thing to do.

Mini Cherian didn't have this problem at all, being a I-hate-Facebook snob anyway. Mini was busy buying up the largest suitcases one could take on board an aircraft. Who knows if she may end up permanently settling in Greece?

And the gods in charge of the destiny department were busy manipulating our paths so that three writerly sister-souls were all headed to a common point to meet up shortly. In the next chapter.

GREECE

12

'I write because I want more than one life.
It's greed, pure and simple.'

'Po! Po! Po!'

Greek taxi drivers can get very angry, very suddenly. And can yell and fling your suitcases out on the sidewalk, mid-ride, and simply zoom away—if you dare to question their dubious taxi meters.

Now what was *that*! This bad-tempered taxi man must be related to the auto-drivers of Chennai; and did he just say 'Po!' which is a kind of 'get lost,' in Tamil? (Later I discovered this was a colloquial interjection in Greek, used to voice angry disapproval.)

I ought to have got pretty mad myself, dumped on a road in a new country. But hey! I was in GREECE!

A manic grin had settled on my face at the Athens airport, where I had arrived in my Emirates flight via Dubai, and even cussing Greeks couldn't dislodge the elation of thinking: I'm here. Really. In *Greece.*

I was scribbling down this intriguing word 'Po!' in my little mole-skin notebook (I'm a compulsive jot-it-down writer), stranded in a random Athens street with my strolley lying on its side, and looked up to the screech of another rattling taxi, coming to a halt before me.

'Hey! Want a ride some place?'

Indians! Indian Girls! The Greek Gods *were* watching over me. And that's how I first met Bobby and Mini.

(When we three are all well past our 80s and cackling away living together in our dream island home in the Mediterranean, we'll go over this moment many times, so I'm giving it some importance here).

Two lovely faces peered at me from the taxi windows. Instinctively I knew where they must be headed too.

'Port Piraeus…I have to catch the ferry boat. Hey, are you both headed for the Writers' Workshop at Crete too?'

The 'YES!' that followed was our moment of bonding for life.

The incredible thing about girls—well not all girls, but female writers for sure—is the amount of information we can exchange in the course of a 40-minute taxi ride. We had so many similar things to say about our writerly-lives-thus-far, and our writing-career-change-dreams-ahead.

As it turned out, Bobby and Mini had first met at the Alitalia flight baggage carousel; with the strong-armed Bobby helping Mini get her two gigantic suitcases and duffel bag off, while Bobby herself had just one sleek cabin bag and backpack. The tinier a person, the more clothing they carry, is a theory of Bobby's.

'I kind of packed to stay on in Greece for the rest of

my life; just in case...so I also have a lot of books and stuff in there,' Mini had apologetically told Bobby. But their writer-vibes had instantly connected, especially when they joyfully discovered the Creative Awakenings Writers' Workshop at Chania, Crete, was in both their immediate destinies.

They'd killed time at the airport lounge together, having arrived from Mumbai three hours earlier than me, so Mini ended up buying even more books—among them a handy Greek phrase booklet. They were heading off to Port Piraeus together, to catch the overnight ferry-boat, mastering their first 10 words in Greek, when they spotted me stranded on that roadside. Ordained by fate to meet up and form the Sisterhood Triumverate that—we didn't know then—would last for life.

As it later turned out, all of us had picked the cheapest option to stay, for the 2-week course duration—Hotel Porto Del Colomba, a charming, tumbledown Venetian building in the Old Town of Chania, capital of Crete. But it was probably the most picturesque of all the hotel options given to Workshop participants, from what we'd seen on the website. And rather than fly into Chania's airport, from Athens, we'd picked the far more exciting route—and definitely at quarter of the cost: an overnight ferry-boat ride to our final destination.

'Oh my God! It's a friggin' *Titanic!*'

Three of us stared at the gigantic ocean liner in front of us. This was our 'ferry-boat'! And here we were imagining that Mini's luggage alone may well sink any boat, during our ride to Crete.

As the 'How to book your tickets to Crete' had told us in the Workshop's website, we had come prepared to buy our ferry tickets right at the harbour itself. No pre-booking needed; tickets easily available even an hour before departure...said the instructions. But at just 36 euros a pop for an 8-hour ocean-ride from Piraeus to Crete, the farthest of all Greek islands, we simply couldn't believe our eyes.

Meanwhile, chaos reigned at the embarkation platform, with a babble of foreign tourists and locals all rushing about on a crowded drawbridge leading to a massive luggage hold. While we continued standing and staring stupefied by the size of our boat, the sun was beginning to set.

A grinning old bearded Greek seaman in a sailor's cap, lazily smoking a pipe, gave us all a welcoming wink.

'Mi-la-te Anglika?' said Mini to him at once, practising this most useful do-you-speak-English phrase mastered in the taxi.

'Mera jootha hai Japani! Beautiful Indian ladies! Namas-they, namas-they...' he replied. It took us a moment to realize that old Raj Kapoor hit films were still the biggest association old Greeks made with India.

'Efharisto!' I said, eager to use my own first word in Greek, which means thanks. 'Can you help us into the ferry, *parakalo?*'

When it became clear that our randy seaman was perhaps imagining getting his hands on us, rather than getting our feet into the ship, we fled in panic to shove our luggage too into the massive hold like everyone seemed to be doing, and with a backpack each, joined the jabbering millions going up the ramp to the ship's deck.

Each of stood on the vast deck, silent and wonder-struck looking out at the endless, fabulous blue Mediterranean beyond that would transport us to a life-changing adventure. 'We haven't taken a single picture yet,' said Bobby suddenly. A Greek teenager smilingly obliged with my cell phone camera; three of us linked arms, and laughed together, leaning against the ship's railings. Behind us the sky was ablaze with sunset colours.

(It is still our most favourite picture of the three of us.)

Mini suddenly noticed a mad scramble for reclining deck chairs. She needn't have worried; I had already nabbed three and flung my backpack, water bottle, and packed sandwiches on them to reserve them…these were going to be our economy class beds for the all-night cruise, out in the open deck. Under the stars!

We soon discovered that this massive ship was not as glamorous as it had looked from the shore; it was actually an old cargo vessel that also ferried budget travellers to each of Greece's several islands, overnight. There were different classes of tickets of course, though who on earth would want to pay 154 euros for a cabin, we wondered, when it was way more fun outside on the deck?

Well, the wooden slats that poked after a while—and prevented all sleep—was the best reason the richer and the sensible paid up 154 euros for a proper cabin and bed, we realized soon enough. But who wanted to sleep anyway? Three excited girls had a my-life-as-a writer-so far narrative to catch up on…

Soon the constant exclamations of 'Really? I too have felt *exactly* the same way!' that linked our different writerly lives became quieter, less frequent, even as the swish-swish-swish of the sea lulled us gently into a blissful sleep...only to be shaken up by a frantic Mini, in the semi-darkness: 'Oh my God! This is our stop! It's Chania! It's 4.30 in the morning already! We gottu RUN girls!'

It's a wonder we all three didn't collapse with heart failure, right there at the harbour of Chania, when the drawbridge dramatically hauled itself upwards—just 40 seconds after Bobby had bodily picked up Mini and leapt out, onto the port's platform. I was already sitting, shaken, amidst our assorted pieces of baggage lying on the ground, flung out by a yelling Greek hand on the ship, for not being ready to hop off at the right time (like we understood a single word of that announcement they made before the trip). I really thought Bobby and Mini would miss getting off the drawbridge, sail away to the next halt in Heraklion or wherever, never to be seen again...

And then we all laughed to the point of hysteria. None of us had any mascara on then, or we'd have created a river of black with our tears for sure, that's how hard we laughed.

Now here's a tip from one of Bobby's notebooks on the joys of travel (boy, was she focused on her passion for travel writing). Bobby wants to point out to you that nothing is more magical about a new city, a new country, than entering it in the very early morning. Much before the city awakes.

We had woken up a sleeping driver from a row of taxi-vans parked near the quay, and showed him the name of our hotel: Porto del Colombo. We could well have shown him a name from a hotel on the moon; he shook his head, and tried going back to sleep, but when Mini woke him up again, he gesticulated wildly, talking in a rapid torrent despite Mini's earnest, *Signomi, ala then milao elinka!* (Sorry, I don't speak Greek). Which is a contradiction of sorts.

Bobby, who had done her homework on the net, knew we should not be spending more than 5 euros to get us from the port to our hotel. She held up a 5-euro note; the Greek suddenly nodded his head, broke into a smile that said, let's go!

And off we went through empty streets, heading towards the charming Old Town as our Trip Advisor reviews had told us, till we came to an abrupt halt in the middle of a deserted market square. Once again, suitcases were brought down to a sidewalk, though by the most smiling driver this time. *'Adio Adio!'* said he, generally waving his hands in a direction down a narrow cobbled pathway no car could go into—and off he went.

What our genial gent had done was: drive us for a distance which he decided was exactly 5 euros worth, and simply gone away after that. With dawn just beginning to break, and not a soul on the streets, we began our hunt for Theotokoppulou Street—as indicated in our printouts. Now this is a great early-morning way to discover a new city, as Bobby would recommend, but not when one of your group is a Mini that has brought along most of her material possessions in life.

'What have you packed in this bag, Mini!' said Bobby, trundling along Mini's gigantic case, apart from her own. 'Some good Indian bricks and cement bags, just in case you build a home here?'

And then 30 minutes later, after a twist in a cobbled pathway, up some flat broad steps and through a crumbling archway, there it was. Our home for the next two weeks.

Ivy randomly climbed up the orange walls of an old Venetian bungalow, 700 years old. A quaint hand-painted signage, supported by two twisted ropes, had a wooden box bursting with bright red geraniums below. A fat cat was sleeping on a little black wrought iron chair. It was all so exactly like the picture each of us had seen on the website! Hotel Porto del Colombo…it was love at second sight.

How many ouzos down so far, koritsi ☺?!

KayKay! My first sms from India showed me that my roaming cell phone was alive and working. It also showed me that my roaming heart was alive and pumping.

'Mini, look up this one in your phrase book. What does *koritsi* mean in Greek?' In a ridiculous way, I wondered if it meant 'sweetheart' or something…then I'd have some detailing to go into, with my two new friends…

But Mini already had an answer. '*Koritsi*! I know that one: it means girl or young lady. You mean you're getting Greek smses already?'

Hmmm…so KayKay had gone into the trouble of looking up Greek words on the internet. My heart did a tiny hopping movement anyway—you must admit *koritsi* does sound a bit romantic.

'It's my ex-boss from Chennai, that's all' I said nonchalantly. But in the next 15 minutes, it had all tumbled out: the dangerous zone our film star boss-tweeter girl relationship had ventured into, the frantic need to get away from it all, not to mention (the delusion?) that Greece would put a firm end to that chapter in my life. It was amazing how comfortable I felt among these women who had been strangers till yesterday. Something inexplicable was making us all seem like long-lost sisters already.

Oh, yes, I also did make brief mention that the arranged marriage proceedings with a certain highly eligible Tam Brahm guy from Finland was well underway.

Which made me remember that I hadn't yet sent off my dutiful-daughter 'arrived safely' message home. With India being two and a half hours ahead of Greece, my parents would've been up hours ago, wondering if desperate unemployed Greek youths had stabbed and robbed me on arrival, so I quickly sent them a picture of me with my two new-found friends taken on the cruise boat. That should keep them calm for a while.

Our comfortable jabber continued into discovering each others' families and their quirks, our work-lives, and the realization that each of us, in some way, was probably 'running away' from something. Each had, it seemed, the Best Job in the World—but was inadvertently searching for something else. Perhaps the Second Best Job in the World! One that wasn't all about money and prestige, but something else that was all about heart and soul…

And we hadn't even had our first ouzo! The three of us were sipping tea in our cosy little room, after a comfortable 2-hour snooze since checking in at 5 a.m. We'd moved one floor up, to the three-bedder sharing option, delighted we'd each save a further 5 euros per night; and even more delighted at the spectacular view of the Old Town spreading out below, and in the far distance, the sea, with Chania's most famous landmark: the old lighthouse catching the first gold of the morning's sun.

The jabbering Greek momma, Helena, and her somewhat sulky teenage daughter who ran this charming hotel, had pointed out Hotel Casa Delfino from our bedroom window: the venue of our Writer's Workshop, just two streets away.

Day One was 'Arrival in Crete, check-into various hotels; and introductions to fellow participants at the Casa Delfino lobby at 6 p.m'.

Ample time to explore the immediate streets leading off our hotel, and discover how close we were to Akti Kountourioti: Crete's popular hang-out street all along the mile-long Venetian Harbour, dotted with bustling open air restaurants.

'Cheers!' we chorused, clinking our glasses of ouzo in Café Konaki. 'You can text your film star heart-throb that you've hit your first ouzo now!' said Mini to me.

'*Former* heart-throb, may I correct you. You forget he may be with a new love now; most probably male!'

'Okay, here's a toast to The New Path in each of our

lives. Amby, may you write the screenplay of your dreams, and fill the void left by Nora Ephron. Bobby, may you write the travel book that gets serialized on TLC to rave reviews. And here's to me—may I experience that torrid holiday romance in this trip that inspires the "Minerva" series, and eclipses *Fifty Shades of Grey* forever!

'Cheers!' said a grinning long-haired gent from the adjoining table, raising his own glass towards us. 'And may I feature in all those works of literature by you three young ladies! India, right?'

'Let me guess: you're here for the Workshop too,' exclaimed Mini.

'Now you're cheating...that's no guess; I just noticed you noticing my course printouts too on my table. So you beautiful young Indian ladies: looks like I'm going to be seeing more of you in the next couple of weeks!' Owen smiled.

And that's how Owen McFee entered our lives. The disarming Irishman whose hobby, he confessed, was eavesdropping on café conversations—how else could a writer improve on dialogue writing?

13

'The world is full of books in search of authors.'

'Tighten, tighten, TIGHTEN your buttocks…now slowly and gently, relax, be easy, chase out the tension, let it go, across the floor, up the wall, and out of the window, and far far away…'

Twenty wannabe Famous Writers, lay on yoga mats on the floor, eyes closed. We had tightened and released, tightened and released various body parts, in unified obedience to the commands of Annabel Keats, Course Director of 'Creative Awakenings'. Apparently, we were undergoing a relaxation technique to make our bodies writer-ready, released of inner tensions.

But a release of tension…from one's buttocks? I knew for sure that three girls lying on the floor may shortly break into complete hysteria like a bunch of school boys, unless we moved on to the next non-funny body part at once.

We were well into the 45-minute relaxation session of our Writers' Orientation session. Hmmm…so this is how Nora Ephron became so prolific with her screenplays, I thought. Or how Bill Bryson became so prolific with his travel books, thought Bobby. Or how E. L. James became so prolific with erotica, thought Mini.

When we finally emerged from our tranced-out state,

struggling to open our eyes from the sleep-inducing method to more creative writing, I saw Owen wink one of his blue Irish eyes at me; perhaps this session didn't have a profound effect on him either.

'Now wasn't that just *bee-yoo*-tee-ful! And aren't we all in that nice happy place!' gushed Annabel. 'Awake, awake, to Creative Awakenings!'

Either we were all extremely polite and well brought up or hypnotized into a state of moronic bliss, because we all broke into claps like a bunch of kindergarten kids.

Standing next to Annabel, in earnest attendance, was her ruddy-faced and stockily built partner with a rather exotic name: Pavol Zavacka, who turned out to be Slav-American. (We very quickly arrived at an easy nickname for him: The Slave.)

Well, The Slave was introduced to us with rather impressive arty credentials: Pavol, declared Annabel, was part of the family tree of an extremely illustrious and world-famous art personality of Slav-American origin. Andy Warhol!

As Pavol Zavacka bashfully smiled at Annabel, she went on to tell us, 'Pavol is part of Andy Warhol's mother's family, the Zavackas, who were immigrants to America from Slovakia. Now we all know of the world's greatest pop art icon, Andy Warhol; well you'll be happy to know that as your art instructor for this programme, Pavol Zavacka will bring an exciting dimension to your lessons on Writing with Pictures. Let's hear it for Pavol!'

The burly Slav with a long flaxen-haired ponytail standing before us looked a far cry from whatever I could remember of the stylish and dapper Andy Warhol. He seemed to be content in smiling and nodding his head to whatever Annabel had to say, suddenly leaping to attention to do her bidding, every time she wanted her notes or a piece of chalk to write on the blackboard.

'Isn't Andy Warhol that guy who made art out of soup cans or something?' wondered Mini. It seemed to her that the ruddy Pavol Zavacka looked rather like a large Campbell Soup can himself.

'Remember this Workshop is all about the Experimental and the Experiential, the Activization and the Actualization, the Visualization and the Validation…' concluded our profoundly articulate writing guru, in her introduction to our 2-week workshop.

And then she told us we could all go away outdoors and return after an hour, to read out 500 words of our first challenging assignment, 'Memories of Childhood'. Wow.

'Maybe this is how true big time writing starts. With the utterly banal!' said Bobby, as we walked to a sunny café for a snack while we wrote our assignment.

'Memories of Childhood! Maybe this is a trick question: maybe we've got to pick some other person or thing's unique childhood, and write about *that.* See? I cracked it! We can't have paid so many hundreds of euros to learn how to write a bloody school essay,' said Bobby.

So that's how we wrote our first assignment on childhood, to Bobby's newly interpreted brief. (Bobby was a true advertising gal; rejecting a client's brief and writing her own was second nature.) So I looked at the first dish to arrive at our table, Bobby's order of Chicken Souvlaki, and wrote 500 words on the childhood of a chicken growing up in Greece. It was an unusual tale and full of pathos.

Bobby wrote about the formative years of a babbling brook in Crete's pristine Samaria gorge, ending in the confines of a bottle of Samara mineral water, placed in front of us in the café. It was a short adventurous travelogue with a twist.

And Mini wrote the innocent beginnings of a sapling before it turned into a tree that turned into paper that turned into a book that turned into an erotic novel. Hopefully her own, said Mini to us, as we'd each finished reading out our assignments in class. A unique reinterpretation of Memories of Childhood!

Our dear mentors, we noticed, had very little to comment on, or add to, or critique as each of our class of twelve did our reading; just a standard 'Oohhh! Wasn't that just WONderful!' so we did feel like it was our first day in nursery school all over again, reciting nursery rhymes. Then they took our assignments and put them into individual coloured files—we wondered if Annabel would correct our spelling and grammar, even the quirky sentences we deliberately put in—and give us marks on 10 and gold smiley-faced stars.

With the three hours of our day's class-time done, Annabel declared the rest of the day to be free, and we set off to explore the island.

'I was wondering if we'd tuned into a blah-heavy TV

conversation between Deepak Chopra and Oprah Winfrey. Experiential and Actualization and Validation...what was *that!*' I exclaimed.

'As for that slavish Slav guy of hers, she's got him jumping through hoops for her', said Bobby.

We were heading off to Foretza Café closer to the harbour, which our Trip Advisor reviews recommended as the best views of the old lighthouse by sunset. We may not have been aware of it then, but 'Rest of the day is free' would turn out to be the most inspiring part of each day's writing programme.

On the way Bobby stumbled upon the famous carpet shop of Mihalis Manousakis that she'd read about in *Lonely Planet*. Smitten by an intricate pink and orange piece, Bobby wondered how on earth she'd take this one back home to Mumbai. '*Kanena provlima*' said the smiling Mihalis. Which we figured was 'no problem'. 'I make the flying carpet too. If I put enough stamps on the parcel, my carpet fly anywhere, to any country!'

Soon our walk to the café was punctuated with '*Hi. Yia sou!*' and '*Ela!*' '*Kali Spera!*' as we began spotting various familiar faces from our Workshop wandering around the harbour cafes and colourful touristy shops. There was Fran and Linda, college pals from Buffalo, taking a break from their day-jobs as Walmart store-keeper and Laundromat owner, to indulge their cravings to become novel writers by night.

We could spot the vivacious Cynthia settling down for a Greek tattoo at a stall run by a rakish ponytailed Greek gent; 'I have NO idea what this Greek lettering means;

κίνδυνος, but I'm going with it as it looks funky!' said a laughing Cynthia, extending a sexy thigh, where she wanted her tattoo of a Greek phrase. Now that says more about the risk-loving Cyn than I could describe in a whole page.

Emerging from a trinket shop with baubles and beads of every colour were a laughing twosome, Stacey and Bonnie. Stacey was from San Francisco, and Bonnie from Melbourne; the fact that both coincidentally had sons named Matt had probably made them instant pals, as we all found out at the introductions session. Life does that all the time, like it makes instant pals of strangers with the same birthdays or even the same sun sign—('You're Aries? Really? Me too!' or 'You're allergic to cucumbers? What! Me too.')

There was the unpronounceable Phoung Trnh, a delightful Vietnamese girl, whose trick was to invent a word if she was stuck for one: and what funny expressive words we would go on to hear from her pieces! Flobitz flobitz flobitz went a guy walking through a slushy mud puddle; coming to a skibbedy-grak halt when he saw a gal…We soon knew all her words but not her name! So she simply became PT for the rest of the course.

And where was our very first pal—Owen the smiley affable Irishman? During the first day's introductions we learnt of the surprising connection Owen had to India: his grandmother was from Coorg. When he said his 'ancestral home' was in Mercara, and he could cook a mean *pandi curry* and promised to demo the Coorg warrior dance to us one night, how could we not like him even more?

As if on cue he appeared before us, laughing by himself at a table in Café Foretza. Till we discovered he was actually on Skype with his MacBook.

'Hi girls! Meet my son Danny. Danny meet three wonderful ladies from India!' An adorable 8-year-old came into view on the laptop screen. 'Hi there Danny! We each said in turn, introducing ourselves, as Owen moved the laptop camera to get us one at a time on screen. 'Hi there…I am in Bangalore!' said Danny to us.

'He's in Bangalore?' exclaimed Mini. That's my city. Owen! How come your son is in Bangalore of all places!'

'He's about one-eighth Indian, remember! So he's holidaying with his Coorg aunts and cousins in Bangalore, and shortly off to Mercara with them soon; where I'm unlikely to get him on Skype easily on those hills, I've been warned.'

As we were to learn later, Owen's wife had died tragically at childbirth, but little Danny and his distraught father had had the loving support of his grandparents living in Dublin. Owen worked as an administrator in a local art gallery, and helped bring great art shows to Dublin from around the world. But Owen's own creative ambitions lay in words rather than pictures. A couple of years ago, his tongue-in-cheek narration of the perils of being a Mr Mom had won him a prize in a local magazine's creative writing contest, and fired up his ambitions to write a whole book some day.

'We Irish anyway have the arrogant belief that we are all born writers—it's only got to surface some day, and then it's time to prepare for our winning speech for the Noble Prize for Literature,' said Owen. Well at least four supremely confident 'born writers' had assumed that—George Bernard Shaw, Samuel Beckett, Seamus Heaney, and William Yeats.

This Greece Writer's Workshop website had apparently ensnared Owen too. And Owen had sent his son Danny off on a holiday with his Indian cousins for two weeks, in the time that Owen would attend this workshop in Crete.

'Danny simply loves India,' said a visibly happy Owen, as we waited for Danny to reappear on screen. He had rushed off to bring and show us an unusual gift he had got from his cousins—and held up an exquisitely carved and embellished knife in a black casing. It was the traditional Coorg warrior knife called 'peeche kathi', and an heirloom that his grandparents wanted him to take back to Ireland.

'Mind you don't keep that in your hand luggage, son, or I'll see you in Juvenile Terrorist Jail,' laughed Owen.

Later, as we walked to explore the local war museum together, Owen filled us on more details of the remarkably inventive Danny. He was busy compiling his own joke book, called *L.O.L. with Danny*. But this wasn't going to be any old joke book. This was a book that made you laugh out loud—while the book too laughed out loud along with you!

Danny's 'invention' was based on a simple observation: every sitcom on TV had a laugh track, that always induced laughter or a smile after every wisecrack. Why not that same idea in a Book? Every page of his joke book would have a tiny embedded chip; one had to simply press it on the page, to have a burst of laughter emerge, as you read each joke.

Danny came up with this idea around age three, or so

claims Danny, Owen said with a grin. A book Danny had then about farm animals had a hidden buzzer, which when pressed, made the sound of that animal or bird. Danny wanted to invent a joke book that would make all sorts of funny laughter sounds emerge, and was already recording various chuckles, guffaws, sniggers, cackles, and even blood-curdling bleats of laughs from his friends, and now even his new-found cousins in India. Now all he had to do was find a clever tech genius to produce his invention.

'And I know just the one!' declared an enthusiastic Mini, totally charmed by Danny's idea for a book. 'My dad knows the ultimate Bangalore tech nerd. I'm going to ask him how to make this work commercially, and then I do know some wildly eager publishers always asking me about new ideas for kids' books.... A joke book that laughs along with you! HOW amazing is that!'

Owen nearly burst a blood vessel with joy. Mini and Owen decided to chat up on Skype again with Danny the next day, and tell him his dream book could actually happen.

'Publishers are always looking out for innovative stuff for kids, Owen. As soon as I get back to Bangalore I am going to do something about this one.' In fact, Mini was already texting her dad, Cheerio, to track down the techy genius for her plan.

So our dear Mini, who'd decided she'd run as far as possible from the world of kids and books and publishers, seemed to have totally forgotten her resolve! Bobby and I exchanged a quiet wink.

Day 3 of our Workshop began again with another elaborate Relaxation Exercise, with our learned guru urging us again to tighten, tighten, TIGHTEN our body parts, before gently letting go.

So this was going to be an everyday ritual, not just something to mark our first day of orientation. We tried hard not to catch each other's eye as we spread out our yoga mats on the floor, or we'd all be giggling helplessly again, recalling what Linda had said over dinner last night: 'It's not the release of tension from our muscles and joints that I'm bothered about, it's the release of flatulence from an obedient buttock that terrifies me!'

After filling 45 minutes of our precious 3-hour class with deep breathing, our Words-and-Art duo finally got around to setting us new assignments; an improvement over the previous day's baby-class, admittedly. The first was Café Writing, where we had to go away and pick out any person sitting alone in a café, and create a vivid story around that person, with a keen eye on how he or she was clothed, what they ate, their body language, and why they were there or what they were waiting for at the café. We were welcome to rely wholly on our imagination, or actually go and interview that person. The point was to make a very compelling story of it, within 200 words.

The other task was the more immediate one, which we had to individually present before the class, after a 10-minute time out to gather our thoughts. It was called the Terror of the Blank Page. Each writer had to come and share tips on how to unblock creativity; any personal experiences we could each share with the whole class.

Bobby was on first. She spoke candidly on what really worked for her: The Positive Effects of Envy. Nothing like a shot of good old jealousy to get something out on her writing pad or comp screen. 'What works really well for me is a Facebook update. Like this status update I once saw of a long-lost classmate from school days, a complete dork as far as we remember. She declared she's written her first book; and smugly invited us all for the launch event. It got me going on my own writing ambitions, like nothing else...'

'Oh, that can be so TRUE, isn't it' said our venerable class teacher, calling out the next name to come up in front of the class.

Stacey, the lovely white-haired lady from California, said she just needed a good, quick 'story-fix' to get her own writing started—and for this she had some favourite websites or books to dip into. One was *The Best Flash Fiction* from around the world: pithy, short pieces often with a dramatic twist to the tale in the last sentence. In fact, she decided to read out her favourite short story for the whole class. It had plot, characters, setting, dialogue, lust, drama, and a dramatic end, all in just 60 words.

The Confession

'Bless me, Father, for I have sinned.'
'How long since your last confession?'
'Two years.'
'What's the trouble?'
'I have wished death on a man.'
'You haven't acted on your wish?'

'Not yet.'

'Who is the man?'

'Someone I know who's cheating with my wife. I wish him dead.'

The priest paled. 'I forgive you.'

I shot him through the screen.

We burst into applause.

'That was WONderful, Stacey!' said Annabel.

Erica, a quiet redhead from Sheffield, urged us all to note down her own favourite website that triggered off a burst of writing: it was called Brainpickings.com. 'It's just my frequent dose of writing tonic. Such inspiring snippets from the world of writers to feed on: you all must subscribe to this one too…'

'Thanks for that WONderful tip, Erica!' cooed Annabel.

It was my turn. After a fair bit of thought, I decided to share an intriguing article I'd once come across in the *Reader's Digest*, many years ago.

'It was called "Throw Your Hat Over The Fence". It was a remarkable one-pager anecdote about a boy and his father taking a walk through a field. Along the way, a very tall fence blocks their path. The father then takes the hat off his son's head and deliberately throws it over the fence. This forces the boy to start climbing over if he really wanted the hat again. The father then uses this incident as a simple lesson in life for getting past unexpected hurdles. By 'throwing your hat over the fence', you were already committed to going ahead to the next stage, instead of stopping or turning back.

'This works for me as a writer, prone to a lot of procrastination: I sometimes throw my hat over the fence, by recklessly bluffing that I have already finished a task, when I haven't even started. Now I am forced to get it done, without embarrassing myself! I wonder if I'm making sense here, but I swear, guilt or the fear of being found out, works pretty well for me,' I told the class.

I got an applause of empathy from a roomful of procrastination-inclined writers (who isn't one? Except Jeffrey Archer maybe, who smugly claims to write 3000 words non-stop every day, without ever goofing off…)

Mini had a curious trick that always worked for her: she would read two pieces of writing by famous people that were the extreme opposite of each other; one which was so original and inspiring, the other that was awfully mediocre and dreadful. This invariably triggered off thinking: surely even I can write better than *that,* and so got her going again.

Cynthia had a very effective, short-cut solution to share. Her slogan was: Weed leads to speed. The best of the world's creative geniuses relied on 'the substance' to keep going; and she was certainly one of them. 'Just light up, and write up folks!' said Cynthia amidst cheers and whistles of approval.

For once, Annabel didn't say 'What a WONderful idea!' as she hurriedly called out the next name. Already the free-spirit Cynthia had shocked the prudish Annabel, when she revealed to us all, the meaning of the mysterious

Greek phrase 'κίνδυνος', tattooed on Cynthia's thigh. 'Danger zone' was apparently what it meant—and Cynthia seemed thrilled she had picked the perfect random word just for its design!

Later, looking back on our session, we realized that our charming Course Director had done little else but scribble notes of what each of us said; with not a single input or insight or advice of her own to give us.

'I think she fancies she's a shrink for tormented or frustrated writers,' concluded Cynthia. 'She collects large fees, gets us all talking, and that's it; thinks she's done her bit.'

'Can't you see? She's using us and all our collective tricks and tips, to secretly write her own bestseller on creativity or writer's manual or whatever it is she's plotting!' declared Mini. 'Did you notice the non-stop notes she was taking all along? Except when Cynthia spoke on doing the deed with weed, of course! She's going to be out with her book with all our collective wisdom in it, most imaginatively titled: 'Some WONderful tips for writers'...

'But I have to admit I found that session useful,' said Bobby. 'Listening to each others' starting trouble was comfort food for my writer's soul. I can see myself dipping often into today's notes to free myself from the blinking cursed cursor on an empty screen.'

'Lucky Amby. At least you've never ever faced the terror of the blank cell phone screen with your worthy professional writing experience in instant literature so far,' said Mini.

'That's only if I continue to live in a country called

Tweetistan, writing for a benevelont handsome Rajah. What about the reality of writing anything that involves more than 140 characters?' I said.

Which led my mind to plummet wildly into past-life regression. Well, the most recent past life to be accurate. How, I wondered, was my handsome Rajah coping without his Birbal? Had he, in a state of devastated misery and pain over the loss of his 'right hand', given up doling out his pithy Tweet-kathas, leaving lakhs of his subjects starved of their daily gyan?

WAS HE WRITING HIS *OWN* TWEETS?

I had to find out. First thing tomorrow morning...

14

'Time you enjoy wasting is not wasted time.'

KayKay's latest Tweet appeared before me on the computer screen, as I sat in Chania's internet café .

With the erratic manner our cell phones behaved on this island, the most reliable way to get into cyberspace was to rush to the 24-hour internet café next to the War Museum, where the randy owner Jose, would always greet us three girls, with 'Hello *amorfi kyrias!* Indian beauties! You're looking like Aishwarya Rai!'

Right now I was looking more like Ash than Aishwarya (and I mean the grey ash here) after our three-nights-in-a-row of crazy partying in several tavernas, and little sleep thereafter. I have this horrendous habit of waking up at 6 a.m. no matter when I go to sleep, and with Mini and Bobby lying dead to the world for at least the next three hours, I decided to catch up on writing mail to my beloved family and friends at the internet café.

Okay, I'll tell you the truth. I was there mainly to cyber-stalk KayKay through his Tweets.

After futile attempts at logging on at the hotel, I had decided to try my luck at Jose's internet café, where the sleepy and cranky teenaged son of Jose opened the door for me. 'Sorry! Sorry! *Signomeen!*' I said, as he pointedly looked at his watch.

'Time you enjoy wasting is not wasted time'. Aha! So KayKay was actually dipping into my own bank of pre-written Tweets that I had thoughtfully put in a folder on his laptop for future use.

Hmmm. Now I had to figure the double meaning in this profound sentence. Was Kaykay *secretly reaching out to me* with this line? Was he trying to make me remember the time we had together That Night in Liverpool? That Stormy Night in Liverpool?

That *romantic* night in Liverpool?

(Now I was beginning to wonder if last night's ouzo was still hanging around my system, making me completely delusional).

With no one in line waiting impatiently for me to finish at the comp, I sent off some quick messages home. Then I walked out of the café and down to a deserted quayside...a perfect setting for nostalgic indulgences, and unabashedly let my thoughts wander off to that magical, mystical tour to Beatles land, some months ago…

'I really do hate you, Amby! You're actually, really seriously going to *Liverpool* next week?'

I could see that Tarun from my gang had never accounted for such unexpected perks to come along with my job, when he had pushed me into becoming a Tweet writer for a film star. Earlier that day, I had been pretty stunned myself, when during a tea break at his film shoot, KayKay had announced quite casually to me: 'You're going on a pilgrimage with the unit next week, Amby. Bring your passport tomorrow for your visa papers…'

Pilgrimage? Was there a shooting scheduled at Tirupati or Manasarovar I hadn't heard of? But why a passport…?

'Amby, for our next sensational song sequence, we are all going to a famous place of worship. You worship the Beatles, don't you?' KayKay's loaded grin made my hair stand on end.

'NO! Can't be. Quit kidding me, Kay!' I said.

'Yes, you Beatle-nut! Liverpool it is. Some crazy throwback to the retro 60s is happening in my next song—where I wear a mop-haired wig and cavort through Liverpool singing to my bouffant-haired heroine in bell-bottoms. I nearly died laughing looking at the song's storyboard in my van this morning. But who's complaining? God bless our wild and wonderful Director saar…'

'Hold on, Kay! Since I am not that bouffant-haired heroine, how am I too part of this trip?'

'Because you have to interview me and write three different versions of an important cover story article for three different filmi mags, my pretty ghost writer. Our PR says these cover stories have to coincide with my film's release. And the deadlines are so close, we have no choice but to force you to come along on this trip, as awful as the idea may sound to you…' KayKay winked, quite enjoying the sight of me opening and closing my mouth like a goldfish with dementia.

'LIVERPOOL! Kay, I've dreamt of going there *forever.* I shall kill you now if this is a joke…'

'Get ready to walk on Penny Lane and Strawberry Fields, and grin like The Fool on the Hill! I've been on a Liverpool trip in my college days, Amby. It's insanely good. But you have a lot of writing work to do after each day's shoot, so don't forget your laptop.'

'She's got a ticket to ride…and she don't care'. Quite appropriately this was the old Beatles' song running in my head as I faced my parents about a couple of hours later.

'Who else is going with you?' demanded my mother. Feck, this was like getting permission for a school trip. Who else? Only a cast of millions who may dance behind the hero and heroine, wearing Beatles wigs.

'But why can't you go to Stratford-upon-Avon instead? That town has so much historical importance…' said my father with inexplicable logic. Why not, Dad? I'll just tell the Director to switch to Shakespearean wigs instead of Beatle mops and create a different dance.

They thankfully never asked me why I couldn't just

finish writing my piece on KayKay within the next seven days itself—the time it took to process our visas and get tickets—but if they had, I would have given them the unconvincing answer that KayKay was way too busy practising his retro dance moves with his leading lady Divyani.

Meanwhile I got pretty busy too—doing intense Google research on the sights and sounds of Liverpool. And also discovered that when the guys in the gang wailed 'Why don't I have Amby's life??' they weren't thinking at all about discovering where the Beatles were born or where they schooled and where they sang and where they ate—but only about the city's famous football stadium which, for them, was the sacred holy ground of pilgrimage, and the sole reason for anyone to go to Liverpool. Beatles? Now, who are they?

I had a well-worked out schedule on how to max out my coming trip to the Mecca of Music, and before I knew it I was far away in England…

And breaking my arm at Merseyside Hotel; not far from Paul McCartney's childhood home on Forthlin Road.

Yes, I broke my arm. A kind of hairline fracture, actually. Thankfully it was only on the last day before we returned to India—well after all the song and dance stuff was over, and well after I'd seen almost all there is to see of amazing Liverpool.

It was our last day there, and the entire unit had a free afternoon to explore the city. I had been rushing down the staircase at our hotel to join KayKay, Divyani the heroine, and a few others waiting at the reception for a general city tour, when I suddenly tumbled crazily downwards along the last few steps, landing with an ungainly heavy thud on my left arm.

I had got up in seconds grinning stupidly and claiming I was completely all right, even as KayKay made a lightning quick dash across to help me up. I felt ridiculous as hell as a whole bunch of people turned, hearing my short scream.

'I'm fine…I swear…how the hell did that happen? Anyway, sorry for holding you up, folks; let's go!'

By the time we were walking into John Lennon's house at Mendips, my arm was starting to swell like crazy. KayKay noticed me constantly rubbing my forearm, and began looking worried. 'We have to check this out, Amby. Let's get to a doctor fast.'

And an hour later I emerged from Dr Watson's near our hotel with my bandaged arm on a sling—'just a hairline fracture on your ulna. It'll be fine in two weeks'—by which time I was pleading with KayKay to go right back and join the unit, wherever they were, for the rest of the sightseeing. (I had noticed Divyani's expression of undisguised annoyance when KayKay had decided to take me off to the doctor).

'Okay, I'll go back to the unit. Anyway, I have been to Liverpool before, remember, and done the whole Beatles' homes stuff, so chill. Now get some rest in your room; and I'll see you later.'

I sat in my room going over all my pictures in my camera…thank goodness I had gone away on my own for the last two days exploring Liverpool! After some genuine attempts at trying to corner KayKay into the interviewing and feature pieces I was supposed to do between shifts, we simply gave up. 'We can do it immediately after our return in a single sitting,' said KayKay. 'Or on the plane ride back. Why waste precious Liverpool time?'

Now that was strange logic, when I was brought along to Liverpool for the main purpose of cracking this story, but sometimes I take weird suggestions from bosses without arguing.

As I had nothing to do with the crazy dance being shot in different locations in Liverpool, I had rushed away in a fit of Beatlemania. I was amazed how many beautiful churches this pretty city had to be proud about, but of course, I began first with my fill of the Beatles and more Beatles.

The Magical Mystery Tour in the famous psychedelic bus was the first on my list; after that, a visit to the iconic Cavern Club on Matthew Street, where the Beatles performed live almost 300 times in the early 60s. And the next day I sang my way through the Beatles Museum where the life of each of the Fab Four unfolded in audio and video.

Sitting now in my room, arm in a sling, I thought it was quite ironic that my pals had said to me before I left, 'Enjoy your trip, Amby!' Trip indeed!

The hotel manager had anxiously dropped in to apologize (just in case his polished staircase had had anything to do with the slip and trip?) and after a hearty room service meal, I was dozing off in my room, when the phone rang.

'Ambujax! Are you awake? Get to my room at once. *Now!*'

I sat up startled. 10 p.m! Why was KayKay calling me to his room at this time? The unfinished article? Or to give him one of my famed neck-massages I used to often boast about. Now I was getting ridiculous. I didn't even have two good serviceable arms right now…Must be to discuss that article, as we were all leaving the next day, I concluded.

Six minutes later, the phone rang again. In that time I had been contemplating how to get into my rather tight jeans again with just one working arm, and rummaging in my suitcase for perhaps a skirt to wear, when KayKay said, 'What's taking you so long, Amby? Hey, just come here in your PJs! You aren't dropping in on the Queen you know…'

So back I went into my pale blue rather fancy silk pyjamas (good packing decision, that). And slinging my MacBook bag on my good shoulder, I walked across the corridor with socks on my feet to Room No. 8 and gently knocked.

'The door's open! Come and sit here fast…you got here right on time.' KayKay was watching TV lounging on his bed, and patting a place next to him, and even propping up pillows for me to lean against.

The thud of the closing door behind me coincided with a peculiar thud sound in my cardiac area.

KayKay in dazzling white linen designer pyjamas. Coooool. Or should that be HOT.

Does KayKay even know what this sight could do to visiting young women in his bedroom?

Well, of course he should know, with that full-length mirror right opposite him, even though he was right then looking intently only at the TV and saying, 'Sit fast! And watch what's coming up just now!'

As I hastily and somewhat self-consciously scrambled onto the bed, KayKay began to smile. 'You faithfully brought your laptop, Amby? Did you think I was calling you here to *work*? Chuck it—I called you here to see the incredible movie that's on just now! Can you guess what it is?'

I looked up at the TV, even as KayKay thoughtfully kept an extra pillow to rest my bandaged arm on. Justin Timberlake and Mila Kunis were on the screen. Hmmm...'*Friends with Benefits*?' I guessed.

'Yes! I know you haven't seen this one yet—but wait for the song that's shortly coming!'

Well, this film was obviously also playing in my room's TV too—why didn't KayKay just call and tell me to switch on HBO there? Why was I sitting within inhaling distance of his Versace Pour Homme with only a pillow separating us? Why was I feeling like watching him rather than some film song he was asking me to see? What was *wrong* with me?

Meanwhile, KayKay was very briefly filling me in on the story so far, preceding the current scene. It was The Grand Hollywood Public Romantic Declaration coming up! Suddenly it had me hooked: I was after all a sucker for these scenarios, and KayKay had been surprised I hadn't yet seen this hit film as 'homework' for my screenplay writing ambitions.

Well, this scene wasn't yet another Airport Terminal scene, where hundreds of star-crossed lovers have dashed to before the gates closed, and declared their suppressed LOVE before a million cheering passengers. It wasn't a gigantic football stadium where the emotional lover pops up on the screen to publicly propose to his girl sitting amidst the audience.

It was the busy New York Central Station and as Mila Kunis enters the terminus, looking puzzled, Timberlake secretly switches on a hidden player, and hundreds of New Yorkers suddenly break into a pre-rehearsed flashmob dance!

And the song?

'It's *"Closing Time"!!'* I yelled.

I was dimly aware that KayKay by now was grinning away and watching only me watching the screen, and rather simultaneously we both joined in the last part of the song we loved so much, and sang away at the top of our voices, even as Justin and Mila were coming closer and closer towards each other…

'I know who I want to take me home…

'I know who I want to take me home…

Closing time…Every new beginning is some other beginning's end…'

'I just switched on the TV and found it was nearing the end of *Friends With Benefits*…and I always did wonder if you knew this song comes in the end. So I asked you to rush here,' said a smiling KayKay.

'I really had no idea—now I have to see the whole film as soon as I return!'

'Oh, you'll love the screenplay here. Not your Nora Ephron, but comes pretty close.'

Now the film ended pretty much soon after that big Hollywood-ending scene, and I should've scurried right back to my room.

But didn't.

We got talking and talking AND talking about this and that and that and this. Leading to our first real big argument. (You notice I said argument, not fight. Friends have arguments, *lovers* have fights…and Kaykay and I were very clearly only *friends*.)

It had started out as quite a simple disagreement when I told him about a quote I had read in the Beatles Museum: 'You should use it as a Tweet sometime, Kay! *'Time you enjoy wasting is not wasted time'*. I immediately scribbled it down in my little notebook. 'It's by John Lennon.'

'No, it's not. It's by Bertrand Russell. I know this for sure.'

'You do? You are so wrong here, Kay. How come it was up on a board at the Museum, Kay? With 'John Lennon' clearly written below it?'

'They got it wrong. Maybe Lennon was quoting Russell. I'm telling you I know this one for sure, because I truly subscribe to this thought.'

So KayKay was getting all literary and show-offy with his knowledge of quotable quotes, was he? And for some silly reason, I felt he was invading my territory. I was the words-expert here. Not only that, I was also the Beatles authority. I knew better. I was right.

And then quite suddenly we went a bit crazy with our arguments after that. Because it was no longer about *who* said this wonderful line, but what that line really *meant.*

'Oh, sure you subscribe to that thought, Kay. You really are wasting your time as a film star right now, aren't you? Anyway so glad to know you are happily enjoying what you are wastefully doing…'

'Excuse me! I'm NOT wasting my time acting. I think I'm doing a pretty good job of it…'

'Oh yeah? Then what were all those true confessions of yours one day in your make-up van about doing this filmi thing just for a lark? Doesn't that amount to a waste of your time?'

'No, it does not!' shot back Kay. 'I said I took it on for the fun of it, but there *is* purpose in what I do, now that I'm in it. I'm giving it all I've got, and in case you didn't notice, have been quite successful too. There's a big awards show coming up, and I hear I'm also in line for the *Filmfare* South Awards…'

'By success you mean the big bucks you're getting, isn't it, superstar Kay? Or are you referring to the "real purpose" you've discovered in what you do, when you cavorted about in that Facebook song prancing with your batty-eyed Shamini, or sang that fabulous Tamil version of "*I wanna hold your hand"* in your big hairy wig today, wooing Divyani in your bright yellow bell-bottoms. Wow, you really should be in the 'Spirit of Achievement' awards list this year.'

'Whoa…watch it, baby. Now that's literally hitting below the belt, when you talk about my yellow bell-bottoms,' said KayKay. I wondered briefly if KayKay was trying to lighten things up a bit, but I was in really no mood to laugh at all now. And so I hammered on…

And as many argumentative people do, we went off the point many times and made wild jibes bringing in irrelevant personal characteristics, misquoted each other several times, and made liberal use of *EXCUSE ME!* and *Can you HEAR yourself here?* Till it all came right back to justifying why we were both doing what we were doing just now, with our lives.

'So your real purpose IS the money isn't it? Come on, Kay! You keep saying you never take your star status too seriously.'

'I don't. Not at all. My directors do, my producers do, my PR unit too. Even my simpering co-stars do! So I owe them all my commitment to the job. The money that comes along is a by-product. And I'll know exactly when I can walk away from it all. After all it's only money.

'Only money! *Only money*! Ha! We'll see about that Mr Pious Sanyasi. We'll get Costumes to keep a designer orange robe and rudraksh malas ready for that big day when you give up worldly possessions. And even have *Chennai Times* cover it, as you walk away into the woods, or Mount Kailash or whatever…'

'Well thanks for thinking so much ahead, Ms Ambujakshi Balan, Tweet Writer. Only you may be out of a pretty demanding job yourself, as there are usually no cell signals in deep forests and remote mountain tops.'

'Oh, did you really think I might follow you there into deep forests like an obedient mindless Sita? That question doesn't even arise, so not to worry about being a jobless Tw...'

'Twit', cut in KayKay.

That did it. I suddenly jumped out of the bed, utterly mad. How dare KayKay make fun of me or my lousy job when it was HIS fame I was writing for? 'You know John Lennon or Bertrand Russell or whoever was right. And the reverse of that is: time you *don't* enjoy wasting is total wasted time. And I have NO IDEA why I'm wasting it here, when I'm dying to sleep, which I was on the verge of doing when you commanded me to come here...'

I stormed off down the corridor, but KayKay had leapt up and sprinted down to reach the door first in seconds, blocking my path. He even made a retro 'Peace' sign à la the Beatles era with his fingers.

'"Don't go to bed mad. Stay up and get even"...now who said that?'

'Some "twit" advising married couples—now if you'll step side, Sir Boss, I have to get into my own room and bed.'

KayKay chuckled. 'Well it's just turning midnight anyway, so run, broken-armed Cinderella. Before your blue satin fancy PJs turn into rags. And hey, is that a pen I see neatly sitting in your pocket? Do you even *sleep* with your pen?'

Omigod, why was he reaching forward towards my breast...er...pocket? Most unnatural thump, thump, thump symptoms in the left region alongside.

KayKay pulled out my trademark black felt-tip pen. 'I've been meaning to write on that white cast of yours—

it looks too clean and needs some messing up. Here, let me autograph it. I do happen to be a very famous film star, you know…'

'I wanna hold your (broken) hand ☺ Love, Kay.

In the dim dangerous light of that corridor, a Beatles lyric was scratched out onto my arm's cast. As he leaned his mid-back against the door, and bent down to write that line, his freshly washed mane of thick black utterly touchable hair blocked my view of what he was writing. If I too leaned forwards (pretending I wanted to see what was being written), I could almost bury my face in that inviting, mesmerizing male fragrance. Tigi Bed Head shampoo?

Now this is so utterly *ridiculous.*

Just minutes ago I was angry and irritated and annoyed and upset and fed up with this very man.

The tips of his hair feather-touched my face as he straightened up. He had finished and looked right into my eyes.

'Bonne nuit, dormez bien, mon ange bleu,' whispered KayKay. I have no idea what that meant, but I guess he was showing off that even his French was better than mine.

I told him so. He grinned, opened the door and the disturbing proximity continued as I almost squeezed past him to step inside. 'Is that a cue to see if my kissing is French too? Sleep well, my Beatle-nut.'

And just like that he kissed me. On both cheeks, as his firm hands cupped my face. The left kiss was exactly below my cheek bone. The right one landed close to my closed right eye.

I didn't expect to sleep at all that entire night—since I had to replay and find the motive for the kiss: As soon as I'd decided it was a mere 'brotherly peck, originating from the planet of Platonia', I would change that to 'Kiss from a guy yet unable to resolve his gay inclinations'—or else why didn't he kiss me on my mouth, full on?

Wait—*why didn't I??*

I had barely snuggled into bed, melting into a state of unabashed physical surrender, when my phone beeped. An sms beep. I jumped up, bolt upright.

KayKay! *'You left something of yours here on my bed'.* Smiley button with a wink.

Jeez. Did I leave a silly white sock behind, Cinderella style?? Nope. Both were on my feet still.

Was it an earring that fell off near a pillow? Always symbolic of A Woman Was Here…Nope. My tiny pearl studs were intact.

So what was that intriguing message? Hah, got it! I haven't really left my *heart* behind there, if that's what you're implying, Mr Presumptuous Man.

Till I realized I had left my laptop behind in his room.

I thought for a full 5 minutes about sending a witty/dangerous/loaded response. But suddenly gave up, and merely sent a smiley button back. The one with raised eyebrows saying a kind of 'Oh!' expression. I swear these emoticons are a useful thing to have in life—both when you have lots to say and nothing to say.

And I must've fallen almost instantly asleep—because I remember lots of wild filmi scene dreams with KayKay playing the lead role. I was the female lead. I was also, strangely, the director.

I had overslept. With a start I realized that it was well past 9 o' clock—how come no one had called me? Then the packed events of the previous day came flooding in.

The fall. The break. The cast. *The kiss.*

I stared at my hand cast, as if seeking proof I hadn't just dreamt up all of the above, particularly the last item on that list. Almost involuntarily, my right arm flew to my face; I touched the two spots where Kay's lips had landed…*why* were they still feeling like two pieces of hot burning *coal?* What would my expression be when I saw KayKay at the unit's buffet breakfast?

What would I say most dispassionately, that would indicate to him that I never thought about it AT ALL, not one teeny bit…that frivolous kiss at the doorway?

What would I blab that would reveal to him that I had relived and dreamt of nothing but that flash of intimacy, all night??

The sharp trrring of the phone cut into my day-dream. It was the Director's assistant.

'Hello, Ambujakshi Ma'm. I have your laptop. KayKay saar has left it with me to hand over to you…'

'Why? Where's KayKay?' I asked, puzzled.

'He's already left for Paris, Ma'm. Change of plan early this morning. He left the hotel at 7 itself…Director saar has announced the unit pack-up and we are all leaving for the airport to go back to India at 1 p.m. as scheduled. May I come and give you the laptop in your room, Ma'm? I could not see you at breakfast today...'

So KayKay suddenly upped and went to France?? Whatever for? How come he didn't breathe a word of this to *me*, his very own faithful shadow? Well that certainly took care of my bashful reluctance to come face-to-face with him!

Arriving back home in Chennai, there was such a fuss made over my broken arm in a sling that even my PR gang never asked for all those unwritten pieces on KayKay. They were so busy being peeved that the usually disciplined and responsible KayKay had suddenly taken off to France, just like that.

Meanwhile I had stuck on a wobbly piece of plaster over the I-wanna-hold-your-hand message on my cast by KayKay (more to obliterate him OUT of my thoughts, apart from blocking it from the inquisitive, disapproving eyes of the family).

By the time KayKay returned to India too, just four days later (the Director saar's special puja to make him come back fast had worked), my 'cool and distanced air' that I had been practising and practising was beginning to feel genuine. Especially since KayKay didn't even bother to ask why his stupid one-liner had mysteriously disappeared from my cast.

So I didn't bother to ask him why he had mysteriously disappeared to Paris either.

'It's all working out just fine, Amby!' said Kavi when I told her about The Liverpool Episode (The one where

Amby and KayKay have a Big Unresolved Argument.) 'Maybe he has a secret Parisian garcon tucked away somewhere too…who knows? This certainly makes your resigning and flying off to Greece easier!'

Did it really make it easier? YES.

'Time you enjoy wasting is not wasted time…'

So why was I wasting time here, sitting in Greece watching the sunrise near the deserted quay, lapsing into a delirious state of nostalgia over a stupid Tweet written by a former boss?

15

'Dance first. Think later. It's the natural order.'

'Oh my Zeus! We've overslept…Amby, whatever happened to that natural alarm clock in your head—it's 8 o'clock already!'

Maybe it was the happy thought that it was our first Day Off today from classes, that all of us had blissed out like lazy lobotomized lizards after the previous night's revelry. But today was our day-long boat excursion and if we didn't hurry up we'd miss our chance to get on that hugely popular cruise to Stavros. The island of *Zorba the Greek*!

Bobby sat up in her bed, fingers pressing down on her

throbbing head. 'Oh noooo, my wretched migraine attack! Girls, I am afraid I have to stay back today; just can't see myself being out in the sun all day: I need to sleep this one out for the next few hours…'

'But what a fine travel story awaits, Bobby! What are you going to do, sitting by yourself all day? Just pop some pills and come along…'

But despite the tea and sympathy we served her, Bobby's head was still feeling as though tiny carpenters with hammers were doing intense renovation work inside her brain. 'If I feel better, I'm going to go over my notes and later begin writing my new travel blog—but I need to weave in the Zorba story too, so take many notes for me!'

Promising to take lots of pictures too, Mini and I hurried down to the wharf of the Old Harbour of Chania, where we saw several doubledecker cruise boats decorated with colourful buntings.

'*Grigora! Elateh etho*! Hurry up and come on our boat *Aphrodite*, ladies!' We saw the crew of the boat waving to us—holding up a board that said Stavros Island Cruise.

Before going to sleep the previous day, we had all collectively racked our brains for scenes we could recall from the 1964 seven-Oscar nominations classic film, *Zorba the Greek*, which, as every tourist brochure of this island would happily ever after declare with much pride, had been filmed all over Crete, the most magical of all Greek islands.

The defining image of the film, of course, was the iconic Dance of Zorba: the robust *Sirtaki* dance on the beach. Played so masterfully by Anthony Quinn.

And it was to this very beach that we were excitedly heading towards; the spectacular bay of Stavros where most of the film had been shot. Cruise-loads of tourists arrive here every single day for the Zorba experience. Something that Hollywood suddenly opened up to the world; making spellbound tourists discover for themselves why the talented Lassally chose this island to shoot, and why he got the Oscar for Best Cinematography.

In many ways, we too had unconsciously been following the film's storyline. A few days ago, we had stood at Port Piraeus at Athens to get on board our gigantic passenger ship sailing to Crete. Just as Alan Bates, the shy, handsome Englishman visiting Greece for the first time, had stood in pouring rain, in the film's opening scene. Awaiting our ship's departure, we had sat in a café, watching gulls swooping down; old Greek *ya-yas* with scarves tied under their multiple chins, and hardy sailors eyeing pretty young *kopelas*...Didn't Alan Bates do the same when he first encountered Zorba at Port Piraeus, fascinated by the laughing, incorrigible peasant? The Englishman's view of life was to change forever with his Greece experience. So too, we were inclined to believe, would ours.

And now, here we were nearly fifty years after director Michael Cocoyannis had directed his story of lust, intrigue, adventure and revenge in a remote Greek village.

Slicing our way through the icy Aegean blue for a forty-minute ride to Stavros Bay, we suddenly came upon the sparkling blue-green bay surrounded by chocolate-brown mountains. Spectacular! This is where Irene Papas, the beautiful tormented widow, fell in love with Alan Bates.

'Oh no, Bobby's missing out on this fabulous travel story! She simply has to hear it all from us, and weave it into her Greek travelogue…' said Mini. 'And hey, Amby! Must say am really impressed with your background dope on *Zorba the Greek*: you seem to know more than our tourist guides here!'

'The truth is I got it all from KayKay and Toni before I left, Mini,' I reluctantly admitted. 'They can spew stuff about Oscar-winning movies at the drop of a director's hat…'

We had two bracing hours to swim, sunbathe, snorkel in the astounding expanse of the bay. Intoxicated with it all, we walked along the very strip where Hollywood technicians must have set up their trolley shot of Anthony Quinn's final signature dance ending the film. A guide told us in charming broken English that Quinn had a fractured foot, but had told no one…instead he had secretly improvised on his dance to cope with the pain.

And that is the very exact dance, step for step, which is a ritual even now at every Big Fat Greek Wedding!

We stood eagerly in a line, random tourists forming an impromptu clique of friendship, linking arms around each other's shoulders. Zorba style. The soundtrack from the film was switched on, from a tinny stereo player placed on the sand. And with the first strains of the santuri, Zorba's beloved lute-like instrument, our tour guide-turned-dance-instructor shouted a full throated *'O-Pah!'*.

The infectious zest of Zorba washed over us. Laugh more. Dance a lot. Live life every day to the fullest.

We willingly fell into step; swaying left, swaying right,

a sudden kick, a slow step back, then working up a steady frenzy...One of those holiday moments that makes one think: what pursuit in life could be more rewarding than travel?

Our obsession with Zorba had really begun on the very first day of our exploring Chania, when we had spotted a gigantic picture of Anthony Quinn, from the film poster. It was hung outside a very large café called Christiana facing the seafront, and had immediately drawn us in; especially since we saw a gleaming Oscar statue in a glass casing sitting proudly next to it at the reception counter.

'Look! An actual real live *Oscar!* KayKay read about this in an article on Crete, and told me to check out if it's true!' I yelled.

Well, it turned out to be only a replica of one of the three coveted statues the movie had won, reminding proud locals of the part their island played in a world-famous movie, besides promoting tourism to Greece. And the café owner never tired of telling tourists that this very café had featured in many scenes in the movie, even seating us where, apparently, Anthony Quinn had actually sat. We suspected this 'exact table' kept changing to suit whichever table was empty at the time, but over the years delighted tourists continue to have their pictures taken here, holding the (real?) Oscar in their hand.

But what really got us even more than the Oscar statue was our chance meeting with the unforgettable Giorgios.

We shot our touristy photos, each holding the Oscar (I even made a brilliant impromptu speech for Best

Screenplay, for my recent worldwide erotic hit called *You've Got Male*). Then we noticed a swarthy gent in a far corner clapping heartily for my speech, exclaiming '*Exaisios!*' from across the café.

'*Kali spera*, Giorgios!' said the hotel owner. 'Beautiful ladies, you can meet famous star of Crete, acting in Zorba movie!' He gestured to the cheering Greek to come on over and meet us. We had no idea then if the conspiratorial wink accompanying this introduction meant it was a merry bluff of some sort.

'Have you seen *Zorba the Greek*? Well, watch it again some day—and look closely for a scene with Anthony Quinn, Alan Bates and an eight-year-old Greek boy. That would be *me*!' began Giorgios, almost in his mid-fifties now, as he promptly came over and sat down at our table.

But what Giorgios had to say next made us gulp in disbelief—mid-ouzo. 'Remember the scene when a delirious Anthony Quinn comes out of a hotel, chased by a lady? Well that's Hotel Contessa. And I run that hotel today!'

We were in no mood to check if this was a tourist trap. Who really cared? But as it turned out (through surreptitious Google searches at Oscar websites, done the next day), what Giorgios said was absolutely true. Hotel Contessa—located just five cobbled streets away from the lively Crete waterfront, was indeed an important location for much of the film's action.

Giorgio told us that his fame in Crete as 'the boy who starred in *Zorba the Greek*—all 45 seconds of it—had continued through the years of growing up, till he and his uncle decided to buy the hotel made famous by the film.

And now here was the very same Giorgio urging us to quit our Hotel Columba at once and move to his hotel instead (with a promise of good discounts too) so that we could even sleep on Anthony Quinn's bed!

While we had no way of knowing for sure if the gigantic bed Giorgio was dramatically showing us was exactly where Zorba's 'night of carnal pleasure' was shot, we do know with absolute certainty that Theofanus Street—just outside the façade of Hotel Contessa—is exactly where Zorba comes lurching out, punch drunk and happy, pursued by a young lady in furs. Frames from that scene were proudly on display at the reception's notice board, and as Giorgio pointed out, the outside façade of the hotel was absolutely unchanged even now.

To have followed the trail of Zorba, from cafés to hotel rooms and then on a boat, all the way to that last iconic dance at the actual beach, seemed to be the most fitting finale.

More exhilaration followed as we sailed on from Stavros to the Lazareta and Theodorou Islands, where through our glass-bottomed boat we were able to see a sunken aeroplane from World War II.

'Oh Bobby, what a day of adventure you're missing!' I sighed, as we swam and snorkled again just before the sun began to set.

Well, I needn't really have felt so sorry for Bobby. For she was having her own unexpected day of surprises back at Chania.

A startled Bobby had jumped up from her contented doze in the reclining chair on the balcony. 'Koritsi! Look, look. You have for you the veesitors!'

Mama Helena stood at our room passageway, gesturing downstairs to the reception. 'Four man friends calling for you ladies!' Our hotel owner didn't look particularly happy about this invasion of strange young men.

Four man friends? Must be some mistake, thought Bobby, hurriedly changing out of her pyjamas into jeans and a tee. And crowding up the tiny reception, jabbering in an unrecognizable language, were four complete strangers. Omigod, had she, Mini or Amby made some wild new friends in the Taverna last night, 'under the influence'? Who the hell were these grinning, weatherbeaten set of guys?

Three blonde heads. One dark head. The dark-haired one, she realized looked Indian. 'Hi! I'm Arvind Seshadri, and these are my pals Dominik, Pavi and Alexis from Finland. Sorry for this sudden intrusion, but we're looking for Ambujakshi Balan…'

Arvind the Eligible! Here in Chania? In pursuit of Amby??

Bobby's face ceased looking a giant question mark. 'Oh, Arvind Seshadri! Of course, she did mention your name…well I'm Bobby Varma, Amby's friend. She's away all day on a boat cruise, and won't be back till 5 p.m. But do sit down…'

Arvind Seshadri turned to speak to his friends in that strange jabber again. Finnish, it turned out. Oh wow. What's with guys who speak foriegn languages fluently…they just seem so cool.

Soon they were all sitting outside on the lawn of Hotel Porto del Columba's tiny garden, as Mama Helena bustled about getting tea and biscuits. 'We are on our annual fishing tour and have been staying at Mykanos island for the past week. The flathead mullet along the coast of Crete is what has brought us here—just on a whim, actually—and we thought we'd look up my Facebook friend, Ambujakshi too. And perhaps get some recommendations on where to stay here for a couple of days. I did send her Facebook messages two days ago that we may just turn up here, but maybe she never saw those...'

Bobby listened to the easy manner of the guy before her—how come Amby had never mentioned that Arvind was a 6-foot-2-inch hunk! Or that he had *long* hair? Hmmmm. So this was her Tam Brahm catch, whose dubious downside however, was that he was a fish-catching and fish-eating fellow.

A recommended place to stay? Bobby could think of just the place: The Contessa! 'Well, there's a great place not far from here we saw the other day, with the owner offering us hefty discounts to move there! I could show it to you...' And despite the fishing gang's insistence that they could easily find their way there, Bobby decided to go along too, as her head had stopped feeling like a beaten up drum.

'Don't know if you've ever heard of *Zorba the Greek* filmed here years ago in Crete—but it was apparently shot here in Hotel Contessa, so it's pretty famous too.'

Half an hour later, the group was totally settled in,

with Bobby having skilfully wangled a discount for them too. After making their arrangements for an early morning catamaran ride out along the coastline to go mullet fishing, the boys had the rest of the day to explore Chania—and Arvind insisted on treating Bobby out to lunch—any place she'd recommend.

Hmmmm. A bit of a charmer, this one.

'You'll never BELIEVE who just landed up here, asking for you, Amby.' Bobby had composed this quick text message on her cell phone, but hesitated about sending it out. First there was little chance she'd get the message out on that remote island, with all the erratic connectivity, but the other reason was, maybe it would be fun to keep it all a complete surprise at the end of the cruise—which was anyway just a few more hours away.

Meanwhile, decided Bobby, this Finnish-speaking Tamilian Eligible with a great voice-over-for-TV-commercials kind of voice, needed some further checking out—for Tam Brahm girl Ambujakshi Balan seeking suitable marriageable boy. Sitting down for lunch with the four anglers at The Dead Fish café, Bobby decided that the Eligible's fish-consuming credentials must definitely be kept secret from the strict vegetarian seeking grandparents…

'So you're in advertising! I really love watching ads, you know; one of those strange people who thinks programmes interrupt commercials!' Arvind was doing pretty well so far. Bobby ticked off a box or two in her head: so he actually loves good ads. Looks dishy enough to even model in them.

Soon they were talking about some outstanding Ikea ads that had won the Grand Prix at Cannes some years ago, and Bobby was beginning to wonder if she was an advertising die-hard after all, and would never ever be able to quit the stimulating world of creating great ads…

'Do you remember that one with an old bedside lamp that is left out with the garbage in the rain, looking depressed and so human—as the owner clears space for a new Ikea lamp? Ha ha ha, that was just brilliant!' Pavi, the Finn who was a cinematographer back in Helsinki seemed to be a fan of advertising too.

Bobby was surprised how fluent they all were in English; though with an attractive accent that was quite unusual.

'So what's made you want to quit advertising?' asked Arvind.

'This!' said Bobby gesturing to the whole wide world before her—the sun, the sea, the sand. 'The great big call of travel! And writing! So much to see and write, so little time…'

'So do they pay you well for this job where one is perpetually on vacation?' asked Arvind.

'Are you kidding me?! I have yet to land myself a visiting card with Travel Writer on it. And that's why I am here spending big bucks on a Writing Programme. And even then, I wonder how one makes a living out of travel writing anyway, or almost any form of writing for that matter—so I am also on the alert for a Greek millionaire, single and marriageable…'

'Well I love travel too, because I long to get away to forget things. And when I reach my hotel, and open my suitcase, I find that I have…' said Arvind with mock sadness. Good one-liner there by Arvind Seshadri; Amby, you'll be pleased to note, thought Bobby.

'And do your Nokia jobs bring with it a lot of travel too?' asked Bobby.

'For our friend Arvind here, yes. For both of us: Alexis and Dominik, no,' replied Alexis a tad sadly. They were accountants in their firm, not like Arvind in Marketing who was always seemed to be off to some new part of the planet every week.

'You call that travel? I call that travail—where you sight-see many hotels, meet new people in conference rooms, and shop in identical-looking airport lounges.'

And soon the conversation led off to what each one really wanted to do in life.

Alexis wanted to do nothing but conduct fishing trips around the world. Dominik wanted to do nothing but cook and eat the fish caught in Alexis's fishing tours. And Pavi made everyone laugh with his secret desire. 'I am a commercial cinematographer, but also the laziest fellow I know. What I want to do is become a mindless wedding video photographer; there's good, easy money there for recording couples dress up, overeat, dance badly, and officially launch the beginning of the end of their lives.'

And what of our pal Arvind? He did seem to have loftier ambitions: he wanted to start an eco-friendly farm. In the Himalayas. Bobby made a huge note of this: wondering if the Rules of Eligibility in the Indian marriage market would categorize this as a good, safe (well-paying) job or a vague, arty (loser) job to have!

'Is that Bobby out there waving to us? And who're those guys with her?'

Mini and I strained our eyes looking at the shoreline at the Chania harbour, as our cruise boat sped towards the end of its tour. Yes indeed that was Bobby, actually looking petite standing next to four rather toweringly tall gents, in Bermuda shorts and caps.

So much for us imagining Bobby still huddled up in bed, a scarf tied tight around her head like a sickly Phoolan Devi. Bobby was grinning away and looking as fresh as a lettuce leaf in Mama Helena's back garden.

As we clambered out of the *Aphrodite*, Bobby came forward to give us a hug of welcome. 'Hiya girls! Look who's here in your welcome-back committee!'

'Hi Ambujakshi, or is that Amby…I'm Arvind Seshadri…'

Ti? Pi-ah? Eh-toh? (That is Greek for a rapid interjection of What? Who? *Here?)*

Later, Mini wished she had recorded this first 'girl sees boy' moment with her camera. Apparently, I closely resembled a large-mouthed bass, a common fish we had just encountered in our snorkelling adventure.

Zeus! A guy who was a much-viewed photograph on Facebook, for weeks and weeks, suddenly standing here LIVE before me. Why was he *here*?

'And these are my buddies from Helsinki, Pavi, Alexis, and Dominik…'

I tried to recover my composure as I shook hands all around, and introduced a crazy grinning Mini to them too.

'We, er, planned this annual fishing trip to Mykonos a year ago, and suddenly decided to take a detour to Chania to say hello—I mentioned it in your Facebook inbox, but I guess you haven't seen that one yet!' Arvind's explanation, tinged with mild embarrassment, put things in perspective, regardless of what Mini's and Bobby's wild imagination may have been concluding…

So he had warned me ahead—only I hadn't seen it. The very very ODD feeling continued, as I tried to make some sense of it all.

'Bobby here has been most kind in helping us find a great place to stay,' said Arvind, smiling with eyes that crinkled almost into smiley shapes. *Nice!* But why was he looking so different from those pictures my family had drooled over?

Long hair! Rather cool and arty, as it had been tied up into a trendy'man-bun', à la Brad Pitt. Hmmm. Double nice.

And what on earth did I look like just then, I wonder. For one, my skin had moved from Warm Cedar to Woody Brown in the shade card. My hair looked like a good testing ground for a new lawn mower. Why did my first meetings with guys always have me looking so horrendously smashing?

The whole group made its way to a new quayside café we'd been eyeing for a while, and sat down to get better acquainted.

Did Arvind Seshadri ensure that he sat next to me, or did my feet just move easily towards the chair next to him? Can't say. But we do dwell on these tiny inconsequential details years and years later, so I should have paid more attention.

The drinks and food orders served as ice-breakers—enough for me to breathe normally, despite not really being pleased at the face that I saw on the polished spoon, as I secretly checked out my flushed face and mad hair.

'So, Amby…or can I call you Ambujakshi? Love the flavour of old Indian names!' began Arvind. 'My own name has 'Arumugamangalam', reduced to a mere A in the beginning. I wish I were called that, though I wouldn't have survived even nursery class with that one.'

He laughed when I told him my family name was a very tribal-sounding 'Maduboosi' which we had detached long ago—and with that I hoped the initial awkwardness had passed.

Well…truth be told. A hint of awkwardness *did* linger on…perhaps more so for Arvind, wondering if he was intruding on my Greek getaway in this unconventional manner; and me? Well I was over-laughing, and over-nodding my head a bit too much, after every sentence he spoke.

The arrival of the food changed everything. Exclamations of *'Mmmm…herkullista!'* interrupted the friendly jabber around the table. Easy guessing that word meant 'delicious' in Finnish—but why was Bobby slyly winking at me, when I too said *'herkullista'* midway through my cabbage rolls with raisins and pine nuts? Anyway, I winked right back.

So what 'compatibility topic' do we move on to next? Do you like cats or dogs? Are you religious or spiritual?

Do you squeeze toothpaste from the front or the back? Do you prefer Mutual Funds or Fixed Deposits? Do you like eating on stainless steel or porcelain? Do you prefer *The Hindu* or the *Times of India*?

Of course we didn't get to providing this crucial pre-marital data to do our analytics with, but I really can't recall what we talked about either. Perhaps it was because Arvind had become so cool and non-fussed and relaxed, I suddenly decided I'd appear cooler, non-fussed-er, and relaxed-er than him. And after returning from the restroom (I HAD to see if my disobedient hair was still standing on end) I deliberately sat on another free chair, and struck up a conversation with Pavi, the cinematogrpaher with the ready laugh.

Back in our room much later that night, a babble of reactions to the arrival of The Eligible broke out.

'So what did you *think*, Amby?!'

'He's got a quiet, wacky sense of humour!'

'His hair is the coolest.'

'He REALLY did land up! Now what does that say…'

'I think that Dominik's taken a shine to Mini, by the way…'

'You got to hide the fishing talent part from your granddad…'

'Hey Amby, those blue eyes of Dominik are killers—think of the babies he'll help make. Just giving you some alternatives here.'

'This mullet-fishing and all is just an excuse, Amby! You're the one this Arvind dude wants to catch.'

And so on. And on.

Mini and I had noticed the easy familiarity with which Bobby had chatted with the group, having spent a greater part of the day with them already. And now Mini was doing her own pairing up.

'Bobby, the two accountant lads are worth checking out further. They're within the Nokia family, they seem pretty grounded—or did you find the more free-spirited Pavi the most interesting? He could be the cinematographer-with-benefits on your travels!'

Well, Arvind Seshadri certainly kept me awake for a while that night. Now this was a pretty unconventional first-meet for an arranged marriage.

Unchaperoned by parents and grandparents, but with two wildly imaginative friends in attendance from the girl's side. A motley bunch of foreigners from a fishing club from the boy's side. And for tea-time snacks, not the ever-favourite *sojji-bajji* sweet and savoury of every South Indian arranged marriage 'seeing ceremony' (usually coyly served by the prospective bride, and proclaimed to have been prepared by the well-trained prospective herself) but *musaki borelki*, *faciio koplella* and *cavito souvaka*—served by a rather saucy waitress gal displaying ample cleavage, who even made eyes at 'The Boy'.

I had to tell Kavi about this very fast. It was a weird feeling: Kavi and I, right through the last week before I left Chennai, had had endless discussions on the 'Film-boy vs Finn-boy' issue of choice as Kavi had labelled it.

(As if either party had actually, formally even *asked* to be chosen by me in the first place, in this grand swayamvara we were inventing in our minds). It was that girly thing girls all over the world do of course: over-discuss a relationship issue to wild extremes.

Kavi had a clear plan at the end of it all for me; and knew where my hypothetical garland would have to land.

'It's the Flying Finn for you, Amby! Only you'll be wrecking *my* own life thereafter, with my parents quite sure that I too should marry the Punjabi equivalent of your Nokia hero, and distribute ghee-laden laddoos to the entire universe at once.'

Kavi's firm recommendation was also to put a certain finality to the KayKay Question.

'Ambujakshi Balan: think very level-headedly about this: can you ever seriously see yourself being *married* to a South Indian film star? Okay, so he wasn't really that white-trousered, white-shoed, oily-haired, chest-hair-displaying caricature that springs to mind, but look where he's quite firmly set his sights: the top spot in the South Indian film industry, then the inevitable desire to enter the race in the Hindi film world too, then all the song and dance that goes with it: practising and prancing at filmi award shows, preening and primping on fashion ramps, sinful and scandalous heroine link-ups. And if all of the above didn't happen, a panic-ridden PR unit that works overtime to see that it *does* happen, till he's so totally into…'

'Kavi! I don't really think he's going to get swallowed into all this. Er, yet. He's got a plan in mind…'

'He's got a mind, but he's also got a handsome mane of shampoo-ad compatible hair covering that great mind, Ambujaks, that's what he's got. The romancing and flirting and texting and Tweeting with you was all great while it lasted, but I think he was only competing with you with your own form of weaponry: *words*. And you've got suckered into falling for words strung nicely together. Look at the rest of the package he comes with: I mean honestly, Ambujakshi Iyer Balan, wife of a *film star*?'

16

'If an opportunity scares you, TAKE IT!'

I was back at Jose's internet café at seven in the morning. As usual, making Jose's son scowl as he opened the door. I was the only creature in the entire island who took their 24x7 signboard seriously.

I had to see what Kavi had to say about the turn of events in my life, after my last quick mail to her sent two days ago. One of those emails that demanded lots of upper case usage.

HE'S HERE KAVI! RIGHT ON THIS ISLAND! ARVIND THE ELIGIBLE LANDED IN CRETE WITH FISHING BUDDIES! More later…

But of course, the first thing I really did was slyly log into Twitter and checkout all the latest Tweets. From KayKay. Some habits die hard.

Seven new ones were out since I last saw this page. Five had been retweeted many times over. Hmmm. Not bad at all. (Confession: I say 'not bad at all' in the same manner that women friends meet and say 'Wow, you've lost so much weight. Not bad at all.' When in actual fact they want to slap them on the spot for having out-slimmed them.)

I went back to the Tweet on the top of KayKay's page. '*If an opportunity scares you, TAKE IT!*' So what's the implied opportunity that may be coming the way of our filmi hero?

Well I got the answer all right, after reading Kavi's mail immediately after.

From: kavisavvy@gmail.com
To: amby8@gmail.com

Dearest Amby

How goes the Greek drama so far! Anything but a Greek Tragedy I bet. I've gone insane waiting for you to say more, after your mysterious THE ELIGIBLE IS HERE!, and More later…More later? Like when, Ambujkashi Hitchcock Balan? Thanks for leaving me in utter suspense. I even snooped in your FB page for possible latest info on your Greece scene, and all I saw was your update ages ago with your new pals Bobby and Mini grinning from a cruise boat—and a 'Like' by our very own Finn-Iyer boy. And so he FOLLOWED YOU there physically after all, not just in an ether form in cyberspace.

So what's he really 'Like', Amby???!!!!!

I hate to say 'I told you so' (that's a lie, EVERYone loves to say 'I told you so') but this Arvind dude was really worth keeping simmering in the back-burner, and now is when you turn on the heat on him, girl! Are you telling me his fishing trip to Crete is a remarkable coincidence? Bollocks! Or whatever they say for bollocks in Finnish. He's only there to catch you, babe. So please render yourself baitable, and catchable, but don't say 'yes' yet (BTW, do the good folks at home know about this?)

And now here are some juicies about your hot ex-boss. Did you know that 'Facebook Kaadal' has just crossed 100 crores?? And 'Raakshasa' *is predicted to be another guaranteed hit. And a news item says that a film about a dance school teacher is being specially written with KayKay in mind. And that KayKay is supposed to be on a HINDI film signing spree, you southies I tell you, how do you all get so proficient in Tamil AND Hindi. Anyway there are rumours (need I say from Vikki-leaks) that a Karan Johar film with Vidya Balan is in the offing (hmmmm. Another Balan?!) at KayKay's own insistence, he'd liked being paired with her, an action film being shot exclusively in Turkey. He's even going off for a recce there, with the director. Vikki got this news from his travel agent pal, who claims to have personally booked KayKay's tickets to Turkey.*

BUT. The Toni-KayKay rumours haven't really gone away either, and Vikki is going to find out soon if Toni too goes along on this recce jaunt to Turkey. Wink.

Now there's more gos to report for sure, Amby. But gotta run now. Hit Reply NOW and tell me the 'More Later…' at once.

PS: Your last big ghost article on KayKay: in the 'Born to be a film star?' feature with baby pix and all, looks and reads

SOOOPerb! Those pix of him taken at the Mutthukadu Sailing Club are sizzling—his 'boy' Toni has done a good job dressing up, or rather dressing down his love interest. Wink.

Love, Kavi.

I walked back to our hotel room slowly with all the news from Kavi buzzing about my head. So KayKay was off to Turkey to further a 'scary opportunity'...with the newest leading lady? Or Toni? Well enjoy, KayKay. After all, it's just one more film. Followed by just one more film. Followed by *just one more* film. Ad infinitum. Ad nauseum.

I had been so right in that war of words we had had in Liverpool. KayKay had lost his focus; and was engulfed in his celluloid world forever. Cheers bye Filmi Hero...And happy romancing to you.

No worries about me. There are plenty of other fish in the sea. Especially fish-catching eligible fish in the sea.

Oh God, WHAT was my scrambled up mind blathering away to itself??

Somehow after hitting the Reply button to Kavi's mail, I didn't seem to get any further than 'Thanks for the goss, Kavi. But have I got a REAL story to tell you, about the rather dishy, swishy Eligible!'

And hurriedly did a back-space on the entire previous sentence, and ended with a tame: 'Hi Kavi! Gos noted ;-). Updates on rather dishy Eligible very soon. Our Writing Course is getting to be really VERY packed suddenly...Luv. Amby.'

And after hesitating for a bit, went to my Facebook page and decided to put up three pictures of all of us sitting with the visiting Finns in the restaurant.

Okay, I admit I also added one more pic taken by Mini I think, of just the Eligible and Me, grinning away side by side—but it's only because I thought I came out reasonably well only in that picture. I swear that is the only reason.

Okay, who am I fooling here?

The boy gang was going away on their fishing trip—and we three girls were at the quay to see them off. Arvind and I kept some negotiable doors open for further '-ings' such as writing, texting, phoning-the usual et ceteras of Stage Two in the Arranged Marriage Game: 'Let's be in touch through email' to 'See you later in India this year'.

(Technically speaking, this was so far neither an arranged marriage game, nor a love marriage game, but a kind of 'like marriage' scenario…The Facebook thumbs up 'Like' symbol, to make things really clear.)

My two new soul-sister confidantes in the proceedings, Mini and Bobby, made it all an utterly self-conscious scenario for me, what with their surreptitious winks and overacted casualness as they shamelessly eavesdropped on our quayside goodbyes. Well, the entire group was all there anyway, getting into their hired fishing boats on the mullet fish expedition. Dominik's handshake with Mini, we all thought lingered excessively. His motives for doing so seemed as clear as his sexy blue eyes.

Arvind, for some crazy reason (okay, you know the

crazy reason...) suddenly appeared to me to be extremely handsome, and uber cool—ponytail and Oakley shades and Giordiano Ts and bronzed muscles emerging from his sleeveless fishing jacket and all. Maybe our first encounter was still at a pretty awkward and self-concious state of banter still (and come to think of it, neither of us had made any attempt to meet up 'alone' for dinner either). But if KayKay was out considering exciting new opportunities in life, why not me??

By now their boat was pulling out of the quay. My eyes were unabashedly lingering on Arvind as he grinned and waved to us, and shouted 'KEEP WRITING!' as the boat zoomed away. But then it could well have been a collective wish for our entire writer-ridden gang...(was it? Or was he saying keep writing email, *only* to me?).

But before I could assess what I was feeling, or where I wanted to take this, the next three days had us working much more than finding new ways to gossip or party. Suddenly, after all the distractions—the hunky Arvind being the most dominant one—Bobby, Mini and I were snowed under with writing assignments. Our laid-back teachers must've decided this group was looking for its money's worth—and was paying more attention to our classes.

Annabel Keats, we grudgingly admitted, had suddenly come up with quite an unusual writing exercise idea, and one that quite caught our imagination. It was called 'In Your Shoes'. It was all about learning how to interview—but with a twist.

We were paired off with different people in the group, and sent away for a whole morning of interviewing each other. And then our task was to write a 700-word autobiographical piece on the other person's life, in any style we felt most comfortable with. Later we would read these essays out loud in class: a most surprising way to hear our own lives unfold before us—only the 'I' in each of our own stories was being narrated by someone else.

'Listen to each other's life stories—and make your judgements and interpretations,' said Annabel. 'You may be surprised how others see you, but that's not the point of this exercise. It is about really getting under the skin of another person, and being able to tell their tale as if it were your own'.

'I am Ambujakshi Balan…' began my paired up partner, the wickedly funny Bonnie Peterson. And I was astonished to hear I was a person who had a secret obsession to be a man-killer! Bonnie's dark sense of humour brought her own spin on whatever I had told her about my life thus far, and I had Bobby and Mini looking at me with a 'Aha! *Now* we know better…' look, as we applauded. *(Spoiler alert to Bonnie's prediction: I was on the verge of turning into a major film star myself; Hollywood, not Bollywood!).*

I, in turn, narrated Bonnie's life story in the form of a screenplay (but obviously) and in a short 3-act play of racy dialogues, Bonnie's life as a loving suburban housewife by day, and a blood-thirsty murder mystery-plotter by night was revealed.

Owen, most unexpectedly, brought tears to our eyes as

he narrated the scars of child abuse, when he 'became' his assignment partner, Beth Mayor, a petite Londoner who seemed to us to have stepped out of a Jane Austen novel. We were struck by Owen's serious, sensitive writing style; and wondered: was this the funny man's real writing voice after all? Beth in turn blew us away by narrating Owen's life in a brilliant Irish accent that earned a spontaneous hug from the laughing Owen. Somehow, a personality switch between the two had happened, with their writing assignments. How amazing.

By the end of this 2-day exercise, it was a most curious and intense bonding that set in between our paired-up classmates; we knew that we'd forever remember the intensity of feeling like and being someone else—a prerequisite for any fiction writer.

Well maybe the dubious Annabel Keats would actually set us up for cracking our first novel. And even while we were debating that, we were launched into creating our own unique books.

With a sniffling and feverish Annabel laid up feeling unwell in her hotel bed, Pavol Zavacka stood before our class, out of his dominating partner's shadow and looking less like The Slave. And eager to get us started on the first of our book-making projects with 'found art'.

'Okay, writers! You are now going to escape a bit from your own overly critical writer's heads, and press a "Refresh" button on your writing skills. And it's called Art.

'Art has a way of combating over-rationalizing, art responds easier to a muse, art gets *something* out on that blank paper far easier than writing usually does. And allows instinct and imagination to take it from there.

'I am going to show you how to take lessons in writing from the world of Art, and see how to stumble upon unexplored images and themes. Most of all, this exercise will keep your writing from getting stale'!

Lying on a table before him were lots of coloured paper, glue, scissors that cut in zig-zag and curly-wurly shapes, ribbons and glitter. We were welcome to help ourselves from this raw material; but the best things to incorporate into our book, said Pavol, would be our own found art from the island: sea shells, coloured sand, twigs, pressed flowers and leaves and so on.

'You have two book-making projects: one is Memoir Writing and the other is Words at Play.

'We're starting Words at Play today. First I want each of you to think of the idea for your book. It must be themed with some aspect of writing, a popular writing technique, anything to do with words, storytelling, even famous books...It can be serious or plain funny, you choose! Next we will turn words to pictures...

'For instance, figures of speech. The idea is to make it all come alive pictorially—where speech turns into "figures" in a very imaginative way. Let's say you take this phrase, "throwing a tantrum". Can you stop seeing it as words, but literally visualize this? How about seeing "tantrum" as a kind of beast that you want to throw over the edge of a cliff!'

Pavol held up a page where he had created a hairy monstrous beast, labelled Tantrum, being pushed off a mountain cliff by a bunch of angry-faced stickmen. It was so visually comic and brilliant.

'The point of this is to make words come alive in your own imagination, especially words that have turned tired with overuse. As writers, you must "refresh" words with your own usage, as you begin seeing them in a new way.

'Meanwhile, see it also as an engaging book-making project, have fun creating your pictures: cut and paste and draw and paint, embellish and decorate; this island is full of stuff waiting to get into your books!'

With the glee of children in a kindergarten art class, we fell on the material on the table. But then we had to get an idea first, so sat and racked our brains for a theme. 'How about Brain-Storming itself as an idea?' said Owen. 'I can visualize an army of ideas making a charge, storming the fortress of my brain…'

'Or, How Ideas are Born. That's it, I am going to show in different ways that when Knowledge and Imagination copulate, a baby called Idea is born…' declared Cynthia.

This was going to bc fun.

As a perfect place to get our project done, Stacey recommended a huge beachside restaurant called Kariatis.

'It's got big tables under umbrellas, overlooks the sea, and most importantly, has the best fresh fillet steaks on the island.'

With plenty of space to spread our colourful paraphernalia, we set about our fun task, cutting and glueing and stitching and fixing. We also discovered a great new art that we officially christened as 'Franning'. Fran from our class had a remarkable ability to make 'pop-up' books—she knew simple tricks of folding and glueing, as well as origami art to make pictures stand up as a page was turned, and create remarkable 3-D scenarios.

The more adventurous amongst us decided to have at least one pop-up creation in our books, and Fran was much in demand as we begged and bribed her with promises of free ouzos and neck massages for the rest of our course, to help us make a stubborn cutout behave and stand up when fixed with her magic hands.

Two days later, we were blown away with each one's hand-crafted book.

Bobby decided to do a take-off from The Slave's example of figures of speech that had got us all going. As someone who simply hated clichés, her book was themed 'Killing Clichés'. We loved her pictorial rendition of 'Flinging Caution to The Winds', where Caution was a peculiar beast being flung from a tree. 'Curiosity Killed the Cat' showed a demon called Curiosity slaying a shrieking startled feline!

Mini showed us her book themed 'Famous First Lines' from world-famous novels. Her first example was from the kind of books she hoped to write in the future: Erotica, and what better than the opening line of the novel *Lolita: 'Lolita, light of my life, fire of my loins. My sin, my soul. Lo-lee-ta.'* A paper cut-out of a rather voluptuous young naked siren popped out. Nabokov would've been proud.

In contrast to this was a demure bonneted and beribboned lass that illustrated this famous first line: *'It is a truth, universally acknowledged, that a single man in possession of a good fortune, must be in want of a wife'.* Jane Austen in *Pride and Prejudice* of course.

A 3-D clock, with movable hands brought alive the first line from George Orwell's *1984*: *'It was a bright cold day in April, and the clocks were striking thirteen'.* Mini Cherian, already the skilled illustrator of her own books for years, brought a professional perfection to her project.

Owen presented his book themed 'Irish Blarney'—and showed the famous Blarney castle's stone that millions have visited in Ireland, and following an old legend, hung upside down and kissed in order to spout wit and wisdom! Owen (with a lot of sneaky help from Mini, we all suspected...) had created big speech bubbles emerging from nutty-looking men, each saying the craziest witticisms—so typical of the humorous Irish.

There were famous book titles as themes. Famous quotes from favourite authors. Some entirely inspired by *Reader's Digest's* 'Towards More Picturesque Speech'.

And mine? Predictably film-themed, of course. I took well-known lines that were written for screenplays; and hand-wrote them into strips of different coloured paper that were tightly rolled up and 'unspooled' out of big movie screens shaped from thin cardboard. Fran helped make my idea work with some deft cutting and pasting. The reader also had to guess which film each quote was taken from. They ranged from the easily guessable 'Frankly my dear I don't give a damn' (*Gone with the Wind*) to 'I'll have whatever she is having' (*When Harry met Sally*) to 'Life is a box of chocolates…' (*Forrest Gump*).

By the end of all our presentations, a high had set in.

It was that tactile joy of creating something with our hands; a return to childhood days of paint and paper and crayons and cutting, to imperfect handmade shapes; an antidote to the world of the computer mouse and ready downloads and Photoshop-perfect imagery that we lived in.

But most of all it linked us closer to our love and play of words, our passion for writing, each in our own unique way.

17

'Lead the memoir life. Remember to remember.'

Maybe it was the exhilaration of being able to say 'I've written and self-published my first book'—twelve wannabe bestselling writers held their arty book creations up for a big group photograph with the Chania lighthouse as a backdrop, as our happy mentor Pavol Zavacka held his camera and said 'Smile! Say Feta Cheeeeeese!'

Our smiles stretched all the way and met up at the back of our heads. This one was undoubtedly going up on each of our pinboards back home.

There was a huge buzz of anticipation and excited chatter as we clambered on board a bus that was to take us to Crete's Heraklion harbour. We had no idea where we were being taken or why.

Days 11, 12 and 13 had been innocuously marked on our agendas as 'Beginner's Luck: Guest Speaker' (Speaker and Venue to be announced).

We were told that after our joint learning sessions, we could get individual time with this Guest Speaker to get advice and feedback into each of our immediate writing ambitions: be it a fiction novel, travel writing, freelance feature writing, screenplays ('and I hope erotica too…' said Mini).

'Pack a change of clothes for 3 days. The whole class is heading off, out of Crete, to a brand new venue for the rest of the Workshop!'

A wild yell of joy had gone around the class when Pavol had made this announcement in our class the previous day. We felt like those dozen finalists at a reality show contest, when told they were being whisked off to a new exotic locale quite suddenly.

What was this mystery destination? As we walked towards the large speedboat at Heraklion's harbour, where a Greek deck-hand stood holding up a signboard with 'Creative Awakenings Workshop', it became clear. A banner hung across the Hellenic Seaways boat announced the boat's destination.

Santorini!!

'Oh my GOD!'

'Oh WOW! FABulous!'

'Really? I think I'm dreaming...'
'Pinch me!'

Terrible. For a bunch of writers who'd just been taught how to keep our expressions fresh, we were all breaking out into a bunch of standard clichés.

We clambered on board with our knapsacks like school kids, almost feverish with excitement. Who was really feverish was our dainty Annabel whose sickly condition had worsened and she had to stay back. 'Good! I don't think I want to waste precious Santorini time tightening my buttocks and exhaling...' exclaimed Bobby. And the good Slave Pavlov seemed happy enough to be our lone supervisor for the trip.

'No, I can't tell you who your new Speaker is or what's up ahead...but I can tell you this: you're shortly going to fall in love like never before!'

Our boat sliced along the icy blue Aegean on its hour and a half trip towards Santorini, or Thira as the natives called it. By ten in the morning, we were disembarking at Port Athinios—and going through another burst of clichés all over again, swivelling our heads to take in the magic of this island all at once.

Sugar-cube white houses with blue rooftops and blue shutters clung precariously to white cliffs. Blue and white. White and blue. Everywhere we looked.

We had never seen a bluer blue or a whiter white, that's for sure.

We recalled so many dreamlike images from the Travel and Living channels. And romantic movies. *Santorini*...we were right here, right now. What a bonus! So this was the 'field trip extra' we had (grumblingly) paid up several extra euros for with no idea what it was for. No regrets here any more.

Pavol was met at the embarkation point by a smartly dressed young Greek woman, Gia, who was to be our guide for our stay in the island. She handed each of us a kit welcoming us to Santorini, the Workshop agenda, and pamphlets to help us sight see around in our spare hours, as we packed ourselves into a minibus.

We were all going to be staying at Fira, the capital town of Santorini. 'Fira is by far the busiest part of the island, and tourists love staying here,' said Gia, as our bus sped off down streets packed with colourful shops and sudden alleyways. 'It is the party place of Santorini and has a great night-life! You'll also be visiting Perissa, Imerovigli and Oia…it will be tough for you to decide which part of Santorini is the most beautiful of all.'

Suddenly Villa Rena came into view. Our home in Santorini. A charming double-storeyed creation rising next to a pool…and painted with Santorini's trademark colours of course. Blue canopies and blue shutters and blue doorways and blue arches set off against the dazzling white walls. The yelps of joy rang through the villa as we rushed to our allotted rooms and clapped and waved out to each other, from the doll-house-like tiny trellised balconies attached to each sparkling double-bedroom.

Wait a minute. We had come here to *work?* Absolutely, definitely, totally impossible.

Half an hour later, our group met up in Villa Rena's small, airy conference room (it seemed crazy and cruel to have an official word like 'conference' intruding into a place so holiday-perfect). As we awaited the grand appearance of our Mystery Speaker, we had some definite plans brewing to either bribe him heavily to cancel all further workshopping for our group or else just quietly kill him in his sleep.

'Howdy, boys and girls! I'm Denis Slater. Welcome to "Beginner's Luck!"'

On cue from Pavol, our special teacher entered the room. A 6-foot 4-inch giant of a man in a red Hawaiian shirt and bermudas.

'Now you know my name, but I don't know yours, so how about each of you come right up here and introduce yourselves to me. I want your name, the country you come from, and the one really sinful, shameful, scandalous unwritable, unprintable thing you've done in your life so far!'

The class burst into chuckles. 'I can see some nervous faces here thinking: Oh no. I've led the purest saintly life,' continued our dramatic speaker. 'Never mind if you've been Mother Teresa's assistant so far and haven't done a thing yet that is sinful, shameful or scandalous—you are creative people. You can *lie*, can't you? Make up something fast, and tell us that one thing that you hope to do!'

All plans to kill Denis Slater suddenly vanished. Our minds were totally engaged in plotting our scandalous introductions.

Did we have any doubts who would come up with the weirdest scandal of all? The man from Blarney country, Owen McFee, of course. Taking his cue, each of us presented a wild side to us we never knew we had.

'Now that kick-off exercise was to prove something about each of yourselves that you perhaps wouldn't put in your resume: you are all born liars! And congratulations on that: because that is at the heart of fiction writing; a convincing ability to make up stuff as you go along...'

Our introductory session had us laughing so much, other guests at the Villa Rena's pool may have thought the international humour society was having its annual meet.

Then Denis Slater introduced himself too. Not anything made up, but the living truth about his life.

'My name is Denis Slater, and I'm from Sheffield in England. My second name rhymes with 'writer' you will notice, but the first, unfortunately, rhymes with a well-known part of the human male anatomy...'

Laughs, hoots, chortles broke out again.

'Now while my parents, in their infinite wisdom, chose to name me after a cherubic naughty cartoon character famous around the world, with a name that rhymed with Menace, a very creative boy in my junior school thought otherwise, and linked my name forever with this Other Word—subjecting me to untold humiliation and cruelty in my formative years.

'Roughly at age 12, I even considered running away with a circus that was in town, having a sex change operation that would release me forever from the hated body part appendage—I mean that both physically, and nomenclaturely—and emerge with a new feminine name. Denise perhaps. It even rhymed with trapeze. *'And now, ladies and gentlemen: it's Denise on the trapeze!'*

'But that seemed like an even more painful option, than the pains of mass ridicule. Besides I was starting to have a crush on a girl in our school bus, and simply didn't want to be a lesbian.

'So I coped in the best way I could. I fought back—word for word. I did Amazing Alliterations rather than Slimy Rhymes, and developed new surnames for boys in my class—announced in mysterious scribbles on the blackboard every day. I had some pretty neat alliterative additions for classmates with first names like Prichard and William. Figure them out: I give you three seconds!

'Okay, the upside of all of the endless and excruciating torture through childhood—it built immunity and character and creativity in me at an early age in life. It was also secretly building my career path. I was going to be the prince of parody. The king of comebacks. Denis the Word-Menace.

'Or you could just say I was just plain and simple "born" lucky. My name, Denis with a single "s" you will note, decided by my well-meaning but clueless parents while I was still a lowly sperm, actually ended up shaping my entire destiny.

'Okay, okay, you are all thinking now…what the Heraklion does this all have to do with your writing lesson today?

'It's about that wonderful thing every single writer has—called LUCK. We're all stepping out now to find it.'

18

'The harder I work, the luckier I get.'

'Beginner's Luck'. Suddenly the title of Denis Slater's opening session was beginning to make sense.

A dozen charged-up writers hit the streets and cafés and tavernas of Fira looking for luck to begin our assignment. 'You are going to use luck and coincidence to jump-start your writing today,' Denis Slater had told us. 'But you are not going to laze under the sun waiting for that opener to come to you out of the blue. It never ever does. You are going to *seek out* luck.

'You're going to look for a trigger, or a sign—that might even be a quirky signpost you see, or a sentence you accidentally eavesdropped upon in a café, or a remarkable coincidence: a cat on a wall with the same face as your landlady? A man in the next table who looks a dead ringer for George Clooney…and it *is* George Clooney? We writers are a bunch of really lucky people! There's ALWAYS something to get us going.

'Your kick-off assignment today is Flash Fiction: a very very short story for around 100 words with character, plot, dialogue, drama, and it's out there waiting for you to discover in Fira's bustling main street, Mitropolios, just 10 walking minutes away. Let yourselves loose there for the next two hours, and come back here with your finished story! 1 pm on the dot in this room. The ones who get here a minute past 1 buy the rest of the class all the drinks tonight!'

We were all raring to go.

'Now how many of you have seen the Master Chef programmes? This is the episode where the participants are led off to an exciting, unexplored town's market square, in a strange new city, with no pre-meditated plan whatsoever, grabbing any potentially good ingredient that comes their way, and rushing back to cook something prize-winning out of it.

'Fira's streets are teeming with writable ingredients; put all your senses on full alert, luck out when you see that tantalizing opening sentence—and GO!'

Late that night, we wondered if Denis Slater had some mysterious powers that had manipulated all the stuff strewn along our path, in the guise of 'luck'. True, there was a story wherever we looked.

Only because, subconsciously, we were training our senses to spot them.

Stacey found a very clear picture of Jesus on the surface of the crêpe she ordered in Kastro café. Her short dramatic story ended with Stacey being canonized and turning into Santorini's newest tourist attraction.

Mini overheard a pretty young lady in the next table ordering a salad, 'Can you bring your dressing separately, please?' She wrote a short sketch about what happened next: the waiter returns wearing absolutely nothing—but with his clothes neatly folded up on a tray.

Bobby accidentally strayed into a photograph being

shot by a Taiwanese tourist. She apologized and stepped aside...but in her story, that tourist was the director Ang Lee, and Bobby ended up being offered the role of a lifetime in an Oscar-winning movie.

Every story we heard that day had us exclaiming with the brilliance of it all. The 'luck' that just happened, just like that. And mine?

I had sat gazing out of my table at the crowded Café Koukoumavlos. Desperation mounting. I still hadn't got a *single* freaking idea. Not any trigger point—anywhere I looked, or heard or touched or smelt. In another fifteen minutes, we'd have to be making our way back to our villa meeting room, and reading out our pieces.

What happened to me? I was supposed to be the jiffy-queen in writing! The proclaimed ruler of 140 characters.

Everyone, I'm sure, was already heroically rushing back with their instant masterpieces. I had to get out of this café maybe and look elsewhere...so I gulped down the last of my lime and mint chiller...and then the thing that has got millions of desperate writers out of starting-up hell, happened: the Immediate Looming Deadline kicked me into writing—and I had this story to narratc:

Eye Contact

I saw him. He was standing right there—across the hall in a black suit. Hair slicked back with gel like Don Draper. I wondered how to make eye contact. 'Look at me, please...just turn around...' my soul willed silently.

But he continued paying rapt attention to the lady in the

red dress. And then it happened. Was it telepathy? The power of positive affirmations?

He turned...and looked right into my eyes. I just couldn't help the quick involuntary wave of my hand.

He suddenly started walking right across the crowded room. And smiled as he reached me.

'Could you bring the bill please?' I said.

The waiter did as he was told.

Applause. Whew. Saved!

Everybody wanted a copy of everybody's pieces. We should compile these pieces into a short book of Flash Fiction!

Such a high could only be treated with some potent liquid nourishment, declared Denis—as he and Pavol handed out glasses, and we said *stin yia sou* as we clinked glasses to our continued writing health.

'The next two days are pretty much free-flowing but I guarantee you this: you won't know when you are having fun, or when you are working hard—because they are both magically the same thing here.

'Now each of you, you will remember, as you filled out your application forms for this course—way before you even came to Greece, you wrote a paragraph about the particular aspect of writing that you most wished to pursue. Some of you wanted to be regular feature columnists, some travel writers, some had their first novel idea already but didn't know where to take it, some wanted to become world-famous with their very first screenplay, some wanted to explore science fiction, some had aspirations for blood-curdling crime thrillers, some had a dozen poems, needing honest critiquing, and some, I am happiest of all to note, wanted to venture into erotica!'

Denis Slater showed us a stack of colourful files on his table. 'Pavol has given me your individual files: it's all in here, along with the writing examples you attached and mailed with your application forms. Also, your other exciting assignments done in Crete. I have gone through them all most thoroughly—and am here to mentor you individually. Just book your time with me for one-to-one personal sessions any time through the next two days…'

Over a big group lunch, served to us on picnic tables set up near the pool, Denis addressed our group again. 'For most of you here, it is about writing that First Novel. The First Screenplay. The First Travelogue. The First Short Story Anthology. And you will always look back at your Creative Awakenings Workshop days as the trigger that said that you *will.*

'Now many of you *already* have it going, I promise you! Even that Flash Fiction exercise each of you turned in today could well lead you to the longer short story, the bigger plot, the pivotal chapter in a fuller storyline. Did you know that the award-winning film *Memento* started out as just a short story? And Nikolai Gogol's famous novel *Overcoat* was just a random anecdote he'd heard at a dinner party.

'Tomorrow I will share with you in a presentation how famous successful writers follow a trick to writing, and sustain that writing: and you too, can choose to be inspired by their methods.

'You will also learn how to discover, capture and nurture your muse. And how serious writers of all types do this all the time—eccentric as it might seem.

'Did you know Mark Twain and Truman Capote wrote best lying down? Ernest Hemingway had to sharpen dozens of pencils to get him going. And next time I feel stuck myself, I'm going to do what the poet John Donne liked to do: lie in an open coffin, before picking up a pen!'

We chuckled thinking of the unputdownable Denis Slater actually lying down dead-quiet in a coffin.

'And there's no escaping the truth of how killing it is to get down to the actual work of writing—but be consoled and even inspired to know that the very best of famous writers had it far worse than you ever will. Plato revised *The Republic* 50 times. And Hemingway rewrote just the last page of *Farewell to Arms* 39 times!

'Did that scare you mindless dead already? Good! And get yourself a custom-built coffin, just in case…'

'I'm a drinker with a writing problem!'

Owen rolled his eyes in mock seriousness with his conclusion about himself. Mini laughed in agreement. They were sitting at the Rooftop Patio with its commanding views of the sparkling night-life of Fira. Sitting a few tables away, Bobby and I were beginning to notice a fine chemistry going on between the sparky Mini and the amiable Owen, and had a knowing 'aha!'

expression on our faces, as we heard Mini's hearty laugh float across to our table.

'Here I am, so perfectly set to devote my attention to an evening of dedicated, steady drinking, but this goddamn writing habit keeps interrupting the flow. Every now and then I feel like taking a swig at my writing pad here, with a thought for a novel I'm about to write,' said Owen in mock anxiety.

'We're addicted!' agreed Mini, downing her margarita. 'We're drunk with new writing powers we never had before. Any minute now I'll get the provocative opening line for my category-defining sex novel.'

'Give it up already, Mini the Kid. Your first short story attempt at the adult stuff came off like a spoof on *Fifty Shades of Grey*. Not its serious competitor! No offence, just your friendly neighbourhood erotica novel reading critique giving you some feedback…'

'But *Fifty Shades of Grey* is its own spoof, I thought. Maybe I should write a counter to it with a novel called *18 Shades of White*' said Mini. 'Well, that's how many shades of white an Eskimo can identify—did you know that!'

'Do that. You can't get too steamy writing about overly clothed Eskimos anyway, so that should suit your pristine U-certificate style,' said Owen.

Mini laughed. 'I never thought I'd carry such a hangover of my kiddie-writing still with me. This Workshop was supposed to change that about me! Oh no. What a waste of finding the perfect name for myself to write under: Minerva. Goddess of Sex. Okay not exactly, but the muse of romantic poetry or something like that…'

'Not easy making a sudden switch from Jack-and-Jill-went-up-the-hill—to You-know-what-they-did-up-there, I should imagine...'said Owen with a straight face.

'Well we do know someone who did, don't we? J.K. Rowling went from writing magical adventure stories for gazillion children fans for years and years, and just one fine day decided to write for adults, *under the same name too*, and just left it there sitting about on bookshelves around the world. I mean there was a screaming F word in the *seventh* page of *The Casual Vacancy*! Hey, there are tiny little *children* in every store picking up and browsing anything you write, Ms Rowling!'

'What's the bet that even if you wrote your great porn novel under your new name, Minerva, or whatever, you'd still have '****' splattered throughout your book like tiny dead bacteria where all the intended erotica should've been. But at least you'd be an immediate contender for the Annual Worst Sex-Writing Award. Ha Ha!'

Owen dodged a flying olive that was flung at him by Mini.

He's right, thought Mini. And as for writing erotica while self-consciously avoiding writing the F word? It's like writing about Neil Armstrong and avoiding writing the moon word. Erotica by Mini Cherian is never going to work. Perhaps this Workshop is also about finding what you *can't* write...

Now, since we are on this very important subject of Mini finding her true calling in writing, I am going to leap forward a bit, and go two days ahead—to the final day in

Santorini. (I blame it on watching too much of *How I Met Your Mother*—where you leap forward and backward and forward again)…

Mini was paying rapt attention to the feedback she was getting from Denis in the final day's individual mentoring sessions.

'Now what I think you should be writing is a screenplay for a seriously good children's film that doesn't talk down to children. Your previously published works are outstanding, and you've found exactly what you are best at. Now writing for children through movies will be the challenge that I think you'll love and excel in. I have also seen your assignments on this Workshop so far, and your ease at writing dialogues and vivid scenarios. I also feel you can think and write more visually than anyone else in this group…'

Mini came away with an odd sense of relief. Maybe she wasn't yet ready to quit what she was best at: writing for children.

When it was Bobby's turn, Denis told her she had her strong advertising writing grounding for being able to write anything she wished—in her case travel writing—without ever boring the reader. He found her headlines, her sub-heads, her last pithy end-line in her sample travel piece, written like an engaging long-copy ad. 'Getting trained in advertising copy is the best thing that happened to you, Bobby! Now I'll be looking out for your byline in *Conde Nast Traveler* and and later on your TV show.' Denis gave her leads to travel essays and travelogue authors that would be her inspiration.

Finally. It was my turn—the very last person to listen to feedback, right at the end of three packed days in Santorini.

When I met Denis on my allotted one-on-one, I went in completely buzzed with anticipation and curiosity. I had even forgotten what I had written in my questionnaire months ago, when we had filled out our forms online. The printout was there in front of us, and under the question: What do you hope to get out of this course? I realized I had typed in: 'I hope to be a writer of…well, I have no real idea yet, but I am sure I will, at the end of my course in Greece.'

Denis greeted with me with a smile of understanding as I went and sat before him.

'So, at the end of this course, what do you think *you* are most likely to be writing Miss Ambu-jack-shi Ba-laan?' he asked, his eyes twinkling with amusement.

Was it: short stories? Really really short stories? Or. That first full-fledged novel right away? Or how about *humour*? I mean I think I could be pretty good at that! (Oh yes, I'd sent many sample Tweets for a famous film star, with my portfolio).

Or hey, would it be advertising? That's it: advertising. (Now that I knew so much more about it all, from Bobby.) The next most logical step from writing prize-winning slogans! (Yes. I put all those gold winnings in my detailed resume too). Yes. Advertising is most definitely what Denis would agree was my true calling…

But wait a minute! *Screenplays!* How could I have even forgotten that? That's what I really always wanted to write. Would Denis agree that I was just made to write romantic, Hollywoody screenplays?

Omigod, was I the most mixed-up, scrambled, addlebrained, directionless, high-strung, everything, but not ONE good thing, person in this entire group??

Okay, I am not going to tell you just yet about which amazing life-changing direction Denis Slater pointed me towards…

But I am going to revert to the *How I Met Your Mother* mode again.

And tell you about Something That Happened in Santorini. Two days before I went in for my way-forward mentoring session with Denis Slater.

Something that was entirely responsible for the rather mixed-up, scrambled, addlebrained, directionless, high-strung state of my brain…

19

'Some people feel the rain. Others just get wet.'

SANTORINI. TWO DAYS EARLIER…

'Taxi!'

Kostos the Greek guide placed two fingers in his mouth and let out a piercing whistle. Taxi? In this narrow lane where the only possible 4-wheel vehicle that could pass, had to be a baby's pram, maybe?

'I get for you, ladies. Taxi right here, parakalo! My own brother taxi—you want? Only 10 euros going up the hill.' It was clear that Kostos, the persistent Greek, was determined to take us for a ride, in more ways than one.

'NO! Signomi! Sorry, no taxi for us. Anyway, how on earth can you bring a taxi into this street?'

We were walking along the narrow cobbled streets of the astonishing village Oia—appropriately pronounced 'EE-Yah!' an exclamation we were frequently breaking into at the beauty of the place.

Kostos didn't give up as he trailed us. His whistle to summon a taxi was heard by his unseen brother, and it trundled up behind us most promptly. 'Here, lovely ladies!' announced Kostas. And standing there was a taxi all right: a stoic donkey with a yellow TAXI signboard tied neatly in between its ears!

Chortles of laughter broke out. No room for four wheels in this narrow pathway maybe, but for four legs—plenty of room.

While we couldn't resist clambering onto this quaint form of local transport, for photographs to Instagram back home, for Facebook updates, and Bobby's next travel piece, we jumped off to allow a sweet old Japanese woman take the taxi further up, as the uphill winding path could prove rather tiring. Donkey taxis were the most sensible thing here for elderly adventurers.

We too, were getting increasingly breathless after a point—but for entirely different reasons.

The view! Or as Owen declared: The Whew!

Santorini offered the best views of its famed caldera—

the massive body of water that had filled in after a volcano exploded in the island 3500 years ago. This became Santorini's greatest ever showpiece and tourist attraction, and the caldera continued to draw millions of awestruck visitors like us; to stand at vantage points along the 'rim' of the caldera, and enjoy the view of the remnants of the volcano surrounded by water.

Suddenly we spotted the huffing and puffing Pavol, waving madly and making our way up towards us. 'There you are! I knew I'd find you somewhere here...I've been looking for your group for the past hour!'

Pavol joined our group of five at the extended balcony of a cliff-hugging restaurant.

'Wait! It gets even better, and that's when the sun sets. And I know exactly that one place where you can get the best view of all!' Pavol urged us to follow him.

As it turned out, there were approximately 200 spots that could be described exactly like that—as the one place in all of Santorini that gave you the BEST view of the sunset. And each new tourist could well find one more to add to the list.

Santorini had to be taken in small, delicious gulps. There was just too much beauty to knock us out, if we didn't pace ourselves.

Earlier in the afternoon, after our first 'Beginner's Luck' assignment and welcome lunch, we had driven 2 kilometres to the north of Fira, to the quiet and charming Imerovigli village. The village residents were lying blissed-out taking their afternoon siesta, finding shady spots to doze off, in white balconies bursting with a profusion of colourful bougainvillea.

We strolled about in wonder, letting it all quietly sink in.

Then it was Oia, about 10 kilometres from Fira. We read from our pamphlets about Oia being the most photographed part of Santorini, or as some feel, the whole of Greece itself. 'You can stand blindfolded just about anywhere, facing any direction, and shoot randomly with your camera. You'll still find you've caught the perfect picture!' Pavol was right about this.

Did somebody whitewash every single wall and building and winding stairway of Oia only this morning? Did every shutter and dome get its touch-up of cobalt blue every single day? Everything was just so pristine clean and sparkling fresh.

We trod our way through grey and white cobbled pathways, stopping at quaint trinket shops, and trying out our newly acquired vocabulary of Greek asking for prices—*poso kani?,* cuddling a little future Greek goddess in a pram—*Omorfos!* So beautiful! Even warding off some amorous attention by rakish teenage *agoris* with a *Signomi! Eho filo*...(excuse me! I have a boyfriend).

Our writerly instincts were full-on, with each of us scribbling down a thought, a phrase, an idea, a piece of dialogue, with the more techy amongst us using iPhones and iPads to record snatches of conversations with the locals, the spontaneous burst of a song, or the buzz and laughter at a café.

We chanced upon friends from our Workshop at many different points of our tour of Oia, and Pavol was busy gathering together as many of us as he could to follow him to his own favourite place—the remnants of the Oia Castle—to watch the drama of the famed sunset at the caldera.

There was a palpable buzz of anticipation and excitement in the air everywhere. The streets were getting more crowded with tourists walking faster and more purposefully to reach different vantage points. Pavol constantly looked around to spot more of us work-shoppers in the crowds, even as we moved on, winding our way upward past the famous white chapel, with its blue circular rooftop, and with a solitary bell—as seen on the covers of so many tourist brochures and guide books on Greece. It was quite a moment actually seeing it for real, right before us.

We were now just a few precious minutes away from Oia's grand show of shows, enacted every evening across the deepening blue waters of the caldera. Soon it would be 7 p.m. *Come grab your ringside seats for today's drama. It's showtime, folks!*

We watched, stunned, as another kind of volcanic explosion surrounded the gigantic caldera's water body…a spectacular explosion of colour that sent fiery streaks of red, pink, orange and gold all across the skies.

A hush fell upon us all, as the sun dipped gently into the sea. And then the silence broke—with sighs, cries, shouts, exclamations. People clapped. People hugged. People kissed. People cried. A thousand cameras clicked to capture the sight.

For many, like me, it was too precious a moment to be

viewed through the glassy restricting barrier of a camera lens; we just had to let the wonder of it all reach our eyes directly.

Life doesn't get more dramatic and heart-stopping than this, I thought.

And then it did.

'Hello, Amby!' said a very familiar voice behind me. I turned around.

And right before me stood KayKay.

KayKay?! Here in GREECE? Okay, this HAS to be a crazy trick of my sunset-affected brain…

'Omigod. WHAT are you doing here?' First Arvind and now KayKay? Was this all a part of a coincidence-ridden Hindi movie screenplay? This was bizarre, totally bizarre…

'Long story!' laughed KayKay.

KayKay in Greece?! By now, my friends were turning around too.

'I've had quite a time sitting here waiting for the sun to go down and for you all to show up!' KayKay continued, his super-white-teeth smile reaching the rest of the curious group too. I thought Mini and Bobby, looking as stunned as I did, may even reach out and touch KayKay to see if he was for real.

Oh, he was real all right. KayKay stepped forward to give me a quick hug. I thought my heart suddenly entered a high-speed lift and went up 30 floors. 'This is, er…' I turned to face the group, who for some reason all seemed to be smiling rather manically at me.

Pavol laughed—and to my complete shock, held out his hand and shook KayKay's saying, 'Hello, Mr Koomar! So you found the place all right!'

Pavol turned to me. 'I sent your friend Mr Koomar here to Oia, to wait here at the castle ruins hours ago, after he landed up at Hotel Rena, asking for you. You had all just left for your walk through Imergovili village. I looked for you in the streets of Oia after that, and when I did find you at the Oia village, I didn't let go—and managed to shepherd you into this place in the nick of time!'

I was jogged into reality by a wide-eyed Mini saying, 'Hey. Aren't you going to introduce us, Amby!'

I remember Mini silently mouthing the word 'WOW!' at me as she caught my eye, even as she stepped aside after shaking KayKay's hand, and I continued the introductions in a dazed state, saying, 'And this is Bobby, from Mumbai...Meet KayKay. He's a friend and er, my former boss.'

'And here, meet Owen from Ireland. And this is Linda, Stacey, and Cynthia and Bonnie and Beth and Fran and PT...all pals from our Workshop too. And Pavol Zavacka, our mentor from the Writer's Workshop, but hey, seems like you already know each other.' It's a wonder I got all their names right.

KayKay shook hands all around and flashed his million-watt smile again. And did his usual trick of remembering each and every person's name as I uttered it, repeating names after me as he shook each person's hand. A small thing but it can be pretty flattering when you are in a big group...

And now can you please explain how on friggin crazy earth did you land up *here?!* I thought to myself, as KayKay chatted, looking as nonchalant as ever, with Pavol.

Must've been either Mini or Bobby who whispered 'major film star from India' to one of the group, who whispered it to another of the group...till a lot of delighted faces took in the persona of KayKay again. The women with open lust, as Owen told me later.

By now, the crowds were beginning to make their way down from the viewing point, towards Oia's many tavernas and cafés. Pavol had useful tips on where we could all go to get a good drink and an early dinner, with everyone quite ravenous after that climb.

'I've been told never to miss out eating at Café Ambrosia while in Oia,' volunteered KayKay. 'I've come here with expert recommendations! Here are other places already circled in on my map of Santorini...'

Curiouser and curiouser. I couldn't wait to sit down in any café, any taverna, anywhere to find out what in the galaxy had brought KayKay here to Greece. *My* Greece.

Meanwhile, why was an object lodged inside my chest doing a ridiculous Zorba the Greek dance? I could even hear the thump thump thump as it banged against the rib-cage.

Even though I made every attempt to persuade Mini and Bobby to join us (more to mask a sudden awkward shyness I felt with my visitor), they made excuses to get away, clearly lying when they said they were heading back to our villa for something urgent. But they managed to sneak in a quick word with me, while KayKay continued discussing the merits of some of the eating places with Pavol.

'He's just drop dead, leave-your-husband gorgeous, Amby!!' whispered the crazy Mini.

'You NEVER told us just how sexy he is in real life...now find out why he's chased you here and tell us every single detail. Later in our room tonight, okay?' said Bobby with a wink.

'Shut UP you mad women,' I whispered back, so afraid that KayKay could hear our nonsensical girl-prattle. 'Maybe he's here for a still shoot. Maybe the *whole unit* is here for a silly filmi song sequence after I raved about Greece so much. Okay, you girls wait up for me till I come back!'

'Be good, and if you can't be, then name your kids after Greek philosophers!' said the demented Mini, in my ear. The group waved goodbye, and made their way down to Oia's main streets again.

KayKay and I started walking towards Café Ambrosia, further up from the Oia castle. And then came my torrent of questions.

No cell phone coverage, no easy access to mails—how did he track down where we were? Even *we* didn't know where we were headed out till this early morning!

'But you are supposed to be in Turkey right now, Kay...'

KayKay stopped in his tracks in complete surprise. 'And how would *you* know about Turkey! You are some sleuth yourself, Ambujax. Your Course Directors told me that you've had little access to any outside information…neither did I mention it in my Tweets or FB: so who told you anything about Turkey! Toni?!' asked KayKay.

Toni? Aha, so was he there too with you in Turkey? I found myself wondering.

'Well I do have my sources,' I replied mysteriously. 'But hey, my questions first! And there's the Ambrosia signboard. Isn't this the place we are looking for?'

We settled into the huge open verandah dining area of the pictureseque Ambrosia. The after-glow of the sunset was still around us; the unforgettable image we had just witnessed was still lingering on magically in the air.

I suddenly didn't want to hear *any* explanation from KayKay at all, didn't want to know a thing about his Turkey tryst, didn't want to know if it was Toni or Shamini or Devyani or whichever new goddamn heroine or whatever or whoever he was currently linked with…

KayKay picked up the drinks menu on our table. 'I hope Greece has cured your addiction to Pepsi—and you are on an unhealthier path to drinking!' smiled KayKay. 'Anyway, it's an insult to the locals here if we didn't have their famed Visanto wine brewed here—I'm sure your good teacher Pavol Whatever taught you all that in your course!'

I too looked into my menu card, as if deeply considering some tough choices, but was actually slyly looking over the menu edge, catching glimpses of KayKay.

KayKay right here in Greece! The reality of it struck

me all over again. That thunderous moment of turning around at Oia Castle and seeing him in his deep blue jeans and ultra white linen shirt—Santorini colours!—and knocking the sanity out of me…

His hands. They seemed tanned and tapered and touchabler, tantalizinger…

Hold it, girl! Why was I over-reacting like this? I tried to recover my cool by talking to the waiter, who'd just arrived at our table.

'*Signomi, garcon! Ena potiri Visanto. Parakalo servira temas grigora!*'

KayKay threw back his head and laughed. 'My my, I'm so impressed, Ambrosia Amby! Let me figure that one…waiter, a glass of Visanto, and serve it fast—isn't that what you said?'

'Clever! Anyway it is the very first sentence everyone learns here in Santorini I should imagine, and since I plan to settle here in Greece forever, I've started mastering some basics.'

'Good! And do these settlement plans include the great Tam Brahm Marriage Prospective from Finland too?' KayKay made that sound just a bit too casual. 'He was here in Greece a while ago, wasn't he…?'

'And how would you know that?' I stared at KayKay completely taken aback.

'To quote your very words, a few moments ago, I do have my sources you know…' KayKay grinned back.

'Wait, Kay! This is going all over the place. MY questions first: How did you even get here?'

'I landed in Crete at around 12 today, flying in directly

from Turkey. Okay, we'll come to the Turkey part later!' said KayKay.

KayKay asked for Visanto too, and continued. 'I knew the name of your course and venue, the PR guys back home had the all details. I went straight from the Chania airport to Hotel Venetia, and met this lady called Annabel something. She looked pretty startled when she came to meet me in the hotel lobby. She said you were all away at Santorini on a 3-day project. I've visited Santorini before, but never Crete, and wondered about exploring Crete a bit till you all got back. But then I saw this cruise boat at the harbour announcing fast rides to Santorini, and boarded it on an impulse!'

And tracking us down after that? 'That was easy: Annabel gave me the address of where you were all staying in Santorini, of course, but again, I reached Villa Rena to find only your teacher guy Pavol, chatting with a very amiable man called Denis...they said you had all gone away sightseeing, but were headed off to Oia for the sunset. Pavol told me about the best view of the sunset—at Oia Castle. And promised to find you some place in Oia's streets and get you and your gang to the same viewing point. Pavol and I decided to spring it as a complete surprise for you!'

And Turkey? Well that was another story. And what a story.

The Turkey plan had been brewing for quite a few months (almost as long as my Greece plan, I discovered later.)

The Food Network Show in London had somehow got wind of KayKay's secret talents in the kitchen, and had called him many months ago to participate in a great new reality show: 'Stars Can Cook'. It was to feature some real big actors from America, England, France, Italy and Spain. Would KayKay like to be part of the show?

Then KayKay heard the names of stars they were planning to sign on. A-Listers from Hollywood.

Top of the list was the man who was actually a practising chef before Hollywood hijacked him: Daniel Craig! Then there was Matthew McConaughey, and Toby McGuire, two aspiring chefs-turned-actors. And upping the glamour quotient even further: two Hollywood actors who had even released their own cookbooks recently, Gwyneth Paltrow and Eva Longoria. Carole Bouquet from France and other big film celebs from at least three other countries were being signed on too, for this sure-hit TV show idea.

KayKay had felt flattered and agreed to be in the show immediately—and no one knew about it except Toni. (*Except Toni?* And why not me too? I held myself from asking this peeved question).

And then came the frenzy of juggling dates and shoots as the taping of the show required at least 20 uninterrupted days every star had to commit to—that's when our dear Director saar nearly collapsed with heart failure, as it came right at the start of the next film he had in mind, but there was no way KayKay was going to miss this opportunity, scary as it was…

(*Hey! That old Tweet of KayKay's: 'If an opportunity scares you, TAKE IT!' Ting! The penny suddenly dropped…)*

But the immediate urgency was the rigorous preparations for the show itself. A briefing from the organizers expected that they master a huge repertoire of Meditteranean dishes for the major part of the competition, plus one signature dish from their country that they had to invent and present.

Then came the many exciting hours of experimentation and practice, with Toni pooling in his own sizable talent in cooking…

Ting. Ting. Ting. More pennies dropped. KayKay and Toni making all those endless trips to Pondicherry. KayKay and Toni forever ganged up at the Beach House. KayKay and Toni arriving flushed with excitement on Monday mornings, discussing what they'd been cooking, all through the weekend…

Toni had nearly blurted the secret to me several times, apparently.

But much before the actual show, all the signed-on stars so far had to land up for a day in Turkey, the venue of the show, to meet Food Network producers, shoot some promo stills and videos for the upcoming show, and also get familiar with the two celebrity hosts. The famous Michelin-starred Alain Du Casse. And the Hell's Kitchen Celebrity Chef with a fearsome reputation, which made him more famous than even his star wife, Emilia Fox: the fiery genius Marco Pierre White!

No one knew that KayKay was taking off to Turkey, on this secret week-long break from his film. Except a rather agitated Director saar, and Toni.

And of course our very own Vikki-leaks. Who told

Tarun who told Lulu who told Kavi. Who told me in that email, just a few days ago…

I wasn't volunteering info on how I got to know the Turkey bit yet. I was so totally hooked to hearing the whole reality show story.

'I heard it got out somehow and was reported in some gossipy film rag, but no one still knows why I had headed off to Turkey, thank God. So if you are moonlighting for Kollywood Kalling or some such thing slyly, I may have to either find out something blackmailable about you to shut you up, or just kill you after this meal…' said KayKay.

So KayKay had finally met Marco Pierre White—his biggest cooking hero. While I, listening with bated breath so far, had to interrupt KayKay rattling off a long list of signature dishes that Marco was famous for, to scream: 'Kay! You actually met DANIEL CRAIG?!'

Midnight was a few moments away. We were walking back slowly down Oia's streets, to catch a taxi that would drop me off at Villa Rena. And then take KayKay back to the B & B place at Fira where he had checked in earlier in the day. The same streets we'd walked through in the afternoon looked so different now. Twinkling lights everywhere seemed to envelope Santorini like the starry cloak of a magician.

It was all so hopelessly, utterly, crazily movie-set romantic.

There was also a fair amount of Visanto in my system.

Many unasked questions remained. (Why wasn't he

asking me *at all* about the visit of Arvind Seshadri? How did he even know about that one?)

One possible reason: I had spent the last three hours or so only cross-questioning KayKay, wanting to know every crazy detail about what Daniel Craig was like in his real non-Bond life, what he had said, what he had worn...not to mention every tiny detail I simply had to know from Gweneth Paltrow's nose to Eva Langoria's toes.)

(And hey. What exactly would my answer be, if he eventually asked me about The Eligible Marriageable?)

And then again, there was all that Visanto.

Like the scene straight out of that old Tamil film, where Kamal Haasan and Sridevi keep walking slowly down a hill, slowly falling into silence, and feel their hands involuntarily, unconsciously brushing against each other...ours did too.

Uncontrollable fingers slowly began twining together, gently, one at a time. They were crushing up together now. His right hand, my left hand. Locked in embrace.

A profound silence took over, as we walked on, down winding cobbled streets to our taxi.

Lying wide-awake in my bed at Villa Rena later that night, the touch, the feeling, the sensation clung on, all over my hand, as it lay cradling my hot face...

Why was this feeling way, way, WAY more sinful and sensuous than that Liverpool doorway kiss?

20

'Don't forget to colour outside the lines.'

'*It's raining men, hallelujah, it's raining men*'...sang Bobby. 'So how many more friends and lovers following you here to Greece are we going to meet, Amby?'

Well, it *was* pretty insane.

Mini and Bobby, sharing my room, had fortunately been fast asleep in our Villa when I'd tiptoed in the previous night, despite their resolve to stay awake and discuss the dramatic appearance of KayKay. But I wasn't spared from their inquisition early next morning, when they found me already up and sipping coffee in our tiny balcony.

'Spill it, you sultry southern siren! By the way, all the women in our class are quite blown away with the looks of your dashing film star *filos*...'

'Filos? You crazy people, he's no boyfriend of mine, I can assure you...but tell me, what did they say?'

'Aha! You'll hear it from them yourself, shortly at class. They simply freaked-out when we told them he's a film star in India! Now you tell us EVERYTHING about last night, and also why you would run away from such a dishy boss to find new paths in life. Now that part we cannot understand!'

'I've seen your KayKay's pictures many times before in filmi magazines—but honestly, Amby, he's *devastating* in real life. Now whatever you say, do not spoil the story with rumours of gay leanings or whatever ridiculous blab you were telling us back in Chania. He is *not* gay. I know for sure…' Mini put a finality to it, as if she had personally done a scientific test on him in some advanced sexuality lab.

Well, I could give her some evidence to support her assumptions (so okay, he only held a girl's hand for a bit, but hey, it definitely *felt* heterosexual) but instead I went right into telling them about Chef KayKay and the whole exciting Turkey story—and that made four eyes widen and two jaws drop.

'Your KayKay's competing with *Daniel Craig*? And Gwyneth Paltrow? Amby, you simply got to get your old job back at once! How can your KayKay not have his faithful Tweeter Girl and Blogging Ghost, not to mention, film-crazy fiend, telling the world about Bollywood clashing kitchen knives with Hollywood!' exclaimed Bobby.

'What's the bet he'll be snapped up by Hollywood itself after this show, with that killer smile of his. Or seduced away by Eva Longoria in the course of the competition. Jesus Superstar Christ. Did you even know he's so world-class good in the kitchen?' asked Mini.

I have to say, frankly I didn't.

By now we were so terribly behind time, and rushed getting ready to assemble again at the conference room with Denis and Pavol. We raced in—the last three to reach the room.

Denis Slater gave us all a grin of welcome. 'I must say

for a group of very creatively inclined people, you are all hopelessly disciplined and obedient; I didn't expect you all to surface in this room for another whole hour!'

Through the morning, we watched a great bunch of videos, and also heard some audio CDs—on the theme of our session: 'How Writers Write'.

Among them were terrific TED talks by authors; including some of our personal favourites: Elizabeth Gilbert. Neil Gaiman. Amy Tan.

We listened. We questioned. We discussed. We argued. We knew exactly what it meant when we heard a good writer being described as a 'gregarious loner'.

In the lunch break came the inevitable leg-pulling that Mini and Bobby had already warned me against. The news that KayKay was a *film star* from India had apparently sent them all in a tizzy over dinner the previous night.

Cynthia said she had already decided that she was applying for her new job—which happened to be my old one. 'Amby! You are looking at your successor to a profession that you so foolishly gave up. I'm going to be your film star's new Tweeter! Whoever knew there was even such a cool job in the first place…'

Stacey regretted not taking photographs of KayKay. 'My neighbour in Dallas is a hardcore Bollywood fan. Now when can I take a picture of your famous and good-looking hunk pal and me? I have to show off when I get back!'

Bonnie, who had done the 'In Your Shoes' writing assignment in Hania, paired up with me, had it perfectly worked out. 'Forget it, Cynthia. No one is more qualified to be in Amby's shoes than me. So since I am already in them, I'll just take the romantic story forward from here…'

Being dark-skinned and all, a blush is not the most obvious thing that shows up…or so I think. At any rate I felt the blood rushing to my face in an utterly silly teenagery kind of way, with all the reactions KayKay was getting with everyone in the class, even as I did the 'But he's here on some work! Besides, we are only friends' spiel with them all.

Oh feck it all, what was the matter with me? Checking and rechecking my certified-dead cell phone for signals and messages, all through the day??

The previous evening at Ambrosia, KayKay had made a tentative plan of meeting up again at the Ammoudi beach near Oia, late in the evening, which was anyway in our to-do list of Santorini's unmissables. KayKay, I knew, was going to be busy all day, meeting up with the famed Chef Nickolas who ran a popular *estiatorio* in Ammoudi village. (Okay, so there was another, and bigger *professional* reason for his visiting Santorini, so why was I kidding myself?).

KayKay had earlier resourcefully made an appointment with one of Santorini's best known chefs and was most excited about working side by side with him all through the day, in a hands-on training stint for the big cooking show coming up.

'I'm learning a variety of Greek desserts from him—Chef Nickolas's speciality. I'm going to knock it with my desserts in the contest, that's what I've decided is my focus,' said KayKay.

Since I, too, had a packed day of sessions with Denis and Pavol back at Villa Rena, we decided not to bank on our unreliable cell phones. So we had a plan. (A date?). 5.15 p.m. sharp at Ammoudi beach, Café Remezzo. One more shot at catching the sunset for sure. And then the rest of the evening for catching up on all the one billion unasked questions.

I had made a rough agenda for the evening (when one is lying sleepless in bed, this can be time usefully spent, instead of letting a delusionary mind run away recklessly down forbidden paths.)

1. 5 p.m. Arrive early in the Ammoudi beach, and walk along water's edge.

2. 5.10 p.m. See many lovers walking along water's edge. Stay unaffected.

3. 5.15 p.m. Wait at Café Remezzo—the meeting place. Make quick check in handbag mirror if Bobby's borrowed blue eyeliner really does enhance my eyes.

4. See KayKay approach. Stay cool and composed.

5. Hug KayKay in greeting. Keep it sisterly.

6. Sit at sidewalk table for two. Focus on Santorini Sundowner, not KayKay's browny drownable eyes.

7. Ask details about Toni/Shamini/Devyani/Any-ani.

8. Get even with Arvind Nokia Seshadri story.

9. Give impression of 'nearly a done deal' with The Eligible.

10. 6.45 p.m. Walk towards sunset viewing point. Remain cool.

11. 7 p.m. Watch sunset. Stay calm.

12. 7.30 p.m. Find suitable fine dining restaurant.

13. 9 p.m. Trade stories of Writers' Retreat workshop with stories of Stars Can Cook workshop

14. 10 p.m. Get dropped at Villa Rena. Shake hands. (Note: not hold hands)

15. 11 p.m. Tell roommates about decision to go ahead with Mr Eligible, not Mr Edible. Go to sleep.

Well, in reality, I got to Item 3, exactly as planned.

But Item 4 onwards everything went haywire…

21

'Find a guy who messes up your lipstick, not your mascara.'

So there I was at the meeting point: Café Remezzo at Ammoudi beach, 5 p.m on the dot.

Wearing Maybelline EyeStudio Lasting Drama midnight-blue-eyeliner/eye shadow, courtesy Bobby. And L'Oreal Luscious Lippers supergloss, courtesy Mini.

My two voluntary makeover artists had earlier headed off to Perissa Beach on the other side of Santorini ('We're dangerous to have around—so we're keeping far away!') and I sat at the semi-open-air café, awaiting the appearance of KayKay.

Fortunately, my over-enthusiastic roommates hadn't tried to dress me up too, approving my choice of a bright multicoloured Balinese sarong, with a flaming orange halter-neck top. But they were waiting like two fashion police lieutenants before they allowed me out of the Villa. 'Lose those demure pearl earrings at once, Amby. Here, you need these golden hoops to complete your glam beach-bombshell look…' said Bobby holding up gigantic circles that looked like I could do the hula-hoop with.

This was getting ridiculous. What a bunch of *females* we were.

Mini was absolutely clear, when she gave me the all-okay-nod to set off on my beach 'date': 'Whether you make it or break it with Mr Hot Bod KayKay tonight, Ambujakshi Sex Goddess Balan, you've got to *kill* the dude with your look. And we trust there's a wildly minimal Victoria's Secret waiting in readiness below that svelte Balinese cover up…Just in case.' Mini nearly breathed her last when I attempted to strangle her neck.

And so I sat, wearing my Joli-type Prada (fake) shades, swivelling my head every 10 seconds like a Havells floor fan, as I wondered which side of Café Remezzo KayKay may walk in from.

A whole half hour went by. I looked again at my watch. Actually only 4 minutes had gone by.

I ordered a long glass of orange and strawberry Santorini Sundowner. It matched rather well with my orange halter-top. The drink was gone in 1 minute and 15 seconds. I ordered another. Another half an hour passed. I mean really.

Okay, girls. I've been stood up at the altar of hope. I have even *dressed up* for this drama of desperation. I've reached catastrophic levels of potential humiliation. I have to stab myself with that stupid toothpick holding up five different chunks of fruit…

'Miss Ba-laan? Hello! I'm Benito! You looka the verry much dee-firent from girl I am searching all over Café Remezzo!'

A rotund, florid gent just a little more than about 5 feet in his beach slippers stood grinning widely at my table. Benito *who?*

The man held out a pudgy hand with a ring in every finger. 'Meester Ku-maar sending me, Senorita! He ask for me to meet you. You can follow me, please, to the Ammoudi village port?'

I hastily paid my bill, and joined the mysterious Benito who continued to smile non-stop at me. 'I see peecture of you in Meester KayKay cell phone' (KayKay has my picture in his cell phone?). You no looka like that, you looka so beautiful *deefi-rent*! Like India Miss World on TV!'

Here we go again, and forgive us all, Aishwarya Rai. Benito continued his explanation as we walked. 'I work for Chef Nicholas, and Meesta KayKay beesy learning the Greek desserts all day. So he send me breeng you to new meeting place…'

I walked quickly along with Benito, further down towards the Ammoudi harbour, where several jabbering gangs of excited holidaymakers all seemed to heading too.

And then I spotted KayKay. Arms crossed over his chest, white tee over khaki slacks, standing next to a cruise boat, one of at least a dozen standing at the quay.

What else can I say—he looked like a *film star*. Thud. Boom. Bang.

Okay, I have to switch now to movie metaphor mode. I felt I was in the film called *Indecent Proposal.* This was like Robert Redford whisking Demi Moore away mysteriously first in a helicopter, and then onto a swanky yacht. This was like Shah Rukh Khan romancing Rani Mukherjee right here in the blue waters of Santorini in the film *Chalte Chalte.*

'Amby, this way! Quick!' shouted KayKay, waving to me over the crowds…A crazy scramble of people getting into boats, and the noise of bargaining boatmen filled the air.

Minutes later, Benito was waving us away in the boat heading out to sea. 'I was just beginning to think you've ditched me, Miss Balan. I sent Benito to fetch you from Ammoudi Beach ages ago…and I was having a hell of a time, holding our places in this boat!'

'Where on earth are we going, KayKay? Your Benito refused to say…'

'We're going sunset chasing, Amby! We're watching yesterday's show repeated—but from a new angle—cruising right across the caldera this time and onto Thirasia beach…'

Thirasia! We'd read all about that tiny uncrowded island lying beyond the volano. The girls would kill me if they knew where I was headed just now!

KayKay grabbed my hand and guided me up past the chattering crowds to the stern of the boat. The red-orange-yellow-pink spectacle in the sky began to unfold its magic. Our boat roared on forwards, like a giant moth being drawn to the flame of the sun.

'Sun touches earth like a lover's kiss,
Sky and ocean are joined in bliss…'

A very old Harry Belafonte song started playing through my head. He was definitely on this very boat at this very caldera when he wrote that one.

The gigantic golden orb dipped gently into the shimmering sea. We gazed, mesmerized. Every sense of mine was devoted to the sight before me.

Not really. A part of it was acutely aware that my hand hadn't left KayKay's since he grabbed it four minutes ago…

'We made it right on time!' laughed KayKay, finally letting go of my hand and reaching for his camera in his duffel bag. 'Mmmmm. *Nice*!' he said, as I heard his Nikon's click capture the beauty of it all.

Okay, I was there in at least ten of the twelve pictures he took. Then there was the one a random stranger took of us both, against the astounding sky. We put our arms around each other for that one. Only because the random photographer thought we were lovers and said, 'Okay, closer now, closer, *erates*. Arms around each other!'

'This is where you get the best Bolognaise in the entire world because tomatoes simply thrive in Thirasia's volcanic soil!' KayKay tossed me a perfect round cherry tomato from a basket at the Yiannis' Café. Every single table here had a wicker basket of bright red tomatoes placed in the centre—a table decoration that diners were welcome to eat up.

I bit into one. So sensational, it was sinful...The Bible could be rewritten starring this tomato, rather than that apple.

An hour ago we had got off our cruise boat at the port of Korfos in Thirasia Island with its tiny population of just 250 people. Thirasia had once been part of Santorini till the earthquake in the 3rd century BC separated it into an island beyond the caldera, and had somehow remained Greece's best-kept secret from swarming tourists.

'Tourists go up to Nea Kameni, the crater of the volano visible in the sea, then go to the hot springs of Palia Kameni—ruins of the lost civilization of Akrotiri, believed to be the Altantis. But most tourists give Thirasia a miss, as there are practically no hotels here to stay overnight, just a few good little eating houses, and that's where we're headed. To Yiannis, who is going to make us an unforgettable meal!' KayKay's cooking buddies in Santorini had certainly briefed him well.

So much for my neatly planned list running to 15 pre-meditated points of action for this evening, to be spent on Ammoudi Beach. I thought I would be holding forth knowledgeably on the charms of Greece through the evening; and now here he was, the authority on Greek tourism himself...*Show-off.* Okay, a very very charming show-off.

Thirasia, to our complete delight, was a mini Santorini in look and feel, and the lingering light of the spectacular sunset allowed a slow walk up uphill to the ancient Kinissi Monastery, Thirasia's best viewing point of the caldera. 'There's a grave of a legendary vampire here somewhere,' said KayKay reading from notes jotted down in his cell phone. 'But more importantly, it has the best viewing point of something few travel books even write about: sun*rise* over the caldera! What a pity we won't be seeing it, as the last boat leaves by midnight from here...'

Then the foodie in KayKay took over as he sought out the little *estiatorio* by the harbour, where Yiannis, the owner and chef, set about making the dish that every chef in Santorini raved about: the world's best Skhara.

'Guess what a Skhara is, Amby?' said KayKay, even as the waiter brought my order first: spinach salad with halloumi—a delicious Cypriotic cheese, and tomato *kef tedes* fritters. Who said vegetarians had no fun?

'Skhara? Sounds like a brand name for a car...' I said.

'It's octopus flame-grilled in Visanto sauce, my vegetarian wonder!' KayKay laughed as I looked horrified at the slithery something placed before him. 'A famous Greek specialty and highly recommended by Spiderman Toby McGuire when I last bumped into him...'

'Name-dropping show off!' I said. 'You dreadful carnivores. There's something eerie anyway about an eight-legged Spiderman recommending eating an eight-armed octopus for dinner...'

'Ha! Ha! But just to correct you—an octopus has six arms and two legs...one of which I could be swallowing now. But tell me Ms Ambujakshi Brahmin Balan, how are you going to cope with your fish-crazed future Finn husband when he brings in his daily bounty from the sea to your kitchen in your home sweet vegetarian home in Crete...'

Husband. *HUSBAND?!*

Just like that. He said it, biting into whatever body part of the horrendous sea monster he had cut and forked.

So just like that too, I decided to play along.

'Hmmm. The matter hasn't actually come up yet in the prenuptials Arvind Seshadri and I are signing soon…but thanks for the warning. We'll work that one in.'

Did I detect the tiniest look of surprise? Couldn't say, as KayKay shot back at once: 'Oh, so Finn boy has been seen, sampled, approved, applauded and signed on. Cool. Cheers to tambrahmatrimony.com or foreigngroom.com or whatever your grandparents and parents dutifully subscribed to, to secure your future…'

Foreigngroom.com? Okay, that really got to me, and even as my fork pierced a chunk of a tomato fritter, I mentally pierced one into our pontificating hero here.

'Foreigngroom.com is where *you* can find a groom for yourself, Mr KayKay or should that be GayGay, I'm beginning to wonder…'

Okay, okay I didn't actually *say* that.

Instead, I was so peeved with his facile conclusions that I went on a reckless binge of bluffing.

'Oh, we never met through any stupid matchmaking site at all, in the first place,' I lied. 'Arvind Seshadri and I were introduced through mutual friends—and then we took it all forward through email, and Facebook and Skype, entirely on our own…'

'And also decided to meet up in an exotic Greek island too, instead of the relatives-packed drawing room of the girl's house?? My my, the modern "arranged love marriage" is finding innovative ways to keep romance alive. So why do I see a bare hand still before me, elegantly holding that fork? Or is there a big ceremonious puja yet to be organized back home when the Finn boy slips the navaratna ring with a vast gathering of Iyer elders blessing you on, amidst Vedic chants?'

Nowjustaminute. Since you're making so many assumptions about my left hand and its ring finger, how come you held it, rather possessively, last night?

'Hmmm...I'll keep you informed, and also invite you to that big pious event, Mr Former Boss,' was what I breezily said.

Four hours later, the free tomatoes were long gone—even the ones in the freshly replenished basket.

Gone too, were the chattering diners in other tables, the genial owner Yiannis, the pleasant waiters, back to their little homes along the hills of the island.

What was also gone was the last boat taking visitors back into the mainland.

What remained was a couple of Indian tourists. Sitting with feet up on the furthest end of the long open patio, in cushioned reclining armchairs that a thoughtful Yiannis had placed overlooking the harbour—for the odd guest or two who simply never seemed to leave.

KayKay and I, a little exhausted after a very very VERY long conversation, which had taken off into bylanes of argument, sarcasm, accusations, assumptions and biased judgement…had at some point drifted off to sleep in our extremely comfortable deckchairs…

Where in the world am I?

I sat up completely startled and disoriented. It was a moonless night and only the faint flickers of light from the harbour reached the patio.

KayKay!! Suddenly in the inky darkness of the night, a half turned head, in supreme peace with the gentle breath of sleep, came into view. Heartwrenching handsome KayKay. An Indian Adonis in a Greek island. Right next to me.

KayKay stirred…a hand changed position, mid-sleep. I froze, wondering if my hammering heart had been loud enough to wake him up.

An errant lock of hair tousled down his forehead. I had to resist reaching out and stroking it back in place. In that moment I wanted to be the heroine of a trashy romantic novel.

I'm insane!

And then it all came back in a flood. The conversation that had turned into a discussion that had turned into an argument that had turned into a fight that had turned into a…

First, there was my ridiculous made-up tale of a huge liaison going on between Arvind and me. The more details I kept adding, the more KayKay seemed to believe it all. I was on a roll! I even made up a fake possible date for the wedding: six months from now, when he'd be next visiting India.

'So how come you haven't splashed it all over on Facebook?' KayKay had asked.

Facebook! (So he'd been stalking me on Facebook and seen that picture of cool Eligible and me in Crete...and the string of comments—18, if I remember right—from my circle of friends.) Damn Facebook!

And when did it all turn into that roaring argument of what we were doing with our lives? Maybe fried octopus makes the eater rather belligerent...

We went right back to that messy unresolved conversation we'd had all those months ago in Liverpool.

I asked him if he'd made up his mind, or rather made up his *body*, on where his sexual preferences actually lay: Shamini/Devyani/Any-ani or Toni?

He asked me if being a dutiful Tam Brahm housewife to a parent-chosen foreign-returned was the one real true calling of my life.

I asked him if signing on film after film after film after film after FILM, lusting after more fame and more money, was the one real true calling of his life.

He asked me to mind my own business, the business of getting married.

I asked him to mind his own business, the rather lucrative business of show business.

The last boat to Ammoudi Beach left Thirasia.

We were so busy arguing, we kept no track of when it left.

The ever-smiling and hospitable Yiannis laughed when he saw us jump and rush madly towards the pier. 'No worries, *koritsi*. An early fisherman's boat leaving at 7 in the morning! Or, you lovers can come and stay at my home in Manalos, maybe?' he winked. 'I make you the breakfast in my home too, and you catch the 9 o' clock local ferry.'

Lovers? We assured Yiannis that we were *quite* the opposite…and besides, we had important work waiting for us the next day in Santorini, not to mention *plenty* of argument left for the rest of the night.

We decided the deckchairs on the extended patio would be a good place to watch out for the very first boat leaving for the mainland, early in the morning.

And also to find fresh salvos to hurl at each other.

And so here we were again on the deckchairs.

When exactly did we drift off to sleep?

'Amby! The Thirasia sunrise! Quick! Before we catch our boat…'

KayKay called out to me from the far end of the quay, where he was splashing his face with water from a basin. I jumped awake from a very deep sleep. The bluey pre-dawn tinge made the entire scene before me so surreal and mystical. I glanced at my watch. 5.40 a.m.!

How was KayKay looking utterly butterly *fresh* still, white tee and khaki?

(And was I looking like something Yiannis's cat had brought in to eat for breakfast?) I hurriedly dived into my bag: popped fresh mints in my mouth, and dragged a brush through my mussed up hair.

No time to think—as KayKay was racing me away from the patio—'Let's catch the Thirasia sunrise, now that we are actually still here'—back to the sunrise viewpoint at Potamos up the hill again.

About 15 out-of-breath minutes later, we were there. Ready for nature's spectacular show of shows all over again, starring yesterday's curtain-call actor, the sun—only in the reverse order now.

Not a single other human being in sight. No clapping, whooping, celebrating sun-worshippers. We waited in the pre-dawn light in complete silence, in profound isolation, for almost 4 minutes...

Gradually the sky eased from inky blue to purple, with licks of blue and pink streaking out in slow motion. And then the shimmering disc of a mix of pink and gold emerged over the sea, with Santorini just beyond.

I felt sudden tears spring into my eyes at the impossible beauty of it all.

KayKay had turned away from the spectacle, and was now looking intently at me. Feeling suddenly self-conscious of my tears, I broke into a completely mad babble of silly exclamations.

And then went speechless again.

Mainly because my mouth was being firmly shut up...*Shhhh!* whispered KayKay as he half turned, locked my eyes into his for a moment, cupped my cheeks in his big, firm, male hands, and kissed me.

What exactly was going on here?

Technically, this was quite immoral on his part, as I had clearly told KayKay I was (almost) bethrothed and bound and banded and belonged to Another Man.

Technically, it was also cheating on my part, as I was very clearly kissing KayKay back.

Technically, this was all pretty contrary, as we'd been quite disillusioned and disapproving and disdainful with each other just a few hours ago.

(Speaking of technicalities, KayKay's kissing technique was so girl-melting, goose-bumpy awesome.)

And then our bodies kissed each other. Hips on his thighs. Breasts on his abs. Shoulders on his chest. The curve of my neck on his biceps. Every soft curve and crevice of my body found a masculine counter in his, to lock into till we had fused into an inseparable one…

'And which Hollywood screenplay moment are you thinking of just now, my dialogue-spouting, movie-mad maniac? Before Sunrise? Or Before Sunset?'

Wait. Did KayKay actually say that? Or did I just imagine he said that?

22

'Every new beginning is some other beginning's end.'

Way past 9 a.m.! I raced towards our room in Villa Rena, hoping like hell that Mini and Bobby were already away at the Villa's buffet breakfast. No such luck.

'Welcome back, lady of the night!' said Mini, as a grinning Bobby opened the door for me. 'I can deduce in single glance that you've been totally ravished by a male of the species…'

'Aha! So the Luscious Lippers and Dark Lashes Drama

did their job!'cut in Bobby, even as I laughed and tried dodging past their torrent of questions .

'Okay, girls. Can you keep a secret?' I asked Mini and Bobby.

'Yes!' they both chorused in high-voltage anticipation.

'So can I!' I said and winked, as I ran straight into the bathroom, and shut the bathroom door.

The yells of protests continued from outside the door, as the girls, in the manner of good friends of the feminine gender all over the world, demanded to know *everything* about my night-long scandalous disappearance.

'It's nothing what you silly girls imagine!' I yelled back through the door, even as I splashed water on my rather flushed face. Scientific fact: Cold tap water has absolutely no effect in cooling down just-kissed faces…

Fortunately for me, Mini and Bobby were off to breakfast, and had their one-to-one feedback sessions with Denis Slater in the morning. So they had reluctantly left the room, by the time I gingerly opened the bathroom door after a shower, and stepped out.

Peace! The time I needed to think sanely about all the crazy logic-defying happenings that had just transpired.

On second thoughts. I felt a wave of delicious sleep hitting me, and hit my bed instead for a tiny 10-minute nap.

I was shaken awake two hours later by the jangling phone in our room. It was Bobby. 'Wakey wakey Sleeping Beauty! You really can't survive on love and fresh Mediterranean air. There's a goodbye lunch over by the pool waiting for us, and also a final writing task we have to do—after which you're the last and only one left to meet up with Denis Slater.'

Final writing task! I was feeling so totally brain-smacked and woozy-headed, I wouldn't be able to write one coherent *alphabet.* And then there was my big feedback session with Denis! All I wanted to do now was just feed—as I raced, famished, to the poolside buffet spread.

I wasn't the only one protesting about the cruel final writing task. But Pavol and Denis only laughed away our collective wails to cancel any further work for us, as he held up a bunch of colourful Greece postcards in his hand.

'You are each going to write a postcard—to yourself!' said Pavol. 'Handwritten! Here, take one each from this bunch: when was the last time you actually wrote anyone a handwritten mail? And if writers don't, who will?

'Now these are "Dear Me" postcards you will write, addressed to yourself, and return to me. A year from now, I shall be stamping and posting them all from Crete, to reach your homes in different countries. You will ask yourself, in your own postcard, how far you have reached in the grand writing plan each of you have made here, even as you go away exhilarated from this Workshop.

'This postcard is your conscience-keeper. Your reminder beep. Your reality check. It is all so easy to go away and become procastinators...but this postcard will arrive one day, out of the blue from *yourself*, from far off Greece. And ask you, 'So how're YOU doing?' And you better *be* doing what you've promised you'll be doing!'

The grand writing plan I had for myself. Well, I had nothing specific to write down yet, on my postcard, as I still had to have my personal session with my mentor. Soon after lunch; the very last person in the Workshop to meet Denis Slater.

It was, Denis said later, the longest of all the sessions he had had. And how did the whole IDEA emerge?

It's that inexplicable aha! moment when many many bits and pieces of thoughts, leads, hopes, suggestions, possibilities, doubts, tips, directions, conjectures, dares, theories, guesses, speculation...dramatically resolve themselves.

The precise moment when the *perhaps*, *could be*, *maybe*, *suppose* and *why-not!* all magically turn into *yes, that's it!*

Denis Slater knew, and I knew, exactly what I'd be going away with from this life-changing Workshop.

Emerging flushed and high as a kite from Denis's session, I wrote me my own postcard and gave it in to my mentor, for posting later.

And then the rest of our Greece encounter zipped by in a happy blur. The final meet in the conference room in Santorini, the toasts to Denis Slater and Pavol Zavaka. And after that, the hysterical *'We're Writer Than We Thought'* song by Mini and Owen, with funny one-liners about each of us, the rush to catch our ferry back to Crete, and then the final day of *real* partying at the Akrotiri Taverna in Chania, when even Annabel Keats let her hair, her inhibitions (but not her skirt) down.

We made those typical sentimental impractical wild promises as we hugged, clung, kissed each other goodbye at the big Workshop close-down party.

'Let's make a pact NOW to return here to Greece, all

twelve of us, every single year! Okay, once in three years for sure. DONE! And we downed our last Cretan ouzos...

Fortunately for seven of us from the group, we had worked in two extra days sightseeing at Athens (how could we not squeeze in Athens and the Acropolis after coming to Crete? It would have been like going all the way to Delhi and skipping Agra and the Taj...) so the madness, mayhem and bonding continued.

We'll email! We'll Skype! I'm coming to India this year end! Catch up with you in New York next March! I'm off to Egypt next year, join me! Don't you DARE get married without inviting me. I've always wanted to visit Ireland! Don't you forget to mail me all your pictures...I love you. I love you too. You're the best. I learnt so much from you. You rock. You're a genius. You're a riot. Take care. Keep smiling. Keep shining.

And the most emotional of all, in a triumvirate of tight, looong hugs at the Athens airport.

Mini, Bobby, you've become my new soul sisters.

Amby, Mini, we three were just MEANT to be. Like Charlie's Angels. Like Rachel-Monica-Phoebe. Or is it the Three Witches of Macbeth?

Bobby, Amby, remember: we have to settle right here in a cottage in Greece, 50 years from now when we are three cackling old ancient swinging-single-again ya-yas.

Don't forget to WRITE!

23

'I write because I'm curious to see what happens next.'

INDIA. THREE DAYS LATER

I saw the news item screaming out of the magazine rack at the airport. I quickly grabbed a copy of the *Chennai Times*, as I waited for my Fastrack taxi to show up. As it is, I was feeling so weird to be back from my Aegean dreamlike heaven, to the reality show of my city's cacophony.

KAYKAY QUITS MISTER-MASTER*! A firm 'no' to Bollywood too.*

KayKay quits?? When did this happen. And how come he didn't breathe *a word* of this to me in Greece, just six days ago?

A smouldering picture of KayKay, white shirt fluttering open against a clean bare chest filled the front page. My heart morphed into a cricket ball and flew out of my rib cage. I read on…

'KayKay is no longer the hero of the much publicized Mister-Master*—a role specially written with KayKay's dancing talents in mind.*

Our sources say a distraught Director Pallanisami still hasn't given up hopes of making KayKay change his mind, ever since he disappeared again after a brief return to Chennai from Turkey. Mister-Master, *a thriller about a staid physics teacher by day, and a swinging dance teacher by night, has already created an unprecedented buzz. Thanks to a very unusual animated pre-trailer created by a fan that has gone viral, getting 50,000 hits already.*

And what about K Jo's attempts to lure this South Indian biggie away to Bollywood? 'It was an offer no star in India would say "no" to. And KayKay has in fact said a firm "No"!' says an industry source.

So has Kollywood, not to mention Bollywood, finally lost KayKay to Hollywood? We know for sure that the mysterious trip to Turkey recently is the reason for the sudden change in plans. A KayKay fan at the Istanbul airport sent us a picture of a foreign film crew seen with the star…and was it the Desperate Housewife EVA LONGORIA that our fan saw, chatting with KayKay in the airport lounge???

Watch this space!

I rapidly changed my phone's sim card and sent a quick sms home to Dad saying I'd arrived and was heading home. And then it was time to call Kavi.

'Kaav! I'm BACK!'

In the space of a taxi ride home, Kavi and I had covered enough news to fill four channels on TV. Only we were rapid surfing between channels as we flipped from a) Headlines on the Eligible b) Kavi dodging a bullet (saying no to creepy US businessman seeking marriage) c) Me finding my true calling at the Workshop. At last! d) Kavi's first online order for her eco-friendly soaps, in her website Eco-nomix) The after-effects of a Greece sunrise/sunset f) An invite for Kavi and me to drive down to Bangalore for Mini's thirtieth birthday bash g) A guru called Denis Slater leading me to The Path h) SENSAtional news about my ex-boss, which Kavi was dying to tell me i) SENSAtional news about my ex-boss, that I was dying to tell her.

The last two items of this list alone needed a whole week dedicated to deep discussion, but I had by then arrived home to a delighted grandfather waving away at the gate, and soon I was swallowed up in a homecoming fit for a hero returning after a space walk.

Two days later: No sms. No Tweet. No email. No FB message. NO PHONE CALL

Okay folks, in this day and age, is it silly for a gal to expect a guy to do any of the above, *first*? But I am a bit old-fashioned about these things and waited for that morning-after call all girls in the history of relationships wait for.

(Did I just say *morning-after* call?? Okay, make that a Greece-after call.)

Strangely, I wasn't a bit jet-lagged since arrival as I went on like a motor-mouth with my family about Greece (Version 1) and with Kavi (Version 2). The two different versions had entirely different heroes in starring roles, of course.

In Version 1, my family grew immediately very

impatient if I branched off into a thrilling Writers Workshop incident, and pulled me back firmly to hear more and more about Arvind Seshadri's appearance in Crete. (Now at this point, I admit, I was so confused with so many wild concocted stories about Arvind and me as a pair—most of which I had invented that night at Thirasia Island to impress KayKay with, I often wondered what was made-up, and what really happened.)

My overjoyed family by now seemed to happily believe that my going to Greece was for the one and only providential purpose of 'seeing the boy'. (It just struck me, what an antiseptic meaning this parental-approved phrase had, as opposed to *us* using this expression, 'seeing a guy'!).

So like a fish that loses its memory every few seconds, and starts all over again, I would be talking in exquisite detail over an intellectually satisfying chat I had had with Arvind Seshadri (*Wait! This was nonsense I had made up for KayKay!*) and then suddenly abandon that story, and resort to a mysterious dim expression and discouraging remarks that implied I really didn't know if Arvind and I were *that* suited for each other...

The latter had as much effect as controlling the Niagara Falls with a teaspoon. The parents and grandparents were gushing away in joy, and were even thinking about renovating our entire house and re-tiling our upstairs balcony where a tea-party could be held when his family and my family formally met up—when the Eligible came visiting India at the end of the year.

And what of that front page of *Chennai Times* that lay

on the drawing room couch, with my dishy ex-boss continuing to hog headlines? Well, I'll tell you.

My mom was looking for waste newspaper to spread below her chappati-rolling apparatus on the kitchen counter. She placed KayKay's torso-revealing picture absent-mindedly on the counter. Then she firmly turned the paper over, where a Pothy's '30% off saree sale' was being announced. And began rolling out chappatis...hmmm. A woman with a rolling pin in hand can be a pretty dangerous, determined person...Turning the page was probably for her a significant sign that I had turned over a new leaf; no more the filmi life with wild star bosses. I was going to marry Arvind Seshadri. Within a year, as predicted by our family astrologer...

But the Greece Story Version 2 for Kavi! It had all the elements of a Greek melodrama. Kavi so far had been my chief cheerleader in promoting my liaison with the Eligible—and so went manic speechless when she heard KayKay *too* had landed in Greece.

'You're kidding me crazy, right Amby?? *KayKay* too came to Greece?'

Even while I was wondering how on earth I'd actually tell her some jaw-drop-inducing parts which involved sunsets, sunrises and a very dark moonless night, Kavi was grabbing her cell phone to show me a news item, exclaiming 'Amby! So did he come all the way there to say goodbye to you?' *(GoodBYE??)*

'Vikki-leaks found out this big news two days ago, first, of course. That KayKay has quit films forever. And going away to Paris for a whole year. But guess you know all that, right? Anyway, the news about Paris just hit *Kollywood Kalling* online—read on. No, you can read that one later...tell me, what did KayKay actually SAY?!'

PARIS? Why, what, when, where...

Strange. Very strange. After sharing a (somewhat) heightened level of intimacy with a guy, here was me, just days after, reading this gossip rag *Kollywood Kalling* like a lowly fan, to know more about Kavi's startling news, in the column 'Remember You Heard It Here First'—

Whoever expected chocolate-eyed KayKay to dump stardom, fame, glamour, adulation, big bucks, romantic link-ups, Bollywood offers...for a new calling?

We did.

Long ago, in these very columns, we suspected KayKay would rather be stirring melted cocoa into beaten egg white than stir up the insides of a moony college girl. We were right! KayKay has officially announced his dropping out of Mister-Master, *and K-Jo's offer in Bollywood too (and in fact ALL future film productions) to chase a personal dream.*

KayKay is on his way to France on a year's intensive chef's course at Cordon Bleu in PARIS.

Dear Distraught Fan, we promise we are not cooking this up.

Hold on till we serve you more sizzlers next week...a little French birdie is on KayKay's trail in Paris, even as we squeak, and we'll be back with more soon!

Confessions and confidences to a best friend (involving palpitations experienced at sunrises and sunsets in Greece) would have to wait.

There was also the underlying humiliation of realizing KayKay had a firm plan all along—to take his cheffing ambitions further—and meeting me in Santorini was just a by-the-way thing.

And even my own best friend might feel inclined to laugh at my delusionary state: attaching serious meaning to dalliances during the rising and setting of the sun.

Suddenly it seemed all so ridiculous that I was devoting so much post-Greece energy to someone else's changed course of life.

When *mine* was poised to dramatically change forever, too.

'Kavi! To HELL with Eligibles and Edibles and marriage-sharrage! *I found what I went looking for in Greece.* I now know exactly what to do with my whole life now. I'm finally moving on to the Second Best Job in the World!'

THE GAP.

That was the working title we gave to the Big Idea. My future path. My creative venture. My new business. My new job. It sounds crazy but it's true…but Denis Slater and I had instantly said 'Let's call it The Gap', *together.*

Somewhere along that enlightening last day that I had had in my one-to-one session in Santorini with my mentor-writer Denis Slater, the whole idea of what I had come seeking in Greece emerged. It was a Eureka moment.

'Screenplay writing, obviously!' Mini had said. 'Anyway you now have enough material to write your own wild romantic screenplay into a hit movie, Amby!'

Mini was both wrong and right here. Because it was all much much MORE than that.

In Greece, right through the 'Creative Awakenings' workshopping; in the little writing exercises, in the big writing exercises, in the art sessions, in the impromptu creative tasks, I thought I had been confused about what writing path I really wanted to focus on.

Perhaps the answer, said a smiling Denis, was ALL of it.

Imagine a Creative Club (well, Institute was too official a word!) where one could go to figure out a life of creative enrichment!

'You mean replicate this Writers' Workshop in my own city?' I'd asked Denis, now fully hooked on.

'Much more than that. Ms Ba-laan! You lead as easily as you write. You inspire as easily as you improvise. Also, my dear girl, don't forget you have a friggin' high falutin' business degree as well as a writers' resume!

'So now. How about starting a kind of finishing school where people come to re-discover their creative side—just as you did, taking a year off from whatever you were doing. This is a common enough concept in the US, where students take some time off, called the Gap Year—when they travel, pursue a hobby, learn a new craft, find voluntary work in places that they enjoy being in, even if they earn no salary…just to explore new paths and discover something about themselves. You told me yourself that a concept like a Gap Year is not really something that Indians are familiar with…now, Amby Ba-laan, you're going to make that big!'

24

'Feel the fear. But do it anyway'.

CHENNAI. ONE YEAR LATER.

'How nice to see that people still handwrite and send postcards from a holiday,' said my dad, walking into my room with the day's post. 'Here. This must be from one of the pals you made in Greece. The handwriting looks so much like yours.'

I had to agree. Since the card was from me.

I grabbed the colourful Georges Meis postcard of a typical blue and white Santorini stairway. Our last writing exercise in Greece: the Reminder Postcards we addressed to ourselves! Denis Slater had posted them back to us—one year exactly from the day the workshop ended.

Dear Me

Kali Mera from your Grecian avatar in Santorini!

Here's a poke across several seas to see how your New Job and New Life is shaping up. 1. Got a name for it? 2. Got a business plan? 3. Got the big bucks to back it? 4. Got the space to run it? Remember Nike, the ancient Greek goddess who personified victory, with these words we all know only too well—'Just DO it!'

XOXOXO

From Me.

What a fine idea of Denis Slater to have our own conscience haunt us with difficult questions with this postcard. To see if we were making the moves we swore we would, after the euphoria of a life-changing workshop.

(Were eleven other Cretan writing buddies around the world going through a stock-taking moment like me, just now?).

Well, it had been a year of real hard work for me, but I was proud to say I could answer Yes, Yes and Yes to the first three Qs on my own post card. But a sad and sorry NO to the last question—of finding the perfect space to run my new dream school.

I had a name for it. A simple, yet profound The Gap. Even though I did consider the one Kavi liked more: The Right Turn. (She felt it suggested a definite turn one's life would take when the right side of the brain was activated).

I had a cool Business Plan in place. Not those dreary tomes with ponderous and intellectual Mission Statements and Vision Statements that sounded like Socrates wrote it, but one that had many fine lines of inspiration from famous right-minded creative geniuses.

It also had a detailed roll-out—with a select band of brilliant, quirky, artistic and inspiring geniuses I knew and already contacted, who were now busy working on what they would teach—some as regular faculty, or as guest speakers.

They were musicians. Actors. Painters. Advertising creative chiefs. Screenplay writers. Photographers. Potters. Gardeners. Theatre personalities. I was amazed how eagerly they had signed on, once they'd heard in full detail about the concept behind The Gap.

Initially I'd take in adults—not just students who might see it as a sort of finishing school before choosing a career path, but also working professionals who felt 'stuck' in their jobs; those longing to pick up a new creative pursuit, improve their writing skills, or go back to an abandoned hobby. So I planned different kinds of time-plans for each creative course: ranging from weekend courses to even three-month long programmes. A year down the line, I planned to expand to take in children too.

I had the big bucks—my well-invested savings from my first Market Research job, plus loans I got for my start-up, thanks to my old ties at Citibank where I once worked...well okay, just for a month! And despite violent protests by the family—you'd think they'd be used to my unorthodox career plans and unpredictable actions by now—I did something to raise further capital for my venture: sold that 'One Kilo of Gold Jewellery' I had won years and years ago in a slogan contest. Cashing in on a month when the price per gram reached a horrific new high, I took out what had just lain about in a State Bank of India locker for over ten years and soon added over 30 lakhs to the kitty.

I took up a small office space in town, and hired a pair of eager beavers to assist me and put it all together, draw up agendas, print out a brochure, make cold calls, contact talent from the film industry—okay, I did have a fair amount of clout in this area! And even had some good feedback from top high schools in the city and many corporates too, about a willingness to join a different kind of School for Creativity.

But the last Question: *Got the space to run it?*

Whoever invented the phrase 'pillar to post' got it so right. I had run about from Chettinad-pillared homes advertised in the classifieds, to post-colonial villas in Chennai's suburbs…but my 'uniquely beautiful space' to run my school for creativity just wasn't falling into place.

It was uncanny that my dearest buddy Kavi should call me just as I wished she were still down the road, to run to and show the Postcard from Me to Me. Kavi was now living far away in Sweden—saving whales, or was it snails? But she never stopped being there for me when I wanted to wail about something.

'Hey, Amby! Pulled off the deal on that villa yet?'

'No, Kavi—the owner changed his mind again!' I said. 'I think I'll give up now, and just set up shop, out in the open air, but maybe on a Greek island…'

'Hmmm…wait, I'll do some Positive Affirmations for you—the Universe just needs to know you deserve a great place for your idea. It'll happen, don't you ever give up…'

True, I wasn't giving up. Especially now that I had all the time to focus on this project of finding that perfect location for my school.

Meanwhile, my parents and grandparents were all off the next day on a six-month tour of the US for my cousin's wedding; and visiting about a thousand Tam Brahm relatives who were already tracing their ancestry to either Bill Gates or Steve Jobs. I did a great acting job of deep anguish that I couldn't accompany them too—but was thrilled to pieces that I now had the whole house, and my entire life, to myself.

A couple of days later I saw a Skype alert coming in for me—from Bobby and Mini! My fabulous writer-soul-sisters from Greece. We never stopped having our 'Awesome Threesome' chats on a fixed day, once a month, and I knew at once they were calling to see if I too had got my Reminder Postcard from Greece.

But first, here's a quick summary on what new turns the lives of Mini Cherian and Bobby Varma had taken, after Crete.

Mini, who'd set off to Greece to change her writing style from innocent prattle to purple prose, was instead firmly and most happily back in the world of children's books and films. Especially after the unbelievable success of 'L.O.L With Danny'—the Laugh-Along Book she and her dad Cheerio had helped produce, for the adorable Irishman Owen's son. The 9-year-old Danny's idea—of embedding chips in a big joke book to provide a 'laugh track' as you read each joke, was successfully made into a prototype by Mini's techy pals in Bangalore.

The book was going into full production soon—and Bobby and I had definite plans to be there for a Dublin launch of the book in the foreseeable future. (Did we secretly hope that trip may also include a wedding celebration of Mini Cherian and Owen McFee? OH YES!).

Even in Greece, we'd all seen the growing chemistry between Owen and Mini, and no one was surprised when we heard she'd made a trip to Ireland almost as soon as she got back from Greece.

Bobby Varma's new blog 'Travaholic' featuring the trip-ups of travel had become so hugely popular, she was sitting up nights keeping it going—especially since she now had a full-time day job with *Conde Nast India* as a regular features writer. Her last trip out of the country was to Finland, to do a story on the unique Santa Claus village at Rovaniemi. And who did she meet up with?? Yes, Arvind Nokia Seshadri, the (former) Mr Eligible in my life!

I had long ago given up the 'imaginary connect' we were supposed to have had, invented largely to keep my family off my back, and I think Arvind and I were both relieved to acknowledge it wasn't going any further any more, after meeting up in Crete.

Much to my parents' dismay, of course. What had become of their sensible, reliable child over these last few years? What was this pattern of behaviour that made her suddenly give up very good things like steady jobs and suitable boys and set off on foolish new paths? Perhaps this is what they asked our family astrologer; I have no idea what he actually said, but his assurances that my *'yezharai naatu shani'* phase, or the rule of a troubling Saturn over my life for the last seven and a half years had finally ended, had sent them home pacified, and filled with new hope. At least that other ridiculous path she took into the *moshamana* bad world with film stars and whatnot had all come to an end, they said to their gods, while at prayer.

Hmm. The rather ego-deflating truth of the matter was—KayKay had quite dramatically vanished out of *my* world; not just from the lives of distraught directors and gossipy columnists. Peeved and bruised for several days after my return to India, I blamed it first on my own exaggerated bluffing about marriage plans to Arvind Seshadri. Then self-flagellation turned into anger—always an easier emotion to unleash, as he hadn't made a single attempt to message me, mail me, Facebook me, Tweet me, WhatsApp me, Skype me, phone me that he was pursuing his chef-dream-plan in Paris. He had obviously had his big getaway plan all neatly worked out when he landed up in Greece. Why hadn't he told me a thing? Meanwhile I had landed up in his arms, and lost my head and my self-respect and...*hey hey hey*! I wasn't going down *that* path again.

The pinga-ponga-alert tune of Skype jolted me back into the joy of connecting up with my writing buddies.

As each of us held up the From Me to Me postcards to the camera, there was understandably a lot of reminiscing and cheering that ensued.

So far, Bobby had already found her Second Best Job in the World, with the dream Travel Writer appendage to her name. Mini and I clapped for Bobby and demanded she take us along as 'emotional baggage' on the next exotic trip she was going to make!

Mini declared herself an utter failure in her dream of

making waves in the world of adult erotica, but Bobby and I exchanged a conspiratorial wink as we clearly saw her heading towards her Second Best Job in the World too, somewhere in a cosy Irish home...(which, without us spelling it out, only meant 'motherhood'.)

I, too, was cheered on by my supportive buddies—for the progress I had made thus far in The Gap. Especially when Bobby and Mini saw their names as Visiting Faculty in my business plan.

'You are getting there, Amby, don't lose heart over finding that villa. And you know what? You're actually going to be making a whole lot of *other* individuals find the job of their dreams!' Mini and Bobby's words did much to reassure my spirits.

'And now enough about our professional lives. Tell us about Mr Dreamy now Amby. WHY isn't he back from his exotic cooking pursuits in France, yet?' asked my well-meaning pals.

'Who knows and who cares...' I said, most casually. Without fooling *anybody*.

'By the way, there was such a buzz in the local filmi goss columns some months ago, which reported that the great KayKay was spotted by some manic fans—riding a bike on East Coast Road near Chennai. Utter rubbish, of course...' What I meant was: if that was true, then how come he never called *me?*

'And my parents and grandparents are far away in California now, to attend my cousin's wedding, and happily off my back for another six months as they visit 10,000 very close relatives all over the States—no doubt picking up matching horoscopes at every point for me!' I said. 'A trusted family astrologer told them I was onto a very good thing with this crazy new plan of mine, as sceptical as they were when they first heard it—and the astrologer even said marriage wasn't on the cards for a while yet, but not to worry, I would most probably marry a man 'coming from the West'. So that's kept them calm and super busy for now. I think I should pay this astrologer guy to keep this going for a while longer!'

I skilfully diverted the topic away from any more talk of KayKay, by showing them plans for my funky interiors—which a bright young architect and I were busy drawing up, even though there was no venue in sight.

We wound up our Skype chat, thrilled to have caught up on each others' lives, thrilled that we had deepened our bonds even more, after our fateful meeting in Greece.

And promised to be available for the next chat, about a month from now…

25

'When you stop chasing the wrong things, you allow the right things to catch up with you.'

ONE MONTH LATER

I should've got an inkling of something brewing when Kavi went mad ringing me at odd hours from Sweden, many times in one week, saying—'Hi Amby! What's up?

No nothing really, just called, that's all...' and then hanging up, abruptly.

And then came that mysterious call. On my office telephone.

An unfamiliar voice with a strong French accent greeted me. 'Bon jour, Ma'mselle, my nom ees Monsieur Vincent. I weesh to parler avec Miss Am-boo-jack-she-Ba-laan?'

'Bon jour. Je suis Ms Ambujakshi...how can I help...er, *Comment je vous aider?'* I said, quite proud of my broken French.

The grateful Frenchman raced away in pure French after that—and I understood nothing.

'Merci, Ma'mselle! Je voudrais vous recontrer pour parler affaires avec vous!'

What was THAT? After going back and forth a bit, I wondered, who is this man saying he'd like to talk about my affairs? *Affairs?!*

'Pardon, I know *peu de Francais*! Very little French—can you speak in English again?'

And then it turned out that 'affaires' in French simply meant a business meeting—which he was interested in having with me the next day. Whew. Some kind of partnership deal...I really couldn't make out, but I ended up saying yes, of course, and agreed to meet up with this mysterious Frenchman at Amethyst at 5 p.m.

Promptly at 5, I walked into the huge open air Amethyst. Sitting at a table not far away was a rather striking-looking gentleman with a suave ponytail, in a smart sleeveless riding jacket and killer-looking shades. Monsieur Vincent. Way younger than I thought he'd be!

He turned and waved tentatively at me, as if to figure if I was the girl he had come to meet.

I waved back, gave him a big smile, and made my way towards the intriguing gentleman.

He got up and reached out his hand to greet me. *'Vous etes absolument magnifique!'*

I stood gob-smacked at this rather supreme compliment from a total stranger.

Did I say stranger? Well, it was the *situation* that was getting stranger and stranger, when the French hottie whipped off his glasses. Reached for my hand. Kissed my fingertips. And broke into a laugh that was extremely familiar…

'Hello, my absolument magnifique Amby! I must say your French had me quite impressed on the phone yesterday.'

KAYKAY!

'WhattheHELLisgoingon…omigod, you look *totally different*, you crazy lunatic man…'

The amused creature broke into another roar. Did I ever mention that KayKay has a laugh that could flatten small trees in its path?

My body had now gone from a state of rigor mortis shock to jelly-belly-wobbly. I had to sit down, or rather collapse in slow motion. KayKay was there in an instant, pulling out my chair, settling me in. Hmmm. Our chef-guy here was also a well-trained waiter, I observed. Only waiters shouldn't wear such sexy, expensive male fragrances.

KayKay sat opposite me, his new face resting on a firmly elbowed fist.

'Well whadayasay, my former employee? Like? Unlike?'

'First of all, you've got to stop popping up in unexpected places and killing me in slow degrees with shock. Second of all, did you go to fashion school or chef's school, since the time you simply vanished without a trace??'

Now that the initial shock had subsided, and we'd ordered our cappuccinos, I looked at him all over again. What is it about some men who manage to look much more masculine and macho by wearing a *girl's* ponytail? His chiselled face had tanned to an incredibly edible honey-colour that seemed to have just been painted over him. And which French haute-couture hanger did that utterly dapper jacket come out from?

He'd become even more of a head-turner now, that's for sure, judging by the subtle yet curious looks he was getting from groups of women going in and out of the café.

Well, that delicious gold-brown tan came from the beaches of Monaco apparently—where he had headed off to lie in the sun for days. A wind-down holiday for him and the rest of his graduating buddies at the Cordon Bleu chef school.

'I'm done with the course, Amby! It nearly killed me with the daily rigour, and I lost touch with the entire world outside of our institute—but what a high at the end of it all!'

But KayKay skilfully avoided any details—he seemed much more interested in what happened to me during the rest of the course at Greece, what Denis Slater had to say about me, and how the idea for a School for Creativity had come up. As usual he listened with full serious attention with his direct eye-contact way—and with a sudden rush, I realized how much I had missed this face. *Unfair.*

But the dangerous twinkle was back in his eyes when he ribbed me lightly with questions about arranged alliances, and though I bounced it all back with some smart ones, I somehow felt he knew exactly what was going on in that part of my life. (The short answer to that one is: Nothing.)

In the next hour of catching up, I was surprised how up to date he seemed to be with my own progress in life—KayKay definitely had a Globe Detective Agency or something shadowing me, wherever in the world I was.

Now there was much explaining KayKay had to do. I was just getting started with some intense cross-questioning, when we got interrupted by a bunch of young college girls, who squeeeeealed and went, 'Aren't you *KAYKAY?!!!*'

A completely embarrassed KayKay laughed, but absolutely refused to sign autographs in their notebooks, declaring he'd stopped being a film star centuries ago—but it certainly drew more attention from other tables, and some whispers and smiles.

'Oh God, I'm glad I'm going to be far far away from Chennai now that I'm back in Chennai…'

What that meant was, he'd be far away on East Coast Road again. Back to his old place by the sea? 'Only until my own restaurant's construction is complete, Ambujax! My own dream restaurant! Yes, right on that beach.'

I let that sink in.

'Hey, are you still open to some freelance social media advertising when I open it in a few months' time? I hear you are quite the expert when it comes to sending out Tweets…' said KayKay, risking ruining his stylish togs with some cappuccino I threatened to pour down his head.

And then all the explanations of KayKay's appearances, disappearances, his knack of knowing what I was just about to tell him—it all came out.

The source, confessed KayKay, was *Kavi!*

Apparently six months ago, on his short, secret visit to India for a week ('You mean all those Elvis-like sightings of KayKay on East Coast Road were true?'), KayKay came just to get the construction of his dream sea-facing Mediterranean restaurant underway, and he also managed to have a secret meeting with Kavi.

'Tracking your best friend down itself took a while, as I've only briefly met Kavi before when you brought her to the film studios a couple of times. Then I tried that public little black book in which anyone can find anyone in this world—Facebook! I in-boxed her to get in touch with me at once, and pretty soon, Kavi did,' explained KayKay. 'Kavi was fortunately in India then too—so we met up for a chat, a high-level summit meeting in a remote restaurant!'

My stupefied expression continued, as I tried digesting this strange back-story. Why this secret meeting with Kavi? To discuss ME? Oh boy, did that traitor Kavi shortly have a LOT of explaining to do…

Maybe KayKay made Kavi sign with her own blood

that she would not tell me anything about this; and so KayKay had got to know quite a bit about what was going on in my life, through the past year. My plans for my own institute, the definite new direction my life was taking, not to mention the direction it was *not* taking—on the marriage front.

A few weeks ago, he even got my office telephone number from Kavi, changed his voice around, and made that Frenchy call to me yesterday. Now it fell into place—the reason why Kavi had so mysteriously been calling me all week, probably curious whether our great meeting had happened.

Wait! Had Kavi also led him to that dramatic appearance at my Workshop in Santorini? 'No, she wasn't anywhere in the picture then,' laughed KayKay, 'so don't take her apart for that too. I was there in Greece to brush up on my dessert-making skills for the TV show—and did my own *jasoosi* on where I might find you on the island.'

'Talking of which! Hey Kay, whatever happened to the *Stars Can Cook* show?'

'I lasted till the third round—a miracle! Such a fantastic experience—and I have many side stories to tell you about the stars, you Hollywood-obsessed thing. The show was a big hit in Europe—and ought to be airing in India soon. I'm actually dreading that—as I'm hardly a star any more! BUT, I can cook, I swear…'

I was interrupted by an urgent call by my hapless real estate broker just then, to come at once to check out yet another bungalow for my new project, and though there still seemed to be a million unanswered questions, I decided to rush away.

The business of tackling brokers and bungalows and haggling with owners would jolt me back to my everyday reality; I needed time to inhale and exhale a bit by myself and *think* about all that had been going on secretly this past year. I also needed to catch Kavi the Informer and subject her to a severe inquisition.

KayKay said in the restaurant driveway—'I'm off to Mumbai early tomorrow, and back in two days, will catch you for dinner and submit myself to further cross-questioning. Deal, Amby?' And then with that smile that melts rocks, gave me a hug that engulfed me with a fresh, spicy woody fragrance...mmm very, *very* nice...and roared away on his old faithful Yamaha bike.

Kavi laughed when I called her the minute I reached home late that night, and accused her of being the new Vikki-leaks in the gang. 'So you met up with KayKay at last, Amby! He got your number from me over a month ago, ringing me up from Paris itself, and I knew he'd be in Chennai around this time. That's why I've been calling now and then, wondering if the great meeting had happened. Now tell me, *what* happened?'

'Not so fast, my whistle-blowing friend! Or drop the "r" and make that "fiend". What extreme confidential information about my life did you pass on to KayKay?'

'Amby, you must actually give me credit for not leaking anything about my meeting with KayKay back to you! Sheer luck I was in India at that time, so we met in a shady café, with your former boss wearing a hoody to avoid being recognized. I felt I was in a movie plot myself…Hey we'll talk about that later, tell me about *now.* You met KayKay!'

'Well, KayKay's got a complete new look that had me totally fooled and is looking dishier than ever—appropriate, since he's all set to dish out the good stuff in his swank new restaurant—by the sea, Kavi! But I had to run away after a while, as I went to check out yet another property—way better than the last horror my broker took me to, so I'm thinking of closing in on it.'

'Good luck there, Amby! I'm in an outdoor location for a meeting here—but we'll catch up again in a couple of days, and you better give me more dope on meeting KayKay, okay?' and hung up.

Well *a lot* can happen in a couple of days…

It began with a series of WhatsApp messages on my phone—along with a cartoon of a French moustache below a chef's cap—KayKay's new profile pic.

The first message confirmed a dinner date on Saturday at 8 p.m. at Patio, Chennai's poshest fine dining restaurant.

Sure thing. Okay. Fine by me.

The next message got me in a complete tizz. I mean, just look what it said:

After dinner, Amby, I have a couple of proposals to make. One of which requires the use of a bended knee. So make sure you are there on time. Kay!

Omigodwhatonearthwasthisallabout.

PROPOSAL? Hold it there, buddy, aren't you presuming *way* too much here? I'm unprepared for this one! (But was that why he was preparing me for it already, two whole days ahead?) Damn KayKay, damn his pranks and his crazy surprises. And the way he simply came in and went out and came in and went out of my life, whenever *he* chose to. And now these loaded, lunatic text messages.

And then on the morning of Saturday, a huge bunch of pink lilies arrived at home. And I read the message attached. On the second breathless reading, it began to sink in. *When Harry met Sally!* That fave dialogue of mine…spoofed here for my benefit.

I love that you know every famous line from every famous movie.

I love that it takes you half an hour to order a masala dosa.

I love that you keep your car's side mirrors permanently closed, as they may hit cows.

I love that you give gifts made with your hands. Especially neck massages.

I love that you get dyslexic over the same words, and always type 'today' as 'toady'.

I love that your most extreme bad word is feck.

I love that you are the last person I want to talk to, before I sleep at night.

Okay, see you tonight at 8 p.m.!

26

'Love is when you meet someone who tells you something new about yourself.'

Which girl takes three hours to dress for dinner? A completely hyper one, who finds every dress in her cupboard seem either like she's trying too hard, or looking like she didn't give a feck…

Finally, I settled for a black and white and red silk ensemble—figuring it came in somewhere in between.

On my dressing table I found Bobby's and Mini's giveaway gifts for me—the night I traipsed off to meet KayKay at Ammoudi beach. L'Oreal Luscious Lippers supergloss and Maybelline EyeStudio Lasting Drama midnight-blue eye shadow and liner. Well, well, look what that led to, I thought, recreating those same eyes.

At 8.10 I arrived at Patio. I scanned the tables, looking for him…now *where was he?* I simply wouldn't be able to take another prank from KayKay now.

Anyway, thanks for the advance notice on your intentions tonight, Mr Presumptuous. Don't think you can take me for granted any more; remember I quit being your 'yes' girl ages ago? So I'm not likely to immediately say any kind of 'yes' to any propo…

A whiff of Eternity from behind announced that he was right at my right elbow.

'10 minutes late!' said KayKay with a grin, leading me

forward towards our table. 'You're not going to believe what they are serving here: Visanto! Unless your *dil* still *mangés* more Pepsi...'

Over the course of the next twenty minutes, I wondered how come I hadn't resorted to heavy drinking earlier in my life. This was amazing! One glass of wine down and I was even able to look at KayKay straight in the eye, in the most matter of fact way, and say, 'Loved the flowers. And the note. Good thing Nora Ephron isn't around to slam copyright charges on you, though.'

KayKay quite missed the sarcasm. 'Wasn't that good?' said KayKay, looking utterly pleased with himself. 'Great that I matched up to your exacting writing standards, Miss Balan. Now I want to match up to your exacting standards for romance...and so...' (*he was slowly reaching forward and holding my hand here, the classic restaurant romantic scene*).

OH GOD! Here it comes already! WAIT. I need more wine now. WAIT. Let's get some food in my turmoiled stomach first. Hey, I forgot my well-rehearsed line; bloody hell, what's my answer going to *be??)*

'...and so let's quit this cliché restaurant scene, soon after this dinner and go somewhere else even more romantic for the dessert. I have a very famous chef lined up to serve us both a very special dish for this significant occasion...'

And so here we were, right near the roaring waves of the beach, twenty-four kilometres out of Chennai down the breezy East Coast Road. Under an almost black moonless night (KayKay apologized that he hadn't been able to fix that one detail); but I was grateful for that, as my carefully coiffeured Dimension's salon hair was now standing up like Percy Porcupine.

After leaving Patio, I was made to abandon my car in the restaurant, and sit on his bike; zooming off on a long unanticipated motorbike ride—to the site of KayKay's half constructed restaurant near the beach.

Wow.

KayKay's grand tour, conducted by hurricane lights, was beginning to shape the fabulous Mediterranean restaurant nicely in my mind. A blue and white Santorini theme! What a hit this would be.

'And here is where I'll be setting up my special Greek desserts counter. All the tricks I learnt from Chef Nickolas in Santorini—plus more that I specialized in Paris!'

I looked around astonished at what KayKay had been meticulously planning in all these months.

'And while I may still consult a world-famous writer I know, who once even worked for me, for the name for my dream restaurant, I do have the perfect name for this Greek Dessert Counter serving some signature dishes. *My Big Fat Greek Pudding.*'

'*Exaisios!* Simply superb!'I said and clapped.

Suddenly amidst all the rubble, I saw a table for two neatly set up, with a wooden crate and a couple of cement bags for chairs. *Had he come here all the way to set this up earlier*? Two sparkling crystal bowls and spoons sat on the table. Gaspworthy.

'And now if you'll excuse for a moment, I'll have my personal chef serve us the finale to our meal…'

Chef??

And then Chef KayKay Konstaninos materialized from nowhere, and served us both Moustalevria, stored in an icebox. A classic Greek grape pudding, and quite unlike anything I'd ever tasted before. 'Mmmmm! *Fantastikos!*' I exclaimed. 'My compliments to the chef.'

'*Efharisto, kyria*! If you like, I'll pass on some kisses to the chef too…'said KayKay. 'I'm glad you could still enjoy the dish, even though it was prepared at least six hours ago, and served without all its trimmings and fanfare. Not to mention special lighting. What I've learnt is food today must not only taste great, it must win beauty pageants too.'

Gulp. A long delicious silence. Then Brownie Eyes wordlessly asked—refill? *Divine.*

And then we sat on the rubble of the steps, leading off to the beach. I was wearing KayKay's swanky off-white jacket, as I was beginning to experience some shivers. And it didn't really come from the cool beach air.

'So when you open your School for Creativity, Ambidextrous Amby, you think I may do some Creative Cooking sessions too as a guest teacher??'

'WHATanidea, Kay!' I said at once. 'However I don't think I'll be able to afford your fancy Cordon Bleu Chef fees…'

'Not to worry. I may even do this for free. Because I owe you big time, Amby'.

For what? I wondered.

I saw KayKay's face in the semi-darkness suddenly turn earnest, almost serious, as he took my hand and spoke into my eyes, 'I have to tell you something, and say it just right. But feck it, I can't even steal lines from famous romantic films here; you're always going to find out. So I may as well tell you I got this from *As Good As It Gets*.

'Here goes...as Jack Nicholson famously said to Helen Hunt: "Amby, you make me want to be a better man."

I looked at KayKay, not unlike Helen Hunt; a bit dumbstruck. I made him a better Tweeter, yes. But a *better man?*

'I've always been the world's laziest laid-back creature, Amby! That's simply because all through my life, things simply came to me too easily. I would study, but never to any extremes of hard work. And then get hugely lucky with question papers. I always got way better marks than I expected, or even deserved.

'Sure, there was some sort of vague plan to be a chef some day, but I did little about that one too, and then drifted into the done thing; sitting for management exams to please my dad, and to my genuine horror got in there too.

'I decided to make good money for a few years from a plush MNC job, to finance my chef school course, but then again, if an easy way out was possible I'd do that. Just as my MBA course was getting really demanding, I quit that happily, getting into films in that freaky way, making myself all the big bucks I needed in a hurry.

'And when I realized that being a film star was a 24x7

programme of hard work too, especially all that PR paraphernalia surrounding a star's life, I didn't want to extend myself—so I preferred to out-source it all away, particularly all the Tweeting Interviewing stuff!'

Ahem. KayKay's eyes danced as he grinned and squeezed my hand.

'Now there I was again, chilling out with the good life, and slowly letting the glam times of a film star go to my head. I was again getting way too comfortable to move on, go forward and do what I really wanted to do in life—till you so articulately pointed it out to me.

'And then I found out by chance about your bigger Writer's Workshop plan in life. I confess I often kept judging you harshly before that (*what's a bright young thing like an Ambujakshi Balan wasting all her writing skills making up Tweets for a faltu film star?*). Knowing that you were off to chase something you were passionate about, jolted me into thinking seriously about my own life too.

'Of course, you took your time telling me about Greece, but I knew you'd be gone out of my filmi life forever—and I may even have manipulated that Liverpool trip with the Director, just to get more of your time with me, before you vanished!'

I listened on—well, a lot of things were falling into place…'Those urgent magazine interviews with you I was to do during the trip! No wonder you were in no hurry to actually do them.'

'After you left my room in Liverpool, after our flaming row on life, it did trigger something off in me. *What was I really doing with my life?* I kept getting tempted to sign the next film, and the next film, and then one MORE film—as you pointed out so succinctly. It was a wake up call. I had to get out fast…

'I realized Paris was just one and half hours away from where we were in Liverpool…I decided I had to check out the Cordon Bleu course and campus immediately. I took the first flight out early morning—before I changed my mind!

'Then later, when you told me you were quitting to chase a writing dream, all I could think of was: Good! Since I'm quitting too.'

'But pause the narration there, Mr Posterboy,' I said. 'What about all those scandalous gay rumours…' (Note: I had clear evidence by now that the heterosexual hand that held mine just now was not faking it).

'Oh, that's easiest to explain! I kept alive those Toni and KayKay rumours only to escape my silly leading ladies and their garland-carrying moms! Toni played along; no worries, he wasn't cheating on his lover back in Mumbai, ha ha'.

I rolled my eyes and felt my shoulders relax in a surge of relief.

'And after my Paris course, I was sure I could return like a conquering hero, with a frying pan and an egg-whisk in my hand, and whisk you off your feet. Till your Facebook updates (I confess, I'm a stalker!) showed you were meeting your Finn Boy Wonder—right in Crete. A mild form of panic set in. That's when I too landed up unannounced in Santorini to check out the situation for myself—using my cooking lessons with Chef Nickolas as an excuse!'

'And meanwhile, I was your Tweet-stalker, Kay, from Jose's internet café in Crete…' I confessed. 'I kept reading all sorts of double meanings into every Tweet you sent out.'

'Touche!' said KayKay. 'Long live social media, for allowing us all to be detectives, without spending a buck…' Both of us laughed together.

'Now once I got to Paris, I had to first see for sure if I even had it in me to be a really good chef, and eventually run my own restaurant. Halfway down my course I began to believe I did—and even came to Chennai during a break to meet my architects to begin work on this lovely piece of land I had bought long ago, on East Coast Road along the beach. That's the trip when I decided to track down Kavi too, as shocked as she was—I simply had to meet up and ask her quite frankly how serious you were with that arranged marriage bullshit with your Tam Brahm fellow. I got a sense from Kavi that it was just a ploy, all those grand plans for your future together you pulled on me that evening at Thirasia—despite succumbing to me later quite easily I thought, Ambivalent Amby!'

'But I went away determined to get my new credentials right, before I did anything else. I felt I had to earn your respect back. I kept in touch with Kavi all along, even when she went away to Stockholm—fantastic that she didn't breathe a word to you—and got your office number.' KayKay's serious face suddenly broke into a grin.

'Of course, that Frenchman caper on the phone was totally unplanned; I thought you'd guess my voice the minute I spoke with that fake French accent, but you believed every word of it!'

'*Ay gamisou Kay*!' I shot back, making KayKay stare at me astonished, and break into a crazy big laugh. 'Gamisou?! Congrats, my pure pure Amby. At last you broke free of your safe, feck-off cussword. Now when did you learn that Greek expression that every normal bad-mouthed teenager in Greece cannot do without?'

My ears and face seemed to burn again, recalling that neat trick I had fallen for, or was that part of a slow delicious warmth that was moving to every part of me; spreading out from the masculine grip that held my hand captive.

KayKay turned dead serious, as his other hand slowly stroked away a lock of hair fluttering down my face. 'I have to confess this: you really had me at "Hello", Amby, when you answered the phone...In French, one doesn't say, "I miss you". One says, *"Tu me manques"*—which is "You are missing from me".'

I doubt if I will ever hear anything more romantic in my whole life.

'And now if you'll excuse me, M'am, we have some unfinished business to attend to,' said KayKay getting up suddenly to go back into the construction site. He returned shortly with a large piece of rolled-up paper.

'Now you can't say "Oh this is so sudden!" as in the standard Victorian romantic novel, as I clearly texted you my devious intentions earlier on your cell phone. I have to make my two proposals now. I'll go with the one that requires a bended knee first…'

The caterpillars in my stomach had fed on the salad leaves I'd had at the Patio and had now developed into monstrous butterflies.

I saw KayKay, grinning his devastating grin, hold the rolled-up paper, and go down on his right knee.

'Amby,' he began. By now he was unravelling the huge sheet of paper and spreading it out. So *that's why* he was kneeling down. 'This is the floor plan of my new Mediterranean restaurant. Now here is my proposal. Would you consider having your School for Creativity on the top floor? I have this very large, sea-facing space above, and no idea what to do with it…'

He had done it again. So the proposal was really a *business proposal* was it? Another prank I'd neatly fallen for.

But what the feck! Here was my dream place at last, in a dream setting, facing the dream blue waters and dream everything. Omigod. NEXT TO THE SEA! No more searching for old crumbling Chettinad bungalows in the city, no more haggling with brokers and owners…

Hold it…where's the catch? And then I remembered there was another 'Proposal' coming up.

'And what's the 'Second Proposal', Mr Smarty Pants?' I asked, crossing my arms.

'Well, it's interlinked to the first one, so if you'll give me a quick, positive answer to the first, we'll move on. But all this rubble is hurting my knees; I'm getting up.'

KayKay neatly rolled up his blueprint, and got up,

giving me time to think...Now he was placing both hands on my shoulders, eyes still dancing with mischief. 'Some day, my dear Amby, I promise to turn into an adult, mature male. This may be around age 64, but if you are in for the long haul, it'll be worth the wait...'

I was so enjoying this little tableau of KayKay—but I knew I had to outsmart him.

'Well, what if I said "Yes" to the first, and "No" to the second proposal?' I asked.

That sent KayKay into complete silence—but only for six seconds. And then he burst into laughter.

'Ha Ha Ha! A "No" to the next proposal would suit me perfectly. Since your superior brain has deduced that the Second Proposal is 'Will you marry me?', saying NO is a relief—who wants marriage these days, it complicates things. As long as you stay right there trapped on the top of my own castle by the beach, I can remain single and carefree, and still have you within reachable, kissable, beddable, make-love-able distance every single day...!'

I made fists of my hands to punch him, but he trapped them in his, suddenly drawing me close to his chest. And after a full minute of simply looking, just looking at each other, we kissed.

Like lovers everywhere. Like lovers who felt they had invented kissing. Like lovers in countless movies...It was all so achingly, impossibly beautiful, I wanted to prolong it. Prolooooong it.

But KayKay was now cradling my face with his big handsome hands. And talking again.

'So I take it the answer is "Yes" to the First Proposal—

the strictly business deal part of this evening. And I think we should seal that agreement, with a kiss.'

So he kissed me one more time. A very long one more time.

And then in the inky darkness he continued. 'And now for the second question. Sorry it's such a cliché, my queen of words, but will you marry me, my gorgeous Amby?'

With my entire body crushed up against his, I felt my heart beat out the answer directly into his. Yes. Yes. Yes. Just-kissed lips just millimetres away, what choice does a romance-obsessed girl have? But wait. I had to live up to my filmi obsession, one last time, before I succumbed.

'Hold on, Kay,' I said. 'I need a screenplay ending for this one. Hmmm...So how about this line by Scarlett O'Hara in *Gone With The Wind:*

'I'll think about it tomorrow...'

KayKay threw back his head and laughed.

Acknowledgements

Writing a second book is no different from having a second baby—you're so exhilarated the first one looks cute, gets compliments and moves about on its own, that you forget all the pain, and recklessly think, why not one more?

So I'll thank my real life babies Kadambari (who I raised to be a writer, but she turned into a banker) and Kanishkaa (who I raised to be a banker, but he turned into a sports writer) for following their own path—the 'message' of this book.

But I must first thank that flattering phone call all writers dream about which started it all. Kausalya Saptharishi, an acquisition editor, rang me up on a day of sudden low self-esteem. (An old friend had just told me he loved my first book, though he doubted he'd actually read it; however Paul Fernandes's accompanying illustrations were absolutely hilarious. Good God, was that why my book was unexpectedly selling well?). Anyway, Kausalya here restored my faith when she said—how about writing another book for me—a funny, romantic novel?

By day's end I was scribbling the synopsis for a story set in Greece—the most romantic place I have ever been to.

A load of gratitude to my dear talented art-buddy Mala Chinnappa, for listening intently to my first outline of what may have been just a fun, ditzy romance, and asking me, as if it were an advertising task, but what is your core IDEA? By answering Mala, I was able to give my book an underpinning of a sound thought—find your true calling in life, young people, don't ever settle. And chase your passion: Create art, finish your book, make music, travel. Bring meaning and exuberance into your life.

Which brings me to the fabulous Sisterhood of the Travelling Writers I made in Greece—at a real-life Creative Workshop in Crete some years ago. Fran, Linda, Stacey, Priya, Cynthia, Shubha…you are all in this book! All the bonding, all the laughter, all the ouzo is right here.

Thanks goes to my action-packed 30 years in JWT—nothing prepares you for a lifetime of writing like advertising. It is also advertising that gave me my up-close and personal brush with Bollywood and Kollywood—during several Pepsi films with Shahrukh, Madhavan, Suriya, Saif, Kareena, Priyanka, Farah Khan (my incurable crush for SRK is probably showing up in the form of this book's heroine Amby, and her film star boss, but don't tell my mother).

A big hug to the funniest email writer on this planet—Priya Madhusudan—she gave me the opening line of the book in a hilarious mail she wrote me once, about her only career option left in life. And another for my author pal, Cauvery Madhavan—I wrote my first chapter sitting in her absolutely magical 'getaway writing cottage' perched high on a hill in Cork in Ireland, while she stirred up delicious Irish potato soup.

Thanks to my truest, closest friends of all—my elder sister Bhanu, for the constant ra-ra from the wings right to the last para in this book, and younger sister Shubha, my partner in crime in countless travels, for a never-ending supply of Greek phrases, giggles and sketches from our Crete writers' workshop, which we attended together. A thank you to my mother Raji, who never fails to appreciate a nice turn of phrase (and made me hurriedly correct some terrible split infinitives; she's such a stickler for fine English). And to my very young father-in-law PVK, still rocking in his mid-nineties, who will probably enjoy reading this breezy romance the most.

Now a return to the studios and thanks to: Kausalya (again)—for rearranging my thinking and chapters so cogently; to Ravi Singh—for taking on my book with his new publishing house, Speaking Tiger, so generously; and to Paromita Mohanchandra—for her sharp editorial eye for detail in the final stages of the book.

Finally, a great big thanks to all the people I've met who follow a passion beyond making a living; and the brave, the adventurous and the honest who quit the safe and boring to follow where their heart took them. And among them are my numerous writer pals. This book is about us. And nobody said it better than Anne Tyler whose quote I have pinned up on my board: 'I write because I want more than one life. It's greed, pure and simple.'